The King's-Horse

Book 1

BY ADAM DREECE

ADZO PUBLISHING INC.
CALGARY, CANADA

ADZO Publishing Inc.

Calgary, Alberta, Canada

www.adzopublishing.com

This is a work of fiction. Names, characters, places, and incidents are a product of the author's imagination. Locales and public names are sometimes used for atmospheric purposes. Any resemblance to actual people, living or dead, or to businesses, companies, events, institutions, or locales is completely coincidental.

WELCOME TO MONDUS FUMUS

This is a world where airships have recently been invented, the first trains have been spotted, and where messages can travel long distances thanks to the revolutionary invention of a man named Tulu Neuma; the Neumatic tube.

Also, this is a world where what we consider to be fairy tales and nursery rhymes are real life events. From the once great secret society called the Tub—led by butchers, bakers, and candlestick makers—to the legend of two brilliant inventors in their twilight years, Christophe Creangle and Nikolas Klaus.

If you've read my series *The Yellow Hoods*, you'll feel right at home. But if you haven't, fear not, for this is a brand-new series.

In the pages that follow, you'll find a continental and regional map for the planet Oerth, where these stories take place. For those who like an introduction to characters and the world before the story starts, I've included a few glossaries as well. Warning: there may be some Yellow Hoods spoilers in there. If you'd like to dive straight into the story, then skip ahead to Chapter One.

With that, welcome to Mondus Fumus, the World of Steam and Fairy Tale.

CHARACTER GLOSSARY

Angelina

Once a mercenary with a kind heart, she became Christina's right hand at Kar'm. At one time romantically involved with Christina, the two remained close afterwards.

Christina Creangle

Former leader of the inventor sanctuary at Kar'm and inventor in her own right. She took Mounira under her wing early in *The Yellow Hoods* series, and the two have been a dynamic duo ever since.

Christophe Creangle

Legendary inventor and father of Christina. Created the King's-Horses with Nikolas Klaus about forty years ago for the King of Teuton. Spent his final days at the Moufan Keep.

Francis Stein, Dr.

Once a medical doctor, Stein became a medical researcher and has been the lead medical scientist at Kar'm.

Jacqueline Benstock

Formerly a professor at a prestigious university, Jacqueline's brilliant and armed with a snarky, sharp wit.

Oskar and Petra

Brother and sister duo with a long, challenged history. She's an antique dealer on the rise in the capital city of Teutork, and he's a scoundrel with some mechanical skill.

Marcus Pieman

Once the High Conventioneer for the King of Teuton, he later became president of Teuton after he helped overthrow the monarchy. He is the father of Abeland Pieman. Marcus was the leader of the Fare until a civil war cost him both his presidency and his hold over the Fare.

Mounira Benida

Mounira's father snatched her and fled north as a civil war broke out. Finding a caring stranger by the name of Nikolas Klaus, Mounira's father left her with him and the Yellow Hoods and went in search of the rest of their family. She then went on to create a rocket-cart with Christina Creangle and save the lives of Mounira's new family, actions that created a permanent bond between her and Christina.

Nikolas Klaus

A legendary inventor long thought dead by most, Nikolas was a close friend of both Christophe Creangle and Marcus Pieman. He played a key role in The Yellow Hoods series and showed that his passion for creating new wonders hadn't dwindled with age. He's known for his kind heart and generous actions, including the creation of a gift- giving celebration at Winter Solstice. Nikolas and Christophe haven't seen each other in a long, long time.

The Mad Queen

Queen Caterina of Staaten and Elizabetina has many nicknames including the Mad Queen and the Queen of Hearts. She was a force to be reckoned with in *The Yellow Hoods* series and may be again one day.

ORGANIZATION GLOSSARY

Fare

The nefarious enemy of the Tub, the Fare was led by Marcus Pieman until he was overthrown by the Mad Queen. Believed to have been folded into her regime.

Tub

Now defunct, it was led by a butcher, baker, and candlestick maker for centuries. This secret society worked behind-the-scenes to guide kings and queens throughout the continent. They were seen as generally benevolent. After being weakened significantly by Marcus Pieman and the Fare, they sacrificed what remained of their order to secure the Moufan-Men's assistance at the fall of Kar'm.

Moufan (Moufan-Men)

The Moufan are an ancient secret society that spread throughout the continent with semi-autonomous affiliates, and they were grudgingly aligned with the Tub. They were founded in a castle outside of Doyono, Dery.

TECHNOLOGY GLOSSARY

Hotaru

The airships created by the Piemans. They are a turbine-based, flying platform.

MCM Engine

The Magnetic-Copper-Magnesium engine is a revolutionary engine created by Nikolas Klaus and Christophe Creangle forty years ago. They are at the heart of the King's-Horses. All the ones ever discovered were booby-trapped, except for one, which was stolen by Abeland Pieman to build his Hotaru.

Shock-stick

A handheld device, usually eighteen inches in length, capable of delivering a shock strong enough to knock out a large man.

Skyfallers

The airships created by the Mad Queen. While not as technologically advanced as the Hotaru, they were faster, easier, and cheaper to produce. They look like sea-faring war galleons held in the air by two giant balloons. They use bat-like wings to catch the air to help them turn and accelerate.

Map of the Continent
Cartographer Megan Beaudoin - 1805

Map of the Region

CONTENTS

ON THE BRINK

Oskar pulled his muddy upper body out from under the carriage. Grumbling angrily at having accepted the job of traveling mechanic for a pompous jerk, he squinted up at the aristocrat impatiently pacing about when something in the sky caught his attention.

"Can we get moving again? We don't have much time." The man glared at Oskar. "Don't just sit there in the muck with your mouth open like an idiot. Say something."

The driver tugged his goggles down and leaped off his perch. Dusting himself off, he noticed the two horses were moving back and forth uneasily. "What is it?" He looked up.

Pointing at the sky, Oskar shook his head back and forth. "Those aren't weather balloons."

The driver's skinny face went pale. "That looks like a … like a war galleon but with two immense balloons."

"And those webbed wings, look at them catch the wind," Oskar said, wiping the sweat from his face and leaving a messy streak.

The aristocrat's gaze darted about, his hands trembling. "I thought we had more time." He punched Oskar in the shoulder. "Fix it. Fix it! We must get to Kar'm before those Skyfallers arrive."

Oskar smacked the man in the face and stepped back, glaring at him.

"How dare you? A man of your station—"

"Where I come from," Oskar interrupted and leaned forward with a scowl, "a man in a forest is no better than the man he is with."

A giant shadow fell over them as the Skyfallers sailed overhead.

"You are right, my apologies. I have urgent information that needs to get to Kar'm."

"What's so important about old ruins? There's nothing there," the driver said.

"Yeah. Are you that in love with history?" Oskar asked, folding his arms and chuckling. "Anyway, that axle is now even more broken, and I cannot fix it."

"You fixed it before."

"True, mister fancy jacket," Oskar said to the aristocrat. "But we were on the edge of a town. Here, what do you want me to do? The front wheels are on the verge of breaking, and the shock absorbers are bent. This thing is done. You had us going too fast, and you rented a carriage that was too cheap and too low to the ground." He shrugged. "Your problem. Now, I'd like to get paid and start heading home."

The aristocrat went to grab Oskar by his shirt collar, but Oskar smacked him away.

"He's right." The driver peeked underneath the carriage. "To make it worse, the back, left wheel has three broken spokes as well. It won't last another mile."

Running a trembling hand through his sweaty hair, the aristocrat glanced at them and then at the horses. "I'll take one of the horses then." He pulled out a knife from a hidden sheath in his waistcoat.

"Whoa," Oskar and the driver said in unison, putting up their hands quickly.

"Out of my way," The aristocrat forced both men back.

Something exploded in the distance, spooking the horses. They moved side to side and tugged at their bits.

"I'll just cut one free. I don't have time to untie it." The aristocrat rushed toward a horse and tripped. His knife brushed across the back of one of the horse's legs as he fell, and the horse kicked him in the head.

As blood splattered, the driver shook out his hands and turned away. "Gross."

Oskar looked down at their dead boss. "What an idiot. You calm the horses down and free them from this thing. I'm going to search the carriage cabin. I'm sure he had something." He grabbed the door and heaved his hefty self inside.

Starting with the curtains, Oskar ripped apart the cabin, throwing things out the door. "Do you want a red cloak?"

The driver frowned. "You mean like spies and couriers used to wear? Wouldn't that draw more attention to us? Everyone knows that after decades of being taught to ignore people in colored cloaks, we're supposed to report them. That era's over."

Oskar threw it out the door. "It is going to take people a long time to start seeing what they have been told since birth to ignore. Hey, there's a sealed letter. It's got some kind of duck pattern in the wax. Ah, feels thin. Too thin to have anything good." He tossed it out the door as well. "Oh, I found something."

"What?"

"Money. The best kind of something." Oskar climbed out of the cabin and whistled at the driver. "Catch." He threw the driver a heavy coin purse.

The driver looked down at his prize.

"That should be enough to get us home, eh?" Oskar said, slipping a wallet of paper money into his vest. He then picked up a pistol and tucked it into the back of his pants.

"Did you already take your share?"

"No, I trust you." He rolled his shoulders.

Two rapid explosions sounded in the distance.

The horses pulled against the reins, and the driver dropped the purse.

Oskar stared at the purse, his eyes narrowing. He glanced up at the driver and then back down at the purse.

The driver tried to calm the horses. "If we head back to town, someone will notice that we're missing our employer. They'll ask questions."

"If we go back about half a day's ride, there's a sign pointing another way back to Teuton. Probably take a little bit longer, but it'll be good. It should be safe." His eyes wouldn't leave the coin purse.

"Here, take this horse." The driver held out a set of reins. "I'll take the other."

Oskar clenched his teeth as he looked at the horses. "You're taking the better one?"

"Better one? They're the same."

Explosions started going off, one after the other, in the distance.

"What do you think is going on over there?"

"It doesn't sound like target practice." Oskar took the reins with one hand and put the other behind his back. "But the good news is that you do not need to worry about these things."

"Why's that?"

He shoved the pistol into the driver's chest and pulled the trigger. As one horse took off, with the driver dragging alongside, Oskar shushed the other one.

Picking up the coin purse, he noticed his boss again and dropped the pistol near the dead man's hand. "There. Now it looks like the driver tried to rob the rich guy, things went badly, and he shot you. Everything solved."

Oskar frowned at all the stuff he'd thrown out of the carriage. He shrugged. *Doesn't matter, no one will care*, he thought.

Mounting the horse, he saw the driver lying in the road ahead. "You were going to do the same to me. I know it because you offered me this horse. But you see, now I like this horse better. Funny thing, I never killed a man before. My old friends in Yarbo, they would have new respect for me." He held his chin high. "They might even invite me to join their establishment."

His expression darkened. "But then, my younger sister, Petra, she would find out. I can almost feel her judgment from here." He waved at the air, and then turned the horse around.

"Now, if you don't mind, I finally have the money to make them see me as the real businessman and inventor I am. No more being a mechanic or repairman."

The intensity of the bombing increased, and he looked over his shoulder in the direction of Kar'm. "Those idiots, wasting so much money. There's nothing at those old ruins."

Christina Creangle bowed her head as the room full of angry men and women unleashed another barrage of insults and fury at her. She grimaced, allowing them to vent, all the while thinking of how the peace and harmony of their sanctuary, hidden in the ancient ruins of the underground city of Kar'm, was a distant memory. Every story has an ending, and she could feel theirs coming.

"We need a new leader! You've made a mess of things for long enough," jeered a man in a red sweater in the back, many around him nodding and raising their fists.

Peering up at the fearful faces, Christina's stomach twisted and churned. She couldn't help but feel she'd spent too much time away helping allies instead of being here, leading and protecting these people.

How many spies and disruptors slipped among our ranks in my absence? she thought. *I can't believe we were wrong to accept every fleeing scientist and refugee inventor, rather than allowing them to be killed or starve.*

Christina stepped to the edge of the speaker's platform. "How have we changed so much in a year? Look at us. This is not who we are. This is the result of poisonous words and deeds by those who want to see us—"

A woman stepped forward to meet Christina and cut her off. "Is it true that the Mad Queen is hunting us? That we've aligned ourselves with the Tub, and she's going to make us pay for that?"

"I heard the same thing," the man in the red sweater said. "Tell us."

How could she know? Christina dug her nails into her hands to stop from reacting. Her mouth slipped open. She wanted to let the words out, to tell them how it had been her actions that likely led the Mad Queen to see Kar'm as no longer neutral between the great secret societies, but Christina couldn't. She knew it would be adding kerosene to the fire, and as their leader, she couldn't be so selfish.

"What were you doing for those months you were away?" a woman with welding goggles on her forehead asked. "Off trying to find yet another of your father's mechanical horses? It's bad enough having that senile old man wandering the halls at night, but without you here to keep an eye on the creepy old nutter, he gets into everything. He took metal from my workshop. Again!"

Drawing in a deep breath, Christina rolled her shoulders, a hint of anger flashing across her face at the disrespectful reference to her father.

Finding him and bringing him to stay at Kar'm had been hard, but discovering that his mind was eroding had nearly broken her. Though they rarely spent any time together, she would sometimes watch him at his work table, putting things together, sketching out ideas on paper. But since his arrival, the old man's paranoia that his inventions and ideas could harm society had consumed her, stealing her time and attention. It was that very thing that had destroyed their relationship long ago, and now she saw it destroying Kar'm.

"This has nothing to do with Christophe. Nothing," she said sharply, her words swallowed by the noise of the crowd. One of her legs started bouncing.

A short man forced his way to the front and raised his hand. "I heard you found an MCM engine. That would make a huge difference in my research if you did." He glanced at the woman next to him who nodded in agreement.

Christina stared at the two of them. While most of her expeditions over the years had been fruitless, she had found a few more of the forty-year-old King's-Horses, though she only had one remaining that worked. Surprisingly, her latest adventure had turned up an unsealed Magnetic-Copper-Magnesium engine in the hands of none other than Nikolas Klaus himself, Christophe's original partner for making the mechanical horses.

The MCM engine was the heart of the mechanical horse. Knowing that the engine itself could revolutionize the world in unpredictable ways, Christophe had booby-trapped each and every one.

Finally, something I can share with them, she thought, the corners of her mouth turning up. *Wait, there's no way any of you could know about that either.* Her face fell, and she narrowed her eyes. She surveyed the crowd. *There's got to be someone in here feeding them this, or maybe two people. Yig, there's too many new faces. I can't read these people.*

Lifting her gaze, she put out a hand and yelled for calm against the roar of the room.

"What about the destruction of the palace at Myke? Is it true that the royal family was killed by the Fare?" a woman in the second row yelled.

Christina's glare silenced the woman. Her fists uncurled into claws. She glanced at the doorway, her heart pounding.

"The Fare bombed them with some kind of new airship, didn't they? Without the royal family of the kingdom of Myke to protect us, we're screwed."

"Look at Creangle's expression." The man in the

red sweater waved his arms emphatically. "Just look at her."

Christina stepped back, a hand slipping to the compressed-air pistol on her hip. She wished she could be closed up in her lab, working on a new edition of her flying contraption. It had been forever since she'd had some quiet and time to herself.

A bald bull of a man pushed off the wall. "Hey, show respect and let her have a chance to answer." His voice boomed and silenced the crowd. He folded his arms, the axes hanging from either side of his belt glinting in the light of the crank lanterns. "You all said you didn't want to deal with me anymore, that you wanted her here, so listen to her. Show some respect."

He looked over at Christina with a warm smile. "Sorry to interrupt."

"Thanks, Remi," she replied, relieved that the crowd was significantly subdued. He was a key reason why Kar'm had always felt like home.

Taking a moment to clear her thoughts, Christina put her hands on her hips and looked up at the ceiling. Then, she turned to the clock hanging like a pendant on the back wall. The messenger was several hours late, and with him, any word about what the Fare's plans for Kar'm were. She was going to have to address that in a minute. For now, she had to find another way to get these people, many who had dedicated decades to making Kar'm the special place it was, to help her turn things around before it was too late.

"We should throw in with the Fare, shouldn't we? They're going to win," the man in the red sweater added.

Oh, for crying out loud, thought Christina. "They'd just kill us all in the end." Her eyes went wide as she realized what she'd said, and the room erupted in yelling.

Putting her hands up and futilely calling for calm, Christina noticed the man with the red sweater slip out of the room, and another man strangely quiet in the middle of the storm.

He was a big man; a dark, loose cloak over him. The hood was back, but it was his expression that held her attention. His brow was furrowed, like he was concentrating on something as he pushed forward in the crowd, but his expression was a demented form of serene. Altogether, it looked almost diabolical.

"Christina," a strong, female voice shouted from the doorway, grabbing everyone's attention. All eyes turned to Christina's right hand, Angelina.

Where many saw Christina as cold, they saw Angelina as frigid. Where many saw Christina as reserved and thoughtful, they saw Angelina as secretive and shifty. Thanks to her sharp, sarcastic sense of humor, there were few who considered

Angelina a friend. Fewer still knew of the romantic history between the two.

"You're needed upstairs, now." Angelina pushed her light blond hair back.

Several of the department leaders immediately protested, their faces going red with frustration. During Christina's latest departure from Kar'm, when the mantle of leadership had once again fallen to Angelina, weapons had been drawn in the heat of the moment at a similar meeting. Christina had thought it had been an exaggerated reaction at the time.

Christina stared at Angelina, dumbfounded.

"I wouldn't be here if it were not *critically* important," Angelina said.

"I can't. I can't be pulled once again. We have to—"

"Christina," Angelina's gaze intensified. "You have to come up. Trust me."

"Don't let her leave. She planned this." The man with the strange expression shoved people aside as he made his way toward Christina.

"Okay. Remi, you're in charge." Christina stepped down from the speaker's platform. "Watch that guy."

"Coward! This is what got us into this mess. We've given our lives to this cause," a woman trying to get around Remi said. "We should have left with the others last week. Stolen whatever rations we could have taken and screw the rest of you."

Christina paused at the doorway as Remi put his arms out wide and shoved the crowd back.

"This isn't your fault," Angelina said placing a hand on Christina's shoulder. "Nothing lasts forever."

"I can't shake the feeling that I'm not supposed to leave. Something feels very wrong."

"It all feels wrong." A shiver went through Angelina. "Now come on. The sooner we're done, the sooner we're back."

Doctor Francis Stein leaped out of the way, clutching his stack of papers, as Angelina and Christina tore around the corner. *The least you could do is watch where you're going,* he thought.

Leaning against the wall of the carved stone corridor, he watched as they continued, unaware of his presence.

Why are you both going the wrong way in such a hurry? He glanced in the opposite direction. *Is the meeting already over?* He pushed his large spectacles up and pursued the women. "Ms. Creangle, if I could have a moment of your time. I've been asking for months. I need more resources for my experiments," his voice lined with desperation.

Angelina glared at him and whispered to Christina. She then broke off and intercepted Stein. "The meeting's still going on, so get down there. This is an emergency," said Angelina, pointing sharply in the other direction.

His face wrinkled up as Christina turned a corner. "How about my emergency? I am on the verge of a breakthrough in fighting infection, but my time is being wasted. Wasted because I don't have the people or supplies I need."

"We don't have time for this, Stein."

As she turned to go, he reached out and grabbed her arm. Several papers fell to the ground.

She glared at him, and he looked at his hand, surprised at himself.

"You keep promising me that I will have time to explain to Ms. Creangle, to make my case, but every time you just tell me to go away. Not this time." He lifted his chin, holding on to the surge in confidence.

Angelina's nostrils flared. "Get to that meeting, Stein. Be where you're supposed to be, when you're supposed to be there. Unless you want me to point out to Christina that you've been derelict in your medical duties lately. Then I'm sure she'd have given you an audience, before throwing you out on your ear. I have half a mind to believe that you're just a con man."

Stein's words failed him, and so he bent down to pick up his papers, his eyes locked on Angelina's. Swallowing, he pushed onward. "I have been here for ten months. Ten months and I am *still* waiting for the very things you promised me when I agreed to lead the medical science and research department here. Maybe it's you who is the con artist? Just where do you disappear to when Creangle's off on her sojourns?"

Angelina folded her arms and stepped forward. Despite being only five-foot-three-inches, compared to Stein's five-foot-nine, he leaned back as if she were a giant. "And what do you feel you've been denied, Stein? Does someone have a nicer lamp than you? All I ever hear about is what more you need, what you don't have. Do I need to remind you that you were lost and running for your life when you happened upon a group of fleeing scientists who were headed here? And despite not having any paperwork on you, we accepted you in as one of our own."

Stein's hands curled into fists. "And I'm supposed to be eternally grateful? I used to be the head of medical research at the University of—"

"I don't care, Stein." Angelina's eyes were cold, the fury and anger in her face disappearing like fire under a tide.

He punched at the air. "There's a girl running around in a yellow hood with a mechanical arm beyond anything I have ever seen." He jabbed a finger sharply behind him. "Where did she get that? I can't believe for a moment that it came from Christophe Creangle himself. Whatever miracles of technology the man once made are beyond the senile, old fool he is now. He couldn't make a shoebox, let alone something like that."

The edge of Angelina's mouth turned up in a smug smile. "Do you think Christina made Mounira's arm? Is that it? Wait, I remember now. She did it in one of those non-existent moments she had to herself."

"Oh please, I think it more than likely that you have some deal, someone else involved that you're hiding from all of us," Stein rebuffed. "Am I to seriously believe that a man who smells constantly like a baby needing a change is responsible for such a miraculous invention as that arm?"

Angelina pushed Stein back. "Now is not the time for your petty squabbling. I've never seen an ounce of the man you claim to once have been. Walk away, now."

He strangled the papers in his grip.

"You know, Stein, you are the biggest obstacle in your life. Now shut up and get down to that meeting, or I'll find someone else to lead the medical sciences team. Someone who actually cares about the team and results."

Stein's body shook with rage as he watched Angelina walk away. His life had been a chain of 'almosts', opportunities he felt had been stolen from him with polite lies and careful smiles.

He'd almost been hired at a university to lead their medical research team, but instead was allowed to rent a lab while they dithered. Then he'd made an incredible discovery, one that would have surely brought him fame, money, and recognition, but he arrived one afternoon to discover the small, one-story building had been demolished. And so on went the chain of events, resulting in him running for his life with other geniuses, hunted as abominators, all the way to the doors of Kar'm. He'd hoped that his lifetime of feeling adrift had come to an end, and it had, but not in the way he'd expected.

Kar'm was a hellish prison for Stein. He was surrounded by brilliant minds with little interest in other than what they were striving for. No one seemed interested in collaborating. Everyone wanted to be left alone with their toys, allowed to display any temperament; everyone that was—except for him.

With a long face and slumped shoulders, he stared at the nearest crank lantern. Unlike its colleagues that all hung on the wall, brightly shining, this one was dim. He reached out, taking hold of its little winding arm.

"Do you need some help?" He raised an eyebrow and leaned in. "What's that? You do? Allow me."

He yanked the handle so hard, the lantern plummeted to the ground and smashed.

"There, how do you like Kar'm-style help?" He gave the broken lantern a push with his boot. "No? I do admit, it was not what I expected either, but better you learn the lesson sooner rather than later." He tapped another lantern. "It's a shame you couldn't find one to complement you. You might have been able to become the brightest of all lights together. But instead, you now hang there, alone, your genius muffled by the cruelty of others."

He slowly headed for the meeting room, his mind going over what he'd wanted to mention. Turning the final corner, he glanced over at the open doorway thirty yards away. There were all manner of familiar voices shouting even more complaints and curses. "It sounds like they're already rabid. Best I be ready for when I enter."

Stein crouched down and laid his papers out. "This first ..." For the next ten minutes, he fussed back and forth with the order of the papers. "Strategy's not your game, Francis. Stop messing with the papers and just get in there. Don't try to be who they want, just be yourself. Wing it." He bowed his head.

Then something caught his attention and he gazed over at the meeting room. His fingers twitched, and his stomach tightened. Frowning, he listened carefully. *Something's wrong. They don't yell like that. That sounds more like panic.*

Standing up, Stein touched his glasses and took a step forward. *What did Remi just say? Did he say—?*

An explosion threw Stein backwards against the wall and scattering his papers everywhere.

His ears ringing, his eyes wide, he stared at the upside-down smoky scene before him. Rolling onto his stomach, he grimaced and righted his glasses.

Later, he would wonder if it was the desire to help or morbid curiosity, but regardless, Stein slowly crawled forward through the rubble, until he collapsed on the floor, his face turned to peer into the bloody scene. His head spinning, he flattened to the ground, and passed out.

2

FALL OF KAR'M

Christina stared at Abeland Pieman, conflicted. She knew he wouldn't be there unless it was something vital. As the right hand of the Pieman empire, a man who could show up out of the blue and have kings and queens surrender their power, he was more than aware of the fuse his presence in Kar'm would ignite among his enemies.

Still, despite how protective of her Abeland had been since they'd first met, he rarely showed up without an ulterior motive.

Abeland bore a striking resemblance to an early forties edition of his father, Marcus Pieman.

"Your nails are scuffed, and your beard's not been groomed in days." Christina pointed at his face. "You've lost weight, a bit too much."

He smiled and stroked his cheek with the back of

his hand. "It's not as bad as it was. Someone gave me an unexpected vacation a little while ago. Terrible accommodations. But, that's a story for another day." He rubbed the brass buttons on the edge of his black coat.

"What are you doing? And why are we meeting in my personal lab?" Christina waved at her messy desk, covered in drawings and engineering instruments. Around the desk were piles of papers and shelves of mechanical devices of all sorts. In the far corner of the room were boxes and a tarp draped over something.

Abeland frowned. "Aren't you going to ask me how I knew about this room? About this entire facility?"

Despite herself, Christina cracked a smile. "Why are you here? This is a very bad time."

"Worse than you're aware, I'm afraid."

As Abeland drew in a breath, Christina noted the trademark wheezing of his asthma. She was tempted to ask if he'd made another machine to exercise his lungs, but as he'd said, such things would be for another day.

Angelina rushed into the room and Christina's smile disappeared. "Sorry, Stein was having a moment."

"Again?" Christina asked.

Angelina rolled her eyes and pushed her light blond hair over her ears.

"Would you mind waiting outside, Angelina?" He pointed at the door, his eyes narrowed.

"I'm not letting you pull another one over on her."
As Angelina stepped between Christina and Abeland,
she felt Christina's hand on her shoulder. "You're not
serious?"

"He's never done us any harm. Moreover, I don't
want anyone barging in here. Stand at the door and
give us the two minutes we need." Christina looked at
Abeland. "I presume we don't need any more
than that."

Abeland shook his head.

Grudgingly, Angelina stepped out of the room and
Abeland gently closed the door behind her.

With a sigh and rubbing his hands together, he
walked toward the far end of the room. Looking at her,
he pointed at the tarp. "I will admit, I was rather
excited to hear the news."

"You mean my rickety old King's-Horse?"

"No, nor the ones you used up helping the Yellow
Hoods." He paused. "It's very noble of you, by the
way. Particularly given your fierce rule of remaining
neutral in this whole Tub versus Fare war."

"I had my reasons and I violated nothing."

"Philosophy for another day. Now, I assume that
under this tarp, behind the lovely last of the
mechanical horses, is the mint-condition Magnetic-
Copper-Magnesium engine I've heard so much about.
Am I right?"

Christina's eyes went wide, and she fell back a step.

"No one knows about that." She glared at him. "No one."

"And yet, I do." A devilishly charming smile crossed his lips. "Nikolas Klaus made it, I presume?"

She stared at him coldly, a scowl on her face.

"My father would be shocked and awed that Klaus eventually came up with a version all himself. We'd all given up hope. Sneaky, old Saintly Nick, always full of surprises." Abeland brought his hands together.

"So, you came here to steal it from me?"

Abeland shook his head. "No. I want to offer a trade. A piece of technology that will be critical to all of us surviving the coming airship war, for the chance for Kar'm to survive."

Christina raised an eyebrow.

"I don't want anything underhanded, and I will say that I came as quickly as I could as soon as I learned you have a plague of saboteurs within these walls."

"What about your spies?"

"They are harmless… to you."

She stared at Abeland, nodding after a minute. "You didn't come by horse; I would have had a heads up. So how did you get here?"

He scratched the back of his neck and looked away. "Rail-raft, if you must know."

"Rail-raft?"

"You've been busy," Abeland said. "When this is all over, let's have tea. I'll explain the future that's coming.

What do you think? I'll even tell you about the brilliant invention of one of our top inventors, Tulu Neuma. We call it the Neumatic tube, and it allows us to send messages long distances in hours. Unbelievable."

"I'm not making any deal until I know what you have," Christina said.

He pulled out a piece of paper from his long coat and handed it to her.

Christina frowned at him as he refused to let go.

He let out a heavy sigh. "You'll need to evacuate all of your people. There are Skyfallers on their way. I saw them a few hours ago, and there's nowhere else I could imagine them coming but here. In the chaos of evacuation, get rid of the people on this list."

An explosion went off in the distance and the underground building rumbled.

Abeland shoved Christina out of the way as a piece of stone fell from the ceiling.

"We're out of time," Abeland whispered.

Christina opened the paper and stared at it. "Oh no." She bolted out of the room. "Angelina, we have to get back to the meeting room. Now." She ran past her.

"What? You're going to leave Abeland in there?" Angelina yelled.

"I'll be fine," he replied with a cheeky smile and wave. "You should catch up with her. Her life might depend on it."

Angelina glared at him and took off.

Stein roused to find Angelina shaking him violently. Blurry-eyed, he could make out her mouth moving, but her words were drowned out by the ringing in his ears. The hint of relief on her face at seeing he was alive confused him. He watched as Christina slipped past them, and Angelina sprang up to stop her friend and leader from seeing the horror that lay inside the former meeting room.

Taking stock of himself first, Stein got up on all fours and then dared to stand. Falling against one wall, he took a moment to steady himself. He stood there blinking blankly, trying to restart the engine of his mind. Then came a loud rumble he felt through the wall and he covered his head as dust rained down. Finally, a thought arrived, and his brain clicked into gear. *I have to get out of here,* he thought, pushing off the wall. Lurching back and forth at first, and then continuing at a clumsy jog, Stein made his way to the stairs.

Arriving on the main level of the facility, he was greeted by a sea of rushing people. He grabbed a man and brought him right up to his face. "What's happening?" he yelled as a rumble shook the corridor.

"The Fare have airships and troops here. They're going to kill us all. We have to get out of here!"

Stein let the man go and stood there for a moment,

watching the people flee. *Why are their hands empty? Where is all the work we've done? How can they abandon everything?*

Raising a hand to his chin, he shook his head, momentarily dispelling his desire to flee. *I'm not going back to a life of nothing. I can't let this past year mean nothing.* He backed away to the edge of the corridor, a doorknob banging into his lower back.

Turning it, he opened the door and entered the room. It was barren, with dull, beige plastered walls, an old kitchen table at the far end, and a window. The scene outside caught Stein's attention, as he witnessed an airship, its bat-like wings grabbing the wind and turning it quickly. He was at once struck by its sense of majesty, and fear as it rained bundles that shook the world around him.

With his heart pounding violently in his chest, Stein's hands went slick. His thoughts started tripping over one another. *I have to go. But I can't go empty-handed.* Standing in the doorway of the room, the panicked river of people now a worried creek, he saw a yellow blur and a glint of metal.

"*Mounira,*" he whispered to himself sinisterly.

As the eleven-year-old girl went by, he grabbed her by the cape and threw her into the room, slamming her into the table at the far end. Kicking the door closed behind him, he looked down at his trembling hands.

His heart was pounding. Pushing up his glasses, he

stared at the mechanical arm and the strange backpack hidden under her cloak.

"Anciano Stein?"

Without diverting his gaze, he reached back and slid the simple bolt lock for the room. Taking a breath, he then straightened up, his mind going a mile a minute. *This is your chance. That arm will make all the difference. You will do far more with it than she ever will,* he thought.

"Sorry, Mounira, but I do so hate that title. My name is Doctor Francis Stein, but you can call me Doctor Stein, for short," he said, his sweaty hands clasped together. "With all the chaos, it should be obvious no one will hear you." His eyes darted about, his hands shaking. "And if we can, I'd like to make this quick and professional. Please give me that arm of yours."

With a jerk of her head, Mounira brought her mechanical arm to life. "You're one of them?"

Them? wondered Stein. He swallowed as he stared at the arm. What he'd thought before was that the arm was a simple skeleton. Now that she had activated it, pieces came out of the backpack and reinforced it. There was a hum from the motor behind her.

Panicking, he rifled through his pockets and pulled out a small knife. "Whomever you mean, no. I know opportunity when it arises. I need the arm… for my research. I don't want to have to kill you, but… but I will." He swallowed hard again, frowning in disbelief at what he was saying. "The difference is simply the amount that you'll scream before giving me the arm."

Mounira clenched her jaw, her short dark hair coming forward to frame her scowl menacingly. "Who said I was going to be the one screaming?" She stepped forward and moved her head to the side, hyper-extended the arm forward and grabbed him by the throat. She threw her weight sideways, sending him into the wall. The arm immediately retracted.

Shaking his head, Stein looked up at her. The fear was melting away, and the indignity of being beaten by an eleven-year-old kicked in. He got to his feet, a sneer on his face. "Impressive. I didn't realize it had that capability. But this only postpones the inevitable," he said, lunging at her with his knife.

Mounira blocked his arm and tried to sweep his legs but slipped.

He pounced.

She rolled out of the way and then, with her feet firmly planted, hit him square in the jaw with her mechanical fist.

As Stein blacked out, he stumbled forward and knocked Mounira off balance, sending her falling backwards into the wooden table.

A few minutes later, a piece of wood fell from the ceiling and smacked Stein on the head, waking him violently.

He rolled around, coughing on the stone dust that was in the air.

A rapid set of explosions went off somewhere down the hall; followed by the roar of part of the underground city collapsing.

Stein squinted at the open door and spotted his knife laying on the floor nearby. He shook his head, tears streaming down his face. "Oh, that was real? How could you have done that, Francis? How could you have stooped so low? You are better than that," he said to himself.

Forcing himself up, his chin quivering in shame, he turned to look out the window but something shiny caught his eye. Stein shook his head in disbelief at the sight of Mounira's mechanical arm embedded in the soft wood of the table. The strange backpack-contraption she'd been wearing was abandoned beside it.

"When she fell backwards, it must have gotten stuck. I must be imagining this." He reached out and touched it. "It's real." Taking a deep breath, he gave it a tug, but it wouldn't come loose.

Frowning, he went to grab it with both hands but stopped, peering over his shoulder, his heart pounding.

He glanced down at the arm and then hurried over to the door. Holding on to the doorframe, he looked up and down the empty hallway.

Sunlight was shining through where the ceiling was broken. He furrowed his brow at the sight of a Skyfaller going down in flames. *I don't have much time.*

Returning to the mechanical arm, he took hold of it carefully with both hands and planted a foot. With some force and wiggling, he finally got it free. He stared at his metallic prize in disbelief. "This will change my fortunes one day. It has to."

"Sir, you need to go," the guard said as she arrived at the door.

Abeland glanced over at her. He was hunched over an engine that was resting on the worktable, under it a sea of papers. "Still in Kar'm uniform I see."

"Yes. The bombardments are only getting worse," the guard replied.

"I can see that, or more accurately, feel it." Abeland pointed with one of the fine tools in his hands at a chunk of the ceiling on the floor. "I'm nearly done. I have to make sure that the chemical controls here are ready for transport." He sighed and slipped the tools into his pocket. "Can you cut up some of this tarp? We need to wrap this engine so that it can properly endure the journey back to our airship factory. It's the missing piece."

"Really?"

Abeland smiled and nodded. A young voice from the hallway caught his attention. "We're not leaving without that," he pointed at the dimly-lit, metal-headed horse statue in the corner. "There's a pull-switch in the mouth that will start its engine. The reins control the direction, the pedals control the throttle."

"Sir?"

Stepping out of the room, Abeland focused on the yellow-hooded girl running from room to room, panic painted all over her face.

"Christina!" the girl yelled.

"You're the one-armed, yellow-hooded girl. Christina's little protégé."

She froze and stared at him. "I'm Mounira."

"Can I help you? I'm a friend of Christina's."

"I don't recognize you, which means that you're not from Kar'm. And that means you're with them."

"Recognizing me doesn't seem to be your problem," Abeland said raising his eyebrows and softening his expression. "I'm not here to harm you. What's going on?"

Mounira lowered her gaze. "I can't find Christina. She's not outside. I've looked everywhere."

"Maybe she got out another way."

"My gut's telling me that she's still here," Mounira said.

The two of them lurched from side to side as a series of explosions went off nearby.

Looking over at the guard as he sliced through the tarp with a dagger, Abeland bobbed his head back and forth as he weighed the issues at hand. "Are you absolutely sure? Have…," he stared at Mounira, his heart sinking, "have you looked on the lower level?"

Mounira frowned. "Why would I look there?"

Abeland grabbed the doorframe.

Before he could say a word, the guard spoke. "I've got this, sir. We'll meet you outside where we rendez-voused earlier."

"Don't be late," Abeland said. "And don't let anyone touch this stuff. Even if you know they're on our side, I'd rather you put a bullet in them."

The guard nodded.

"Why would I look there?" repeated Mounira angrily, pulling on Abeland's arm.

He looked at her, swallowing hard. "Because that's where she was going the last time I saw her several minutes ago."

Christina knelt down, staring at Remi's face, once so full of life and strength, now bloody and with a dead-eyed stare. Her entire body was vibrating, from her quivering chin to her shaking hands. Her mind still unable to grapple with what she was seeing. She hadn't noticed Angelina running off, or that parts of the ceiling were falling down around her. All she could see was the loss of one of her best friends and bloody failure everywhere.

At the back of her mind, she heard Angelina's words from minutes ago. *Did she say something about people tackling a man with a bomb? And there being only a single survivor? One survivor. One.*

Christina's chest heaved, and her hands shook as she reached out and ran a finger along the side of Remi's face.

The room shook, and a two-foot chunk of ceiling came crashing down in front of her. She didn't move, not even a flinch, as the dust shot into her face.

A voice inside screamed for her to leave, if not to help the others, then for her own survival. The voice was drowned out by the crashing waves of guilt and regret.

"You shouldn't have let me in that day," she said to Remi's blank gaze, tears welled up in her eyes. "You shouldn't have listened to me. You weren't giving me a new world, I was infecting yours with my past." She swallowed hard and gestured about. "You trusted the wrong person to listen to. Why?" Her hand hung in the air, as if to smack him in jest, and instead, crumpled to the ground. The anger and rage she craved wasn't there.

Christina rubbed her nose and stared at the broken ceiling, swallowing hard. "I deserve this, not you. You should be towering over me." She bowed her head. "For once, I'm thankful that our interests were opposite, or we would have undoubtedly married and had a child. And right now, I would be grieving over them too."

For the first time since she was little, a tear escaped her emotional clutches and rolled down her cheek. She breathed in deeply and tried to push the sorrow back down, but there was too much of it.

Staring at the center of the blast, her head wouldn't stop shaking. "I should have seen this. The man with the cloak and that look, that strange look, it must have been him. It's so obvious now. How could I have been so distracted? How could I have not said something?"

The room shook violently, and wooden support beams crashed down around her. She coughed from the cloud of dust.

Closing her eyes, she laid down on the ground beside Remi and pulled his arm around her. "Can we stay like this, one last time, pretending there are stars above us, and we're wondering about the world?" Her chin quivered.

"I'm sor—" the word froze in her throat, refusing to come out. Another tear slipped out. "I failed all of you."

She drifted into a strange slumber, with crashes and bangs happening all around her. She thought of Mounira, rushing around in a panic, yelling. There was someone with her. She couldn't tell who, but she was certain he would take care of her.

Then she felt strong hands grab her and lift her up.

Her blurry eyes opened, and she stared at the bearded figure in confusion. "Abeland?" She passed out.

3

THE LITTLE MOUSE

In the Past
Thirty Years Ago

Christophe Creangle's gaze fell on the old grandmother clock atop his lit fireplace's mantel. His fork clattered onto the edge of the black-and-blue china plate and his chest tightened.

"Oh, my goodness, I have to go. It's nearly eight o'clock." He yanked out the napkin that had been tucked into the neck of his shirt and threw it over the top of his half-eaten meal. "I'm going to be late. I can't be, not this time."

He dashed over to the coat hooks by the door of the single-room apartment. "My apologies, Kolas. Enjoy the rest of the dinner, and feel free to leave everything.

I shall clean up when I return home." He started fighting with his coat, dancing around and cursing.

Nikolas Klaus stared at his close friend in a mix of confusion and amusement. "Christo?" He ate the bacon-fat glistening piece of broccoli that hung on the edge of his fork.

Finally, with his coat on, Christophe felt his pockets. "My notebook, where is it? It has a new story for her." Spinning around, he bolted over to his bedside table. "Ah, I found you."

"Wait, Christo, what are you doing?" Nikolas asked in their native language of Brunne. He knew it always had a way of calming his fellow inventor down. He waved his hands at the hourglass-shaped table he was still seated at. "We have plenty of food, and there's no Conventioneer meetings tonight. So, sit, yes?"

Christophe stood by the door, his face long and drawn, his eyes filled with terror.

Nikolas straightened up. The last time he'd seen that look on his friend had been three years ago. He'd stumbled upon Christophe cornered by a group of hooligans intent on beating him senseless for the crime of being a genius not in the employ—and following the rules—of the crown.

Each kingdom had their own Order of Conventioneers, run by a High Conventioneer who reported directly to the monarch. Their chief responsibility was to make sure the scientists and inventors under the crown's employ didn't contradict the beliefs or edicts of their divine leader.

Nikolas, who had himself been saved by another conventioneer, a young Marcus Pieman, had intervened and saved Christophe's life. Nikolas had then convinced Marcus, now a senior Conventioneer, to bring Christophe into the order.

While Christophe and Nikolas got along fantastically and pushed each other's inventive brilliance to new levels, Christophe constantly bristled and rebelled against the ignorant limitations that came with the title of Conventioneer and having to serve at the leisure of the king.

Christophe finally got his coat on. He pulled out his pocket watch and set the time to match the grandmother clock.

Nikolas waved him to come over with one hand as he used a napkin to wipe his mouth with the other. "A minute ago, we were talking about an *even more* revolutionary edition of our Magnetic-Copper-Magnesium engine, and now, you look like a man who is trying to outrun a raging river. Sit."

"I can't," Christophe replied. He put a hand over his eyes, a habit he had when trying to focus. "I'll need to hire a horse to get me there in time. The guards at the edge of our Conventioneer's villa complex will change in four minutes. I can still escape."

Nikolas got up, his hands out reaching for his

friend. "Escape? We are not in prison. Are you having an attack again?"

Briefly glaring at Nikolas, Christophe shook his head. "I love you like a brother, Kolas, but you are naive. This is a prison." He went for the door, but Nikolas grabbed him by the arm. "I will return in a few hours."

"No, wait. You keep disappearing, and I wasn't going to say anything, but even if it is a lady friend, it will be noticed."

"Kolas, I must go. Enjoy your gilded cage alone for a few hours until I return." Christophe pulled his arm away.

Nikolas put a hand on the door. "Whatever it is, tell Marcus. He can make it official. Look at Isabella and me, we are courting, and it's accepted. We have our outings, as long as they are planned and approved. You could do this too."

Christophe put a hand on the door handle and started opening it. "Out of my way."

"No," Nikolas said as he pushed the door closed. "I say nothing when you and Marcus argue. I say nothing every other time, but now... now, as your friend, I say enough."

"You say nothing? I bite my tongue every time you laugh and smile with that venomous demon. I can't understand how you can be so blind to Marcus' ambition and deceit. And Isabella," Christophe stopped himself, his fist clenched. "I…"

Nikolas' chest was puffed out, and he was glaring fiercely at Christophe.

"I am not trying to insult you," Christophe bowed his head, his words slowing down. "I must go now. I made a promise that I cannot break." He grabbed Nikolas by the arms. "You know me, Kolas. My sense of duty is everything, is it not? You know I will return out of my sense of duty to you, yes?"

With a furrowed brow and awkward sigh, Nikolas stepped out of the way. "Go."

Christophe put his hand on the handle and there was a knock at the door. The two men looked at each other.

Nikolas shrugged.

As Christophe opened the door, the chilly evening air came into the room, along with a captain of the guard. Two sergeants stood behind him, their hands on the short swords secured on their belts.

"Good, both of you are here," the captain said. "By order of the king, you are to come with me to court immediately."

"Now? No. In the morning, fine. The king won't even arrive until morning. He's not going to waste our time again." Christophe tried to push passed them but failed as the guards closed ranks and blocked the doorway.

"The king is already there, waiting for you."

"What is this about, Captain?" Nikolas asked.

"You are both under arrest. I don't have any more details than that." The captain's beady eyes shone from beneath his gold and green helmet. "And you will come with me, Creangle, conscious or not."

Christophe shivered as they walked passed yet another row of Conventioneer villas, his arms tightly folded. He could feel the eyes of his timid colleagues in their homes, watching.

Will none of you take a stand? Will you all hand over your ideas to the enemy who has killed your families and burned your communities? Of course you will, cowards. You are tinkerers and dabblers, he thought.

The piercing creak of an iron gate sent a bolt of fear down Christophe's spine. Looking about, he saw armed guards with crossbows at the ready, the tips of the bolts glinting in the moonlight. His fanciful ideas of a harrowing escape melted away.

He shifted from side to side as he stared down the long, walled path to the palace. He'd watched too many good men and women go down this lonely road, never to return.

Christophe swallowed hard as a sense of doom came over him. Closing his eyes and putting his hands to his forehead, he fought back the tears. *I meant to keep my promise this time, Meeshich, I swear it. I will find a way. I will be late, but I will come.*

Glancing over at Nikolas, he saw the worry, tainted with hope, on his friend's face. *You believe that Marcus will save you, don't you? How can you not see him for what he truly is, Kolas? Is it naiveté or hopefulness with you? I never know.* Christophe's lips curled up at the edges. *I pray that you are right. You deserve it.*

"Pick it up, it's not getting any warmer." The captain waved over his shoulder as they headed onward.

Christophe's shoulders drooped as he thought back to the thrill he'd felt over a year ago. He'd convinced Nikolas to throw caution to the wind and work with him on a secret project. For the first time, they would ignore Marcus' stifling advice and stay true to their revolutionary ideas.

Once it came to life, however, when the manifestation of their imaginations and hard work stood before them, Christophe had been unable to stop himself from showing it off to the king. He'd convinced himself it would humble the king's arrogant ignorance and have him toss aside Marcus, his principal advisor.

Now, in the cold, with the midnight ground crunching beneath his feet, Christophe wondered if his real goal had been to sabotage himself and his one true friendship.

Nikolas' expression had soured further. It reminded Christophe nothing of the look he'd had the day they'd set up shop in an abandoned warehouse on the edge of the city. Or when they'd found a retired blacksmith keen to help forge the gears and metal casing they would need. They'd thrown the dice of Fate, and now Christophe couldn't help but feel they'd come up snake eyes.

Christophe swallowed hard and glanced up at the full moon as they stepped up to the mouth of the palace. *Please, let this be just a chastising. Let me get to her, let me keep my promise,* he thought.

He turned to Nikolas as they walked past ornate statues and fine paintings. "I know you wanted to talk about your Solstice celebration idea tonight. I'm sorry I didn't let you. I think it's a very noble idea. Making presents for the poor children once a year, giving them something to look forward to, it's a good thing. You're a better man than I, Kolas."

Nikolas smiled appreciatively and then shook his head. "One day, we will have such a celebration."

Christophe's stomach turned at the thought that his actions and influence may have signed the death warrant for such a saintly man. He knew Nikolas made him a better person. His stomach twisted even further at what type of person he'd be without Nikolas around.

As their heels clicked and clacked against the

marble floor, Christophe felt his chest tighten. Then, in the middle of a thought, he stopped and looked about nervously.

"Just a moment, Captain." Nikolas reached out and gently took Christophe's hand, giving it a squeeze. "Christo, are you there?"

Christophe stared at him and then at their clasped hands. With a sigh, he nodded, and they started walking again.

"Thank you," he whispered to Nikolas.

Nikolas patted his friend on the shoulder. "There is no better way to walk through the gates of the damned than with a friend at your side, yes?"

A timid smile appeared briefly on Christophe's face.

The grand, red-and-yellow doors to the court opened, revealing a checkered marble floor leading to a platform four steps up. Upon it was the king, sitting on his large, stone throne, with a gaggle of sycophants around him. Several feet away, but still on the platform, stood Marcus Pieman, his head bowed. Midway between the king and the entrance door stood the king's aide at the ready.

Banging his six-foot gold-and-silver staff on the floor, the aide drew everyone's attention. "Captain, do you have Conventioneers Klaus and Creangle in your custody for the King of Teuton?"

"I do," the captain replied with a bow.

The aide turned to the king. "Then, Your Majesty, I present Klaus and Creangle."

"Thank you, Captain." The king stood up and glared down at his new audience.

He was a tall, heavily-bearded man with a notorious, omnipresent scowl. His family had been feared by their neighbors for generations for their ruthlessness and opportunism. The king's grandfather had engaged in long and bloody wars upon his rivals, wearing them down until they simply couldn't afford to fight anymore. Many saw the current king as the spitting image of his grandfather, in temperament as well as appearance.

He was dressed in a frilly collared shirt and dark purple robe that flowed down to the floor.

"Did you mistakenly say Conventioneers, Aide?" The king scoffed. "Conventioneers are to follow the will and edicts of the king, guided by the High Conventioneer." He shot a sideways glare at Marcus. "While other kingdoms have had frequent problems with Conventioneers misunderstanding their role, we have had remarkably few. But you both were the first to ever show a king that he demanded too little from his leashed geniuses. And yet, after you show me, you then refuse to show me more."

He descended the steps of the raised throne platform and gradually approached Christophe and Nikolas, two elite guards stepping out from the sycophants and following two paces behind him. "I brought you before me so that I may hear your answer directly. Will you build the weapons I have asked of you? Will you bring Teuton into a new era of strength and help keep our enemies at bay?"

Christophe stared at the wall-mounted crank lanterns he'd designed. "We have no enemies, but such actions, they will bring some. Is that what you want?"

"Ha." The king came right up to Christophe's face. "There's that inability to understand one's place. Is that what led you to sneak away from the palace, to steal from the treasury, and make the pieces for the mechanical horse you showed me?"

Anger flashed across Christophe's face. "We didn't steal a thing. Neither time nor money...," he bit his tongue. "I am guilty of many things, but in my duty to society, I would never steal from the people or its ruler."

The king stood there, studying him.

Christophe nodded at Nikolas. "Kolas knew nothing of the deceptions that were done over the weeks of our work. He thought I was informing High Conventioneer Pieman," he said, swallowing hard and glancing over at Marcus.

Nikolas raised a hand in protest, but Christophe caught it and pushed it down. "It's okay, Kolas. I might as well give him everything, it's what he wants."

"It isn't, but you're amusing me," the king said. "I'd

offer for you to continue, but I have to know, is all of this a feeble attempt at humor? Hmm?"

The king smirked and folded his arms. "I am not an idiot. You could not have made the engine, never mind the rest of that horse, in weeks. My advisors tell me that it was at least a year, if not two. And that would be more than enough time for Klaus to have mentioned something, anything, to someone." He pointed at Marcus. "And I doubt his words; I find them hollow and unconvincing."

Christophe shifted his weight from side to side. He was hot and sweaty, his heart pounding. *Please let this end with words of warning and quickly. I can still make it before she's asleep. At least let me keep the spirit of my promise.*

"No, I believe that young Conventioneer Stimple had the right idea about you two. You worked on your *four* King's-Horses for a year, showed me one in the hopes of diverting attention, and then planned on selling the rest of them to our enemies."

"King's-Horse?" Christophe frowned at the king.

"Yes, of course," the aide interjected. "Such a thing is only fine enough for a king. In the spirit of all things considered the most elite, the most coveted by the king, he has graced it with this name. Like the king's-men who serve as His Majesty's most trusted advisors and emissaries among the people, it will have the hyphenated name to signify its greatness."

The king smiled and ascended the stairs to the raised platform. Pausing for a moment, he looked down at Christophe. "I felt it was only fitting. I admit, I enjoyed the roar of the mechanical beast, its speed, its power, very much. Not since I was a child have I found my imagination so awakened."

He brought his hands together in his lap. "You once said to me that you wanted to show me what you were capable of and then you did. And when I asked you to now engage that capability, to help the people of Teuton by creating the instruments of protection that I asked, your bravado evaporated. Am I a fool for not having seen you as a fraud, or are you foolish to be playing a dangerous game with the king?"

The room was silent, save for the sound of the king's fingers drumming on the arm of his throne.

Christophe stared at his boots, his mind racing. His clothes clung to him, and his throat was gummy.

"I was already of the mind to hang you both in the square, as traitors to the nation, but I was told to consider otherwise." The king glanced at Marcus Pieman and then pointed at him, shaking his hand. "He told me it is better to offer you a carrot, to give you an opportunity to reconsider your misguided and inappreciative answer, rather than beat you with the proverbial stick."

The king smoothed his beard. "He was right on one account. Hanging you would have brought no good to the kingdom. That said, I believe Pieman is wrong. Living in the darkness of a dungeon has a way of softening a man's politics, reshaping his obstinance into compliance. My stick to his carrot."

Christophe's head lowered a bit further. When they'd started, Nikolas had committed himself to follow Christophe's lead to the bitter end if needed. He couldn't believe that Nikolas had actually meant it, but there he was, standing beside Christophe, not saying a word. He looked at his friend out of the corner of his eye. *Why can't you just agree? Marcus will protect you however he can. Don't do this to yourself,* he thought.

The king moved to the edge of his throne. "Tell me, will you both perform your duties, create whatever I ask, and return to your life? I'd even be willing to forgive this transgression." The king glanced at Marcus again.

"I have remained true to my duty," Christophe snapped, glaring at the king. "My duty is to society, to make sure that my ideas do not bring about the pain that men like you inflicted upon my family and village." The words shot out before he realized it.

The king's face first went red with rage and then he erupted in laughter. As he laughed, the tension in the room rose and rose until even the aide's hands shook.

"It's like…," the king tapped a finger to his chin, "it's like you are a barbarian from a distant land with no understanding of our ways and customs."

The aide raised a finger.

"Yes?" the king said, amused.

"Barbarians live in tribes, do they not?"

"Excellent point." The king laughed again. "Tribes have chiefs, and barbarians show them respect, don't they? No, Creangle is a savage from a foreign land, painted in our color of skin and fluent in our language. You can dress a savage up, but his insolent, corrosive soul will show, won't it?"

Christophe's breathing had sped up and he stared at the ground with wide, panicked eyes. Every time the idea of submitting rose up, images of the death and destruction he'd witnessed beat it back down. "I am a man who was hunted by the ravenous dogs of mad kings, drunk on power and ego, armed with the weapons made by people like me."

The king glared at Christophe, sending a chill through him. Christophe raised his gaze to meet the king's and said nothing.

"Your friend has some sense. He knows to remain silent when his betters are speaking to him, and he is silent in loyalty to you, though I see it as foolishness." The king rubbed his hands together, the scowl back in full force. "You should know that my men found your workshop. We have all four King's-Horses. I turned three of them over to Conventioneer Stimple." He smiled at the shock on Christophe and Nikolas' faces.

"You may be marvelous at building all manner of

contraptions, but you have no understanding of what it is to hold power."

Christophe caught Marcus giving the king a menacing glance.

"And each of the engines they have opened has rendered itself completely useless, haven't they?" Christophe smirked.

"Is that so?" The king looked at Marcus. "Have you heard anything?"

"I have, Your Majesty." Marcus rocked on his heels.

"And?"

"It has not gone well, Your Majesty."

The king glared at Marcus. "Speak."

Marcus scratched the side of his face and slowly looked up at the king with a steely-eyed gaze. "It has been a wasteful mess, to be honest. Stimple, in his eternal over-eagerness, ignored my advice. All three of the engines' booby traps were set off, and their chemical and mechanical secrets ruined." Straightening up, he looked at the two Conventioneers. "Perhaps had I not been sidelined and made to witness the horrors from afar, we could have had—"

"Enough. You will not have your hands on a single one of these so long as I live," said the king, his face twitching.

He moved his purple robe around. "Any more philosophy or proclamations, Creangle? Please, speak now like you were talking to a god in your final moments." He gestured toward the ceiling. "I heard it's needed by the condemned."

Nikolas stepped forward.

"I have no interest in what you have to say." The king waved a dismissive hand at him, which was copied by the aide. "Pieman has spoken more than enough on your behalf, and I care not to hear another word of how you had no involvement in the engine itself."

Christophe lowered his gaze and ground his teeth. Out of the corner of his eye, he saw Nikolas shaking his head in disbelief.

"Any more words of wisdom, Creangle?" the king boomed.

Clenching his hands into fists, Christophe took a deep breath and lifted his head. As the words organized themselves into a final blistering attack, he saw a giant, looming grandfather clock in the corner of the room.

I'm supposed to be there. My promise is broken. Christophe's face went pale. *I've failed.*

"In your tiny cell, you should pray, Creangle. Pray for the wisdom to change your mind or that my Conventioneers cannot figure out your little miracle. For if they do, then you are of no value to me alive." The king waved at a crank lantern. "As with all things, they will figure it out in time. And so, I ask this final time, will you, Christophe

Creangle, make what I ask of you without question?"

Christophe looked up, his head held high. "No."

"And so, we finally come to you, Nikolas Klaus. Will you build whatever I ask, without question?"

Nikolas straightened up. "Since I was rescued off the streets by Marcus, I have helped invent many things. Yes, I am like Christophe in many ways, but I cannot make the types of things you ask."

"Yes or no," the king bellowed, his face red.

Nikolas clasped his hands together and looked down at them, silent for a moment.

Christophe swallowed hard. He leaned over. "Don't follow me. Please."

Nikolas shoved him back with a shoulder. Staring at his hands, his fears played out on his face. "Weapons and instruments of pain... I will not build these things." He lifted his gaze and stared at the king. "I cannot. Even if it means not seeing my beloved again."

The king shook his head and glared at Marcus. "And here I thought you would most certainly be wrong. But once again, you are right where my other advisors are wrong."

Marcus offered a tight-lipped smile. "May I say something to them? To him personally, Your Majesty?"

With a nod from the king, Marcus hopped off the platform and came up to Christophe. Looking him right in the eyes, Marcus whispered, "Your greatest achievement in all of this was you prevented me from helping you in any way. Despite all of this, I will try my best to see you both released."

"We both know you mean you will help Nikolas, and that's okay." Christophe shrugged passively. "It doesn't matter."

"I mean you too, you idiot." Marcus glared at him and then stepped aside, following Christophe's gaze to the clock.

The guards came and took Christophe and Nikolas by the arms, hauling them away.

I'm sorry, Meeshich. I did my best to see you. I hope one day you will understand. Duty to society above everything, even one's own heart, thought Christophe.

"Christina, please close the window. It is bitter cold, and you need to go to sleep," the innkeeper said as she folded the last of the towels.

She stared down at the four-year-old girl, who like her, was dressed in a brown bonnet and dress with a black apron. The old woman could hear the little girl's teeth chattering, but she knew that Christina could block out the world if she needed to. The candles mounted on the wall threw shadows about as if there were other children there lending Christina their support.

Christina's elbows were propping her up on the white window sill, the rest of her body lying on her bed. For over an hour, she'd been eagerly gazing out the second-floor window into the solemn darkness of the night, her heart slowly sinking.

"I can't, Auntie. He hasn't come yet. Papa always comes every second Tuesday. This is the second Tuesday." She raised a finger. "And he promised he wouldn't miss any more."

"Christina Creangle, your words. There are so many of them. How do you know so many things?" Auntie let out a heavy sigh and picked up the towels.

"I hear them when we work. They just make sense to me. Like the little things I can fix."

Auntie's attempt at a smile soured as she glanced out the window. She'd hoped she'd be wrong today, that for the first time Christophe would show up as he'd profusely promised two weeks ago.

Sadly, since Auntie had gotten up that morning, she'd known how the day would turn out. To distract herself, she had helped her sister to prepare a new edition of the argument they threw at Christophe every few months. They couldn't understand why he wouldn't take Christina with him to live in the palace, as they'd heard that other Conventioneers had family in residence with them.

"Auntie?"

"Yes, Meeshich?" She tapped Christina on the nose.

"Do you call me *little mouse* because my Papa does? Or does he call me *Meeshich* because you do?" Christina took the towels from her auntie's arms. She then scooted to the end of the bed and ran over to help put them on the shelves.

With the job done, Auntie sat down on the edge of the bed. "Sit with me. Come."

Christina hesitated. "Is it okay if I stand? I'm taller this way, and maybe I can see Papa when he comes."

Auntie put her loving arms around the little girl who had been dropped into their lives three years before. Christina's mother, a close friend, had died, and Christophe came to the inn with the two-year-old and a million promises.

"I see the clock you made last week." Auntie pointed at one of the two objects that decorated Christina's room; the other being a black, wooden horse the little girl had made herself. "And I think of all your words, and I wonder how all of this can be in such a small girl." She rubbed Christina's belly, making her giggle.

Christina smiled at the clock, its second hand going around backward, a particular delight for the little genius. "You know, I made it from three broken ones."

"Oh, I know." Auntie's heart warmed as she saw the ever-rarer triumphant smile on Christina's face. She laughed and planted a kiss on the top of Christina's head. "You have told me almost as many times as my sister has told me. And it is the best clock I have ever seen. It is so beautiful."

She turned her head away from Christina and braced herself. "I don't have my glasses. What time is it?"

Christina thought. "Eight forty-two."

The old woman didn't want to ask the next logical question. It would be knocking over the final domino, but it had to be done. "And when is your bedtime?" She rocked Christina gently back and forth, her gut twisting with anxious anticipation.

Auntie felt the little girl's body stiffen and her body suddenly heat up.

Gently pushing the woman's arms away, Christina raised her little square-jawed face. "He's not coming." Her voice was soft, almost like hearing a breeze, but the words were wrapped in a lifetime of pain and disappointment.

As Auntie ran a soothing hand down Christina's back, she thought of how each time Christophe didn't show, it stole another piece of Christina's soul.

Putting aside her smoldering rage at the man, Auntie took Christina by the hand. "It's time to get ready for bed now."

Christina nodded.

Without another word, Christina washed her face, got dressed in her simple nightie, and got the candle for the final part of their day. "I think I have no stains today. I was very careful."

"Let's check," Auntie said as they laid the threadbare clothes that Christina had worn that day on her bed. She kneeled, her knees cracking and her face twitching, then took the candle from Christina and started the inspection. They methodically passed the candle over every part, and finally, Auntie leaned back.

"You did a very good job, Christina. Very good. These can be worn tomorrow."

They folded up the pieces of clothing and put them on the night table beside Christina's bed.

"I am proud of you." Auntie gave Christina a warm smile.

The little girl was once again staring out the window, her gaze forward.

Pulling the covers back, Auntie patted the bed. Christina reluctantly climbed on to the bed and crawled across to the window.

Watching Christina's reflection, Auntie's heart broke as she saw the quivering chin and tears pooling on it.

Christina grabbed the sides of the window pane and slammed it down, throwing the latch and pulling the curtains.

Auntie bit her lip instead of scolding the little girl. Telling her to be careful with the window wasn't going to help matters. "Come here, come to Auntie," said the old woman, reaching over, tears rolling down her own cheeks.

Christina didn't move.

"He loves you, I know he does because he has told me many times." She scratched the side of her nose and glanced away. "And I am certain he will be here next week."

Christina allowed herself to be pulled into Auntie's embrace. She rubbed her face quickly, hiding all evidence of any emotions.

"You know, sometimes Christophe gets mixed up, Meeshich."

As Christina had too many times before, she curled tightly into the old woman's embrace and cried.

Auntie rocked her back and forth, but to her surprise, a minute later, Christina pulled away. "It's okay. You can let it all out."

"No," came the little voice. Christina gave Auntie a look that chilled her to the bone. "No more crying. Ever."

Christina gazed about the room, her fingers twiddling.

Auntie reached over and held Christina's hand.

"Will you always tell me the truth?"

Swallowing hard, Auntie let out a hard sigh. "Yes. Yes, I will. You deserve that." She squeezed Christina's hand.

With a scowl, her little eyes darting about again,

Christina sat on her legs, her hands at her side. "Does Papa really live in a big castle and have to escape the dragon to visit me? Will the dragon eat people if he doesn't return or if he tries to bring me?"

Bending over and letting out a pained sigh, Auntie slowly shook her head. "It is... complicated."

Christina showed no sign of recognizing the response. "The note you gave me, was it really from him?"

Auntie nodded, relieved that it was indeed the case.

"It said that he promised tonight to take me to see a wonderful thing." Her eyes lit up. "It's a special horse that is better than all of the others and fit only for the greatest of kings." She beamed with pride at her auntie, bringing new tears to the old woman's eyes. "And I thought it was only in the stories he told me, but he said it was real. He calls it Black Beauty."

Christina stopped, the momentary joy dispelling, leaving behind a red face and watery eyes. "Is it real? Have you seen it? His King's-Horse?"

Auntie put a hand against her chest and grimaced. It took everything she had to continue gazing into the little eyes. They were so filled with pain and torment that for her, Christina was the embodiment of injustice.

"I can't answer these things...," Auntie's words slurred and she slumped against the wall.

"Auntie?" Christina tilted her head, her brow deeply furrowed.

The old woman swallowed hard, her eyes bulging. "Get... get my sister. Quickly."

"Auntie?" Christina screamed.

"Go Meeshich. I will be fine." She tried to pat her but missed completely. "Get her now... please," she said, drawing in a sharp gasp.

As Christina tore out of the room, the old woman lay down for her final rest.

4

GEARS THAT GRIND

In the Present
Six Months Later

An adult Christina stood, leaning against a four-hundred-year-old stone archway on the southern side of the Moufan's compound. She stared blankly at those passing by in the drizzling rain. Occasionally she noticed the brilliant, emerald moss that lined every stone and fixture, but instead of allowing it to remind her of playing in the backyard of the inn long ago, she bristled and shifted her position.

She'd explored nearly everywhere in the compound, regardless of whether or not it was officially permitted. It was the spy in her, as well as the survivor. Unfortunately, her mind was so muddled lately she couldn't keep straight what was where and didn't care.

The compound was set on a hill, with nearby lakes and the outskirts of the capital city of Doyono visible on a good day. It was the oldest of the Moufan tribes, and the root of the tree of their beliefs and customs.

Christina wondered if the only thing that had kept them together had been their allegiance to the now defunct Tub.

Surrounding the facility were high, stone walls that had stood the tests of time and turmoil, with arrow slits everywhere and guard towers at the corners. The north side housed the only official entrance, with a converted courtyard that was used to host merchants and traders. The Moufan rarely, if ever, received guests other than from other Moufan tribes, and usually they only sought a few days of hospitality at most.

Christina stared out at the smallest of the compound's three gardens, arms folded tightly. Over on the east side was the largest of the gardens. It was shaped like an amphitheater with the tomb of the founder at the base of it. She'd noticed suspicious comings and goings from there in the twilight hours when she wandered around, unable to sleep. She took shallow comfort in the idea that it wasn't her place to say anything.

Mounira's laughter drew her gaze over to the garden's wrought iron gazebo where her now fourteen-year-old protégé was spending time with Christophe.

They had cards in their hands and three chess boards stacked on bricks, with pieces setup in a pattern that only made sense to them. Christina had marveled at the evolution of their strange game over the past few months. She wondering if it made any sense, hesitant to ask and find out that it didn't.

Mounira glanced up at her and waved, but as she'd done since the first day they'd arrived, Christina shook her head and kept her distance. Taking a breath, she shifted her shoulders and leaned against the wall. She looked forward to dinner, when she and Mounira would sit down, and she would be bombarded by her young protégé's recounting of the events of the day and the million questions she'd come up with.

Christina bowed her head and smiled. She was proud and thankful that Mounira could both engage fully with the apprentice Moufan and still have the time and energy to sit with Christophe.

"Come over," Mounira mouthed, waving for Christina to join them.

Christina shook her head and straightened up.

Mounira turned a hand up.

"You know why," Christina whispered to herself. She shook her head again and Mounira returned to the activity.

For the first time in a long time, Christina hadn't

had to fight with herself, tooth and nail, to get out of bed. Her dreams were no longer haunted with the final images of Remi and instead the familiar ghosts and fears of her childhood had returned. Breathing was becoming easier and her soul lighter.

A grey-hooded figure exited the building from the door behind Christina and came to stand beside her. "Xenia Creangle," he said with a partial bow.

"Deputy Leader."

He followed her gaze. "Your father, Xenio Creangle, seems well today."

Christina looked at him, her steely face and eyes offering nothing. She found it strange that the Moufan used their word for *invited stranger*, Xenio and Xenia, all the time. It seemed like, under the guise of being polite by offering a Moufan honorific, it was actually a way of reminding everyone that the person was not truly welcome and, most importantly, was not one of them. Every time she heard it, it reminded her that one day she and Mounira would need to leave, and what then?

"I saw him the other day, he was... less well," the man said.

"Today seems a better day." She changed her position and then returned to leaning against the archway. "But tomorrow? Who knows? Who knows indeed?"

"It saddens me that such a mind as his is rotting away, with no salves or remedies able to do a thing."

Christina bristled at the remark and straightened up, her cheeks going red.

"I meant no offense," he said, raising a hand. "But, my leader and I, we have a deep appreciation for what he did for us and our cause." He folded his arms. "We were boys, hiding in an abandoned home on the edge of a town. He was walking by, a pack on his back, and noticed us. A day later, he left us with a working stove. Because of him, we survived the winter and discovered a Moufan tribe in the spring. He also had two occasions where the life of a Moufan was in his hands, and both times, he showed mercy."

Grinding her teeth, Christina nodded, listening. "He was a different man to different people," she said, grimacing painfully. She glanced at the embroidery on the trim of his cloak and the markings on his red sash.

"Honoring our personal debts, as well as our collective ones, has been a core principle of the Moufan for centuries."

Christina glanced at him. "And what of Rumpere? I've heard grumblings, I've seen gatherings; is it not a principle to clean out the infection before it consumes the body?"

The Deputy chuckled. "Stronger men than him have tried to disrupt our ways, he will fall away."

"Will he?" She waved a finger about. "The world's

changing, and there seems to be an appetite among your people for change to come here too, regardless of whether or not it's for the better." Her words came with an immediate pang of regret. *You weren't going to get involved. Don't start now,* she reminded herself.

"Men like Rumpere just test our resolve and dedication," the Deputy Leader said, puffing out his chest.

"There's a lot to resist, what with the lands, titles, and incomes the Moufan extracted from the Tub for helping at Kar'm."

As he glared at her, she looked away. "I am not one to argue about what happened," she continued, "it saved many lives. But those things, money and power, they have a way of changing people."

"You have an important perspective. Will you reconsider and join our ranks?"

She kicked at the dirt and shook her head. "Will I join to back your leader in a political war that we both see coming? There's no point. No matter what I do, I'll be an outsider and my voice, if anything, could poison the support you'll otherwise have. Right now, I have not the heart or energy for battle. I am slow and sloppy; my mind's still distracted by the ghosts and sins of my past."

He put a hand on her shoulder and squeezed it. "You are formidable, and we could use you." Gazing out at the gardens, past the gazebo, he drew in a deep breath. "In my heart, I feel change is coming but I don't know which way the winds will blow. It would be good to have you with us."

"I have to focus on letting my soul heal and on those most important to me." She waved a hand at Mounira and Christophe. "If you'll excuse me, I need to walk about." She stepped into the drizzle.

"Would you like a cloak? The rain has just started."

"No, thank you." Looking at Mounira, she turned back to the Deputy. "I did want to say, once again, how much I appreciate you taking Mounira in as a trainee. I know that no outsider has ever participated before, and it has meant a lot to us both."

"I have heard that they give her no quarter."

"None. I believe they made it as hard for her as possible, but in her own words, she doesn't need friends here. I think the classes have given her balance, perspective. Not everyone is your friend, and those who oppose you aren't necessarily your enemy."

"That is good to hear." He started walking with Christina. "I am relieved to hear her fighting ability has improved so quickly. I was concerned having one arm would limit her."

"Mounira would argue it's everyone else who is restricted. She has made me look at a great many things differently." Christina smiled.

The Deputy laughed. "She most definitely would. I've heard much from her professors. She pushes them to the edge of their patience with her questioning, but most of them come away quietly appreciating her for doing so."

Turning, he looked in the direction of two posted guards at a set of large, steel and wood doors. "Some have mentioned that they'd thought putting her in the dungeon would soften her rebellious streak. But some people become all the more resolute from such things."

Christina looked at him and stopped. "Was Rumpere ever one of those men?"

"He was in and out for two years, but... the last time caused a small uproar." He pulled his hood back and stared at her, his soft brown eyes kind and concerned. His hair was braided in concentric circles. "We need more allies on the council."

"The others wouldn't accept it."

"Is that fear or your political savvy speaking?"

"I don't know," she said, looking at the red flowers in bloom at the edge of the path.

"Consider it."

"That I can do." Her words barely audible. "And thank you for the company." She turned on a path that would bring her back toward the gazebo.

"There's something else that I thought you should know," the Deputy said. "We received a confirmed report that several of Pieman's airships, called Hotarus, fought the Mad Queen's Skyfallers to a draw over the capital of Belnia. The kingdom is in ruins, and the lands are being carved up by both the Piemans and the Mad Queen. I would guess that her ambition is stalled, for now."

She stared at him, her pulse racing. "And what of Abeland Pieman's manufacturing facility? I know you are aware of it, I saw you carrying a report the other day."

He narrowed his eyes at her.

"You know something else," Christina said.

The deputy nodded slowly. "It would seem that the Mad Queen learned of it first. It has been completely destroyed. The Moufan tribe sent scouts to investigate. They said there was nothing left; just charred remains and skeletons."

Christina rubbed the bridge of her nose. "And what of the Hotarus that fought over Belinia?"

"To the best of our knowledge, they were destroyed."

She looked at her father in the distance and let out an uneasy sigh. *Abeland wouldn't have had time to perfect the process of making more MCM engines. At best, a handful of people would have understood how they worked. He would have had them working around the clock.* "How was the manufacturing facility destroyed?"

The Deputy scratched his chin, his hesitation palpable. He leaned toward her. "The locals say that Skyfallers appeared, attacked, and left quickly. I interpret that as an ambush."

"Good." Christina ran her hand through her hair. *Abeland's not changed since I met him decades ago. If there was a traitor, he'll find them and destroy any signs of my father's technology.* She sighed again and straightened up. "Thank you. I fear what comes, though. While the Mad Queen bides her time, everyone will be racing to find an edge, to build up their strength."

"That's what we're seeing," the Deputy said. "But you should also know Marcus Pieman revealed two critical things to the world as part of this. There's apparently a system for sending messages from city to city, a labyrinth of machines and pipes. It's being called a Neumatic tube, after its inventor Tulu Neuma. There's also a system of rails with a muscle-powered craft, called a rail-raft. It would explain how the Piemans were able to communicate so quickly and move their airships about by land…"

Christina stared blankly at him, having known of the rumors for years, but never having seen proof. "This will change everything."

"It will. But with that, I must take my leave." He pulled up his hood and left.

She stood there, staring at the ground, her mind going a mile a minute with the implications of these two inventions having been made public.

Wiping her wet face, she continued walking toward the gazebo when she overheard someone yelling nearby. She turned to see three men clustered together.

"You will listen to me and you will do as I say," Moufan-Man said as he put another one up against a tree by the throat. Two others were flanking him, watching for unwanted observers. "You will do as I say or you will be on the list of those we will hunt like dogs when my day comes."

Christina clenched her jaw, and she narrowed her eyes, as she recognized the ruffian's voice. It was Rumpere. *I can't get involved. Whatever happens, Mounira and I will likely be long gone when this all explodes. We're just guests here.*

The short aggressor's hood slipped back, confirming it was Rumpere. He noticed Christina looking at him and shot her a glare. Holding it for a second longer than she knew she should, she then looked away.

"Know that if you stay, your time will come," Rumpere said.

As Christina headed for the gazebo, she rubbed the back of her neck. It didn't matter what her gut told her. For once in her life, she could just wait out the problem, couldn't she?

"Ah, for crying out loud," Oskar grumbled as he looked down at his manure-covered shoes and then glared at the horse and cart trotting down the street.

"These are still new. Have you no respect?"

Glaring at the people around him, Oskar pulled sharply on the sides of his oversized jacket, and there was a loud tear as several stitches came loose.

Hot and grumbling, he marched over to the corner of a building and leaned against it. He scraped the manure off his shoes as best as he could. With a satisfied smile, he stared down at them and exploded into a barrage of curses. The shoes were now covered in scratches.

The town clock tower gonged in the distance.

He immediately perked up. "Already?" Giving his shoe another rub on the wooden sidewalk, he glared at a couple that were shaking their heads at him. "What? You would do the same." With a dismissive wave and loud curses, he hurried off.

Stopping at a corner and noting the street sign, Oskar pulled out the letter he'd received the day before from his sister, Petra. He stopped and read it again.

He scratched his head. "Why would I go and see an antiques client of yours? You're a day away by coach, you go see if he needs someone to assemble furniture. I don't need your pity, your charity." He crumpled up the letter and threw it away. "And how did you hear that I was looking for work anyway, Petra? Do you have spies?"

A finely dressed man as Oskar nearly banged into him absentmindedly. "Watch yourself."

"Yes, so sorry. My brain, it is very full. So many ideas," Oskar replied.

The man took no notice.

Oskar turned about and found himself at the very place he needed to be. Before him were familiar, grand, black doors with gold trim. Swallowing and lowering his eyes, he climbed the steps and gently took hold of the gold knocker, shaped like a monkey's paw.

His stomach turned. How could things have gone so badly, so quickly?

Banging the knocker twice, he turned around and gazed down at the street, soaking in the misplaced admiration from the few that offered it. "It's a good club. I've been coming here for a long time," he said, an unconvincing smile on his face.

The door opened, and the butler's warm expression transformed into a dark scowl. "Oskar." She let his name hang in the air like a foul smell. "I will admit, I'm surprised to see you have returned. Have you come to pay your outstanding balance?"

She was over six feet, and her hair was in braids that encircled her head, making her seem even taller. As always, she wore a starched high collar with a fine, long, black jacket that went down to her knees and black trousers.

Oskar grabbed his own collar and pulled it forward. "I... I will get the payment. This is all a misunderstanding. You see, I've been helping my sister with her antique business. Very important business, growing very quickly. Have you ever been to Teutork? What a city. She's just outside of it, very famous. Just down on her luck, so I'm helping her. I'm good for it."

"You were deemed *good for it* for the second month fees, but then came the matter of the third. Then there's the matter of your fine for brawling. This is not a low-class tavern. This is a place of opportunity, relaxation, and diversion. Behavior like yours would not even be fitting for those criminal organizations that call themselves *establishments,* let alone for a gather place of elites like Abeland Pieman."

"He's here?" An excited smirk appearing on Oskar's face.

She glared at him.

Licking his lips, Oskar rubbed his hands together. "There's no need to talk like that. I'm a good man. A man of class." He smoothed his shirt. "I'm just helping out my sister."

The butler looked down at his shoes and wrinkled her nose. "A hypothesis sadly not supported by the evidence. Good day, Oskar."

She went to close the door and he put his hand up to stop it. "No, wait." He brought his face right up to the door, inches from hers. "I was asked to come to fix the furnace," he whispered.

"I am well aware." She glared at him, her scowl making him recoil. "And as you should be well aware, this entrance is for members only. The one in the back is for services and staff."

"Please, I won't stay. Just let me walk through." He smiled awkwardly. "You know, I almost met Abeland Pieman once before."

She shoved the door closed.

Oskar stood there, glancing about, sweating profusely. He hit the door with a fist and then scurried down the stairs and around the corner.

"Well, it's been a while," a well-dressed woman said. Behind her were several men and women, all dressed in what they claimed was casual, but to Oskar seemed opulent.

"Oh, hello everyone." He pulled at his collar and brought his together in front of him. *What's her name again, this talkative one?* thought Oskar, looking at the woman in the front.

He'd met the group on his first day at the club, and they'd taken a strange liking to him. He'd only managed to financially survive hanging out with them for a month before his fortunes had started to sour. Alcohol, and the easy acceptance of promissory notes, had stretched out his time with them for a bit longer.

A gentleman in a top hat took it off and stepped forward. His short, auburn hair was slick, almost painted on his head. "Coming to the club today, Oskar? We haven't seen you since that bout of fisticuffs you had with that other inventor. What was his name again?"

"Marconi, I believe," another man said.

"Yes, Marconi. Brilliant fellow. He called you a fraud, if I recall."

Oskar stared at the ground and nodded. "He did."

"Good for you, standing up for your honor, fine be damned." The talkative woman glanced and waved at her crew. "Don't you think?"

Many of them nodded.

"That was the most fun I've had at the club in quite some time. I must say, what you lacked in technique, you certainly made up for in gusto."

"Thank you." Oskar drew his eyebrows together and then flashed an awkward smile at her.

"What's wrong with your attire? You look a bit rumpled," one of the men said. "Busy night?" He gave a wink.

"Ah." Oskar looked down at himself, unable to see anything wrong. "A story I can't tell." He grimaced. "What do you call it? Gentleman's honor?"

There was a laugh from the crowd.

The talkative woman shuffled forward a step. "Listen, what you should do is pop home and change and then join us at the club."

"I'd listen to Mariana," a woman behind her added.

Oskar rubbed his chin and then folded his arms in

tightly. "I was there earlier. I spoke with Abeland Pieman."

"The former President of Teuton's son? I thought he was in hiding," the first man said.

Mariana's eyes went wide. "That's remarkable that you were able to talk to him, Oskar. Bravo. I've heard it's nearly impossible to get through his entourage these days. Fear of assassination and all that."

Oskar swallowed hard.

"Say you'll join us. We'll even order you a drink. What would you like?" Mariana asked, taking Oskar's hand and giving it a pat.

He stared at her. "Ah, sadly, I cannot... Maria?"

She raised a disapproving eyebrow at him, as the man with the top hat leaned forward. "Mari*ana*."

"No." Oskar let the woman's hand go and pretended to look through the crowd. "I thought I saw someone waving at me. A friend, Maria. Never mind."

"Oh, my apologies," the man said.

"So, what do you say?" Mariana asked.

"Sadly, I cannot." Oskar offered the group a wide smile. "I have a client commitment. A very important client, terribly important. They have asked for my expertise in a matter of machines, and I cannot keep them waiting."

"Ah, our work never ends, does it?" another woman said. "Those lesser people, always in need of helping. Sigh. It is our way. By the way, how are you doing with that horseless carriage venture of yours?"

"Huh?" Oskar frowned at her and then his eyes went wide as he remembered the lie he'd spun last time. "Oh, well."

The talkative woman turned to the rest of the group. "Did I tell you I was recently approached by someone looking to build a plant for making horseless carriages? She's already making two a year and believes she can get it up to ten by the end of next year. She wanted to set up shop south of here." She turned to Oskar. "Do you know her? Her name's Harriet Ford. Maybe I should connect the two of you?"

"Ah, no." He looked away and scratched the back of his neck. "I bet she's using one of the older designs, a lot of people are using those. They change a door, change a wheel, but it's still based on an old design. My design, very revolutionary."

One of the men scoffed. "Old? The only person to have one that I've ever heard of was President Pieman himself. Now there are a few, but still, old?"

"Mine will be revolutionary," Oskar's face lit up, his nostrils flared.

The group glared at him quietly.

"But I can still bring you all in as investors. There's not much time left." Oskar bowed his head and leaning forward.

"Well, we'd love to Oskar, but I think I speak

for all of us when I say we can't do a thing without a prospectus. Our accountants won't release a penny. I'm sure yours is the same way," Mariana said.

"My wife won't allow me to leave the house without a prospectus," the top hat man quipped, getting a laugh out of the others.

"Yes, of course, a ... prospectus." Oskar rubbed his hands together and looked away. Pulling out his pocket watch, he snuck a glance at it. "Ah, I am late. I must go. Have a good day." He lowered his head and started walking.

"Get that prospectus done and bring it to the club. We'll be regularly at the club from two to five for the remainder of the week," said Mariana. "Won't we?"

Everyone murmured their agreement.

"Yes, of course." Oskar hurried around the corner. As the services entrance came into view, he stopped and looked down at his pocket watch, still clasped in his sweaty hand.

For a week, it had read the same time. Its once-shiny gold color was looking more red-brown, and the glass on its face appeared foggy from the constant rubbing inside his vest pocket.

Stuffing it back into his pocket, he walked up to the lightly-stained, wooden door. Above it was a sign that read Services. Beside the door was a small silver bell and a hammer on a chain.

Oskar looked around and then rushed up to the door and hit the bell with the hammer.

He stood there for what seemed like an eternity, the bell of his misfortune ringing in his ears.

The door opened, and the butler's voice bellowed. "Enter. I've been informed if you get it done within the hour, they'll remove an additional twenty off your outstanding debt of three hundred and fourteen."

He grimaced painfully, twisting his head from side to side in an ambiguous nod. "Okay," he said, wondering if they had something he could set up to break while he was in there. Maybe if he was lucky, it'd be worth another twenty to fix tomorrow.

5

WINDS OF CHANGE

Mounira looked up from her sketchbook as a tall, grey-hooded figure approached. She was sitting on a wooden bench, shaded by a large and fragrant orange tree, at the southern-most end of the compound. There was a gravel walkway between her and the ivy-covered stone outer-walls.

Picking up a cloth to wrap the piece of charcoal she'd been using, she studied the gait and then shoulders of the approaching person. Even without looking at the informative trim on the edge of the hooded figure's cloak, she figured out who it was. Mounira smiled. "Good afternoon, Professor. Did I miss a history lesson?"

"You, miss a class? I doubt it." The woman came right up to the bench and gazed about. "This is a beautiful spot you've found. I can't say that in all my years here, I've sat here more than once or twice."

"The ivy and blooming flowers remind me of home. At this time of year, my home city of Catalina is covered in them. Have you ever been to Augusto?"

"To be honest, I've never been to any of the countries on that part of the continent. I heard you escaped at the start of the civil war."

Mounira's joyful facade slipped and she turned to look at the wall. "We were at a royal parade. Me, my parents, my siblings, my aunts and uncles, all of us were there." She scratched the side of her head. "I remember all of a sudden people started falling down and red was spraying everywhere. My little mind couldn't understand it, I was only nine."

She sniffed and shook her head. "I remember the expression on my father's face, the horror. He then focused on me, grabbed me, and ran. I got shot in the arm as we fled."

"I had no idea," the professor said. "And you lost it then?"

"As my father and I traveled north, I got sicker and sicker, until an old soldier forced him to cut it off." Mounira hung her head. "Sometimes, when my mind gets too quiet, I feel terrible for him having to do that."

The professor glanced at the other Moufan around. "For what?"

"I know my father," Mounira said, her cheeks red.

"He is the kindest, softest soul there is. My mother is the whirlwind, moving everything to get things done, her morality firm but focused on the greater good without question. For him to have to do what he did, I know it ripped his soul apart."

"Not as much as having you die would have."

Mounira nodded. "True."

"I heard you'd been left with a family in Mineau. Is that where you met Xenia Creangle?" asked the professor.

Taking a breath, Mounira stopped herself from correcting the small details. "Yes. Christina and I met, made a rocket-cart, and saved some friends. It was very exciting. Later, we went to Kar'm, and that's where Anciano Creangle made this."

Mounira showed the professor the picture she'd drawn. "He doesn't remember making me the mechanical arm, though he smiles when I draw pictures of it."

"What happened to it?"

Making a fist, Mounira swayed her head back and forth, remembering Christina's warning about not over-sharing with anyone at the compound, for their first loyalty was always to the Moufan.

"I fell backwards into a table, and the arm got stuck in the soft wood. I had to abandon it. I came back later, but it was gone," Mounira. Said, smiling at the picture. "Sometimes I try to design a new one, sometimes I draw it."

"Do you miss it?"

Mounira shook her head slowly back and forth. "No. But I am curious about it. My mother would say that my days with this thing are not done, and this is the way of Fate telling me." She smiled.

"I've never had a student like you. You fight with the written word, but it doesn't matter. You absorb everything else, and you reflect on it. You'll be a remarkable woman. I wish I'd been able to teach you for the rest of your time here."

"What do you mean?" Mounira asked.

"I'm retiring."

Brushing her shoulder length hair in front of her eyes, Mounira stared at the shadowy face hidden under the grey hood. "I overheard you two months ago, telling another professor that you were retiring in two years."

The woman turned to look in the opposite direction. "Written words fatigue your mind, but you catch everything else, don't you?"

Mounira noticed the professor's chin was up and casually glanced in the direction it was pointing. There were two Moufan-Men hanging around suspiciously.

"Walk with me to the southern garden?"

"Certainly, Professor."

They stood up and started walking.

Mounira scratched her arm. "May I ask you a

question that has been bothering me for some time? I feel embarrassed for not knowing the answer."

"You shouldn't. You're vanquishing ignorance. So please, ask."

"There are men and women Moufan, correct?" Mounira glanced at the professor, and to her relief, saw no judgment.

"There are." The Professor smiled. "But your real question is 'Why do we sometimes say Moufan-Men and sometimes say Moufan, but we never say Moufan-Woman?'"

Mounira nodded.

"That has to do with our legacy. Our way is that of the Moufan. Long ago, we were rebels with a way against that of an oppressive region. And the men in Moufan-Men does not refer to males, but rather it refers to those who embody the spirit and learnings of the Moufan. So, I am a Moufan-Man, or you could say I am of the Moufan. Or if I were a guard, a Moufan-Guard or a Moufan-Man standing guard."

"Huh." Mounira smiled. "Language is a funny thing."

"It is indeed, as is politics." The Professor ran her hands along a patch of purple and white flowers. "The winds of change are strong and have come faster than I had hoped, and my poor little boat has been blown ashore, I'm afraid."

"Professor?" Mounira shifted the sketchbook that

was under her arm and snatched a low hanging orange as they passed by.

"Oh, I love your innocence Mounira, but I know you know. I could see it in your eyes when I asked you to walk with me."

Mounira grimaced. "Christina says I need to be careful with what I see and more so with what I say." She looked at the Professor. "Did you come to warn me?"

A nervous laugh escaped the professor. "And here we have the other side of the enigma that is the one-armed girl from Augusto. An innocent question on one side, and the sharp insight on the other."

The Professor rubbed her bony hands together. "I did come to warn you. There's a man at the center of this political storm, Rumpere. He came to us from a north-eastern Moufan tribe; a tribe that was wiped out. It's said there was one survivor, a young woman a few years older than you, they call her the Fox. Some believe that she foiled Rumpere's plans, and that he destroyed the tribe in retaliation. But what's true, and what's story, I have no idea. Then he came here. I've heard it said that he sees a lot of the Fox in you, so be careful. If given the chance, he will come after you. The only saving grace is that he is rarely impulsive. He will make sure that his actions will have enough support, that they will be seen in the right light, and only then, will he come."

Mounira stared at the professor in disbelief. "Why is he allowed to be here? He sounds terrible."

"These things are just rumors. Should we judge people without proof? Those are the acts of tyrannies."

"No." Mounira furrowed her brow and stared at a newly planted tree surrounded by bushes. "It's because he has friends in high places here, isn't it?"

"Enough to have opened the door for him, and then his words about a new era for the Moufan have charmed the hearts of enough to tilt any judicial decisions in his favor, save for the gravest of crimes. For all I know, it might be for the better."

"But you don't believe that, do you, Professor?"

The woman shrugged. "I have seen a ship in the sky. Something that I thought to be utterly impossible just a few years ago. So, what do I know? I'm just an old woman."

"You're a great teacher," Mounira said with a spring to her voice.

"Promise me you will be careful, Mounira. Don't give Rumpere, or his people, any excuse to act against you or the Creangles. Rumpere is not a man to ever forgive and forget, regardless of what he says. Now, I must leave you."

"Will you still be around?" Mounira asked.

"You'll always be able to find me in the gardens in the morning. I'll be retired, not excommunicated."

"Thank you for the talk, Professor."

As the woman walked away, Mounira noted all the hoods turned in her direction. She could feel them whispering.

Glaring out at them all, she bit into the orange and spat out the chunk of peel.

Jacqueline Benstock clutched the edge of the worn, wooden counter. She glared at the stained and crumbled stacks of papers in front of her, her nostrils flared.

"You have an obligation to file my patent," barked the rotund man across from her. He thrust his large belly into the counter and stuck his nose in the air. "Do you even understand your job as a clerk? I have never been so rudely detained." He jabbed a finger in the air and glanced about to see who was watching.

Rocking back and forth, Jacqueline then let go of the counter and grabbed a towel she kept just below view. Wiping her hands first, she adjusted her spectacles and shook her head. "I have an obligation to provide a modicum of critical thought when accepting a patent application, which I believe is more than you have evidently put into whatever this heap of mess is supposed to be," she whispered to herself.

"Excuse me? What did you say?"

Ignoring the man, Jacqueline glanced over her

shoulder at the office manager in the pony-walled area deemed to be the back office. He was staring at the ceiling and muttering to himself. *Wondering if it's a water stain again, are you?* she thought.

"But even with only a casual glance at this upside-down supporting sheet of maths and physics, I can tell that yours has no merit whatsoever." She pushed the papers back toward him. "Now, if I may offer some advice? I recommend you consider enrolling in the elementary school down the street where you could learn both an adequate level of penmanship for writing on grownup paper, as well as the basic mathematics of multiplication."

The man's plump face went red, contrasting sharply with his tight, white, curled hair. "I will have you know that I am a professor."

Jacqueline's head twitched as she glanced downward. Shrugging off the reminder of her recently lost position at the University of Doyono, which had forced her to seek other employment in the city of Plance, she narrowed her eyes and grimaced at the man.

The man shook, his face going red. "Did you hear me?"

Peering over her spectacles menacingly, Jacqueline leaned forward. "Do you know how many idiots come in here and inflate their credentials, never mind their level of import? It would be enough to blow your mind. Why, I'm certain even a small one like yours would make a decent popping sound."

"This is unbelievable." The man laughed angrily. "Unbelievable." He slammed his hands on the counter and looked past Jacqueline. "Sir. Sir! I demand an intervention. It is not right that I suffer such abuse at the hands of this meddling clerk." His spittle went everywhere.

Jacqueline bit her lip hard and grabbed the edge of the counter. She knew she'd gone too far, but she didn't care.

It wasn't right that the royal family of Dery had been able to oust her as a professor so they could install a king's-man of theirs, simply because she'd had no royal support. It wasn't right that she'd been forced to leave the city she'd always considered home because her brilliant reputation fanned fears of inadequacy in potential employers.

Then there had been a glimmer of hope a month after her arrival in Plance, just when her finances were running out, with a job at the official Dery patent office as an analyst. But when she'd arrived for her first day of work, the manager had had a familiar look. Despite all of his bungling and excuses about there having been a mix-up about what position was actually available, Jacqueline knew it was because he'd expected J. Benstock to be a man. He wasn't courageous enough to have a woman analyst, not in Dery. It had made her blood boil and made her wish once again she'd had the finances to move westward, where no one cared about such petty things.

Despite her loathing of dealing with people in stressful situations, she'd argued with him to no avail. In the end, she'd taken the lesser position out of necessity. Every day since, she watched with fury in her eyes as the manager drowned in his pitiful and prideful attempts to handle the work that would have been second nature to her.

The client pulled on his tight collar angrily. "I demand satisfaction."

"I'm coming," the manager replied.

Jacqueline picked up one of the man's messily-written papers and slapped it down in front of him. "If you would kindly look at your summary trajectory calculations, you would see your ineligible and very odd Neumatic device, if we are to be as gracious and forgiving so as to call it that, is only capable of pushing a standard Neumatic message cylinder an inch, not a mile as you've claimed." She straightened herself up, claiming every part of her five-foot, five-inch height.

"What seems to be the problem?" the manager asked, coming around beside Jacqueline and leaning an elbow on the counter.

"Decimals, I'm afraid," Jacqueline cut the man off before he could even get started. "Those notoriously evil little creatures seem to have ruined this poor man's day and wasted my time."

The man pointed a fat finger at Jacqueline. "This infernal woman has done nothing but insult me. I have every intention to send a letter to the High Conventioneer of Dery himself and notify him of this."

Jacqueline touched her spectacles. "Well, by all means. I'd love to see what you consider a full sentence."

The manager put his hand on her forearm and she fell silent. "Miss Benstock, I do believe you are due for a break." He nodded at the customer, his eyebrows up. "I'll complete this transaction."

Folding his arms, the customer put on a sour face. "I suppose. It's small compensation for being assaulted in such a manner. These types of things have a way of spreading out into the community. And for what? For the crime of picking the wrong line?" He nodded his head at the other line, where Jacqueline's co-worker was motoring through papers and clients.

"You do realize she has no idea what she's doing, don't you, sir? She'd stamp a small child if she was presented with one." Jacqueline's fists tightened.

The manager glared at her. "Miss Benstock! I …," he laughed nervously. "I do believe that your employment with us is at an end. You may come in the morning for the monies owed to you, but I need you to depart immediately."

The customer nodded, a satisfied smile on his face this time.

"You're dismissing me? In favor of morons who will only create absolute chaos for our legal system in the years ahead because of their overlapping, non-sensical, illegitimate patents? You do realize the obligation we have to protect society from this sad sack of meat, don't you?" She shook her fists violently.

The manager banged his palm on the counter and flashed an exasperated smile at the customer. "It isn't for you to judge them. You are to process them."

"I was to judge the worthiness of their applications," she corrected. Claiming her purse from under the counter, she drew in a deep breath and closed her eyes. Opening them, she then smoothed her silver and blue dress. Slowly, with her head held high, she made her way to the hooks by the door where her feathered, wide-brimmed hat awaited her.

Unable to help herself as she left, she glanced at the people in line, clutching their applications. She stopped and tapped one held by an old, frail woman. "May I see that? From what I could read of it in your arms, and upside down, it seems interesting."

"What's she doing?" the irritated customer who had cost Jacqueline her job asked.

Without a second thought, the old woman gave it to Jacqueline, who sped through the papers. "Hmm. This has merit." She handed the application back. "Be careful. These men have a habit of losing our applications. And then, a few days later, by some miracle, one of their friends files the very same thing, and someone's got a bit of extra pocket money."

"Miss Benstock," the manager said.

With a final, stabbing glare at him that made the man recoil, Jacqueline exited the building and headed down the flagstone path to the main road and sat on the bench at the end.

She took off her spectacles, bowed her head, and rubbed the bridge of her nose. "Oh, goodness, Jacky, what have you done now?"

Her leg bounced up and down as she considered, rejected, and then reconsidered the humiliating prospect of going back into the office and apologizing so she could make rent.

Looking up and putting her glasses back on, she gazed at the flurry of people moving about. Her eyes set upon a man very much out of place.

He was a tall, thin man with sunken eyes. His hair was thinning and his clothes, though seemingly of good quality, were very dated and clearly had been mended several times. Over his shoulder was a single-strap backpack and in one hand, he had a medical bag that, even from fifty yards, had also seen better days. For some reason, he reminded her of a lost puppy, a noble spirit down on his luck.

She folded her arms and leaned back. She watched

as the man entered one place of business after another, each time coming out with a little less hope on his face.

As the man crossed the street, she felt someone watching her. Turning around, she saw the applicant she'd argued with inside.

"He's granted me my patent already," he said, thumbing at the office. The man walked away laughing.

Jacqueline screamed, noticing the attention of the stranger she'd been observing. He seemed to be keeping a polite distance.

"Tell me, good sir," she said, looking at the stranger with an exhausted and pained smile, "are we meant to waste away our days in service to our lessers? Are we meant to forever be in the shadow of the greats like Klaus, Creangle, and Neuma and beholden to royalty, king's-men, and their friends?"

The stranger scratched his thick beard, his eyes sliding back and forth as he reflected on her question. He walked over to stand beside her.

"I hope not, but I haven't seen any proof to the contrary," he said. "My name is Doctor Francis Stein." He put his hand out.

She looked at it and then studied his face. "A doctor of what sort? No offense, but I haven't encountered any doctors in such ..."

"Deplorable conditions?" he asked, glancing down at himself. "No, I suppose not. While I am trained, my credentials are of no value. And my hand isn't as steady as it once was. I hadn't noticed I'd developed a familial tremor over the past few years, until …," he put his hand against his chest.

"And how would you fail to notice such a thing?" The corner of her mouth turning up.

"I was a medical researcher … but the facility where I worked was destroyed."

Jacqueline's eyes went wide. "Oh my. A wrong experiment?"

Stein stared at her, his lips breaking into an all-out smile. "To be perfectly honest, it was bombed to pieces by Skyfallers. Some problem between the management and the Mad Queen, I suppose."

"I suppose so," Jacqueline said with a laugh.

"Would you mind if I sit? I've been on my feet since I arrived by mule-pulled cart this morning."

"Please." Jacqueline moved over on the bench.

"May I inquire as to your profession? Miss …"

"Benstock. It was once Professor Benstock, but being without privilege, my title has gone amiss."

Stein raised a finger and chuckled. "Well said, Miss Benstock."

"Ah, a man of wit." She gazed out at the carts going by, a grin on her face. "I was working at this patent office, but my employment was cut short."

"Oh?" Stein looked at the office. "What was the reason?"

Jacqueline turned, leaning an arm on the back of the bench. "As it happens, I am uncontrollably allergic to morons and this place is infested."

Stein burst into laughter, his hand over his mouth.

As she smiled, he went silent.

"May I ask you something, Doctor Stein?"

He nodded.

"That backpack seems out of place, as much as you seemed out of place in the crowd. I figure you have the medical bag to make the first impression and help establish credibility as a medical doctor, but why the backpack?"

Stein slid it off his shoulder and put it on the bench. "When the research establishment was destroyed, it changed me. I used to be someone who was afraid to speak out, and instead I bottled everything up. Then, I did something so out of character it shook me. I've learned something about myself through all of it."

"A man with self-awareness and humility?" She leaned in and stared at his face. "Hmm, you do not seem to be a woman. Maybe you're simply a rare form of man, at least for Dery. I've heard the Frelish are rather more open-minded and egalitarian. Anyway, go on," said Jacqueline.

"Well," continued Stein, giving Jacqueline a quizzical look for her remarks, "I've realized my problem is not in finding opportunities, for I am rather persistent. But when I have them in my grasp, I fumble them."

Jacqueline straightened up.

Stein lowered his gaze. "My apologies for sharing all of this, but your demeanor … it's rather disarming."

She laughed. "I do not believe anyone has ever accused me of that. Can I admit something?"

He nodded.

"I hate talking to people," Jacqueline said. "Not the likes of you, you're just fine." The corner of her mouth twitched into a smile and then back. "It's the in-the-moment dynamics of a hostile conversation, all of the elements at play, I usually get flustered and—" She stopped and looked at Stein. He was sitting there quietly, his eyes and face telling her he was engaged but not eager to take over the conversation.

"And then I unleash whatever searing comments are on my brain and the entire situation melts down. However, if you give me a moment to plan, to strategize, I can work miracles." Jacqueline sighed and they both stared at the street for a while.

Pursing her lips to the side, Jacqueline gave Stein a good, long look. There was something about the man that intrigued her. "Might I inquire as to what's inside the backpack? I find it's rather out of place."

"Oh." Stein glanced about nervously. "I haven't shown anyone, save for a few I'd hoped would invest in it. Again, a fumbled opportunity. And there used to be a mechanical backpack that operated it, but I had to sell it for parts. It was heavy, and sadly, I needed to eat."

"What is it?" She raised an eyebrow as he handed the backpack over.

"It's a mechanical arm that was made by Christophe for a girl at my facility."

She undid the leather strap of the backpack. "Christophe? That's an unusual last name."

"No, sorry. Christophe Creangle."

Jacqueline's hands stopped in mid-air as she was opening the top flap of the backpack. "You do realize there's a famous inventor by that very name."

Stein nodded and pointed at the bag.

"That would be impossible." Her expression twisted. "Are you a confidence man? Or did someone send you to mock me?"

"Nothing of the sort." Stein sat up straight. "Please, have a look. If you know his works, then hopefully it will speak for itself."

She laid the bag on the ground and opened it, allowing the sunlight to pour in. Carefully, she pulled out the arm and inspected it. "I do not mean to offend, but my sense of humor is rather dulled, particularly having worked here. Is this for real?"

Stein nodded.

Jacqueline narrowed her eyes, but after several seconds when his expression showed no change, she returned to examining the mechanical arm. "This is impossible. When did you get this?"

"A few months ago."

"Whoever made it replicates the style and brilliance of Christophe Creangle perfectly. If he hadn't died a long time ago, I'd have even wondered if it was by him."

Stein's eyes went wide. "Died?"

"Yes." Jacqueline leaned back. "What is it?"

"While he didn't have all of his mind, Christophe Creangle was with me at Kar'm."

"What's Kar'm?" Jacqueline put her hand over her eyes for a moment. "Surely you don't mean the old ruins in Myke? Are you saying you were visiting them and Christophe Creangle happened to be doing the same?"

Stein waved his hand. "Never mind. The point is, I was working as a medical researcher at a place where he would roam the halls and complain a lot. A shell of the legend, I'm afraid."

"Really?"

"Truly."

"And you are certain it was him and not potentially someone who looked like him, or coincidentally having the same name?" asked Jacqueline, carefully putting the mechanical arm back in the backpack like it was a newly discovered ancient relic. "And I remind you, I have no patience for pranks and the like."

"I am positively certain it was him. His daughter was there as well. Her name was—"

"Hold on." Jacqueline turned to see the manager storming down the flagstone path.

"Miss Benstock! Miss Benstock!"

To her surprise, before she could do anything, Stein got up and intercepted the man.

She scratched her head as she watched the two of them talk, at first loudly and with big gestures and then at a reasonable volume, and ending with a firm handshake and smiles. The manager returned to the office.

Standing up, Jacqueline frowned at Stein as he returned. "What did you say to him?"

"Nothing new, really." Stein glanced over his shoulder at the office.

"I don't believe that. I know that tone of his, he was ready to unleash some fury."

Stein nodded and then put his hands together in front of him. "What if I told you he'd like to offer you a contract position as analyst, starting tomorrow?"

"I'd say that you have a very cruel sense of humor." She waited, but once again, Stein's expression remained unchanged. "Is this for real?"

"It is. Is an analyst position good? I haven't the foggiest as to what it means."

"I do." She scratched the side of her head. "If I may,

how did you manage that? I thought you didn't do well without a plan."

He offered a boyish smile. "If I may be so bold, you inspired me. I didn't even think about getting up, I was just there. Before I had a conscious thought, his anger was gone, and we were negotiating terms."

She laughed. "Can you remember what you said?"

"Something about being a doctor, and in my professional opinion, you were simply the smartest woman I have ever met."

"Did you now?" She raised her eyebrows, her smile widening.

"I told you I was inspired."

"Well, Doctor Stein, will wonders never cease?"

"You may call me Francis, if you like."

She took his arm, her smile positively glowing. "Well, Francis, I do believe we are at the beginning of a most exciting enterprise."

6

ON THE SHOULDERS OF GIANTS

In the Present
A Year and a Half Later

The dusty, battered horseless carriage coughed to a halt between the front steps of a collapsed palace and its once-manicured garden. The overcast sky gave the ruins an eerie glow befitting their importance in Teuton's history.

"I have a much better design for a horseless carriage than this," Oskar said, looking about the inside cabin of the carriage. "This one is falling apart. And this ride? It has been a beating on my buttocks. We would have been better to save the money and come by horse."

"Where's this better design? As always, I see nothing," said his younger sister, Petra. She pulled on her high, dark brown boots and tucked her light beige pants into them. "Hmm?"

Oskar rubbed his face vigorously, shooting her a nasty glare.

Freshening up her ponytail, she stared back at her brother with the same fierceness. "Don't make me regret asking you to come, never mind covering the expense."

He puffed up his chest and was about to offer a sharp reply when he let himself deflate and nodded. "Though I am a very busy man, I always have time to help my sister."

"Nice words, but they have worn thin over the years. Screw me over again, Oskar, and I will shoot you."

He scoffed.

The driver banged twice, and Petra opened the door. "Do we understand one another?"

"Yes, yes." Oskar folded his arms and put his chin on his chest. As Petra climbed out, he continued. "You weren't going to shoot last year, and more importantly, you didn't need the money like I did. Look how much you waste on luxuries like this horseless carriage."

She waited until he was out before pulling on her brown leather gloves. "Waste of money? Did you know there's a new law here in Teuton that requires all coach companies to keep a record of who is transported and to where, for five years? But, strangely enough, if you have enough money, or influence, to allow you to register a horseless carriage, you're fine. Care to guess why?" She smirked at her brother.

"Because they aren't considered coaches. It is obvious. Stupid, but obvious." He scanned about. "Are you saying you have the money, or the influence? Because I find that hard to believe. Yes, you have more money than me, but this much?" Oskar tapped his nose. "Something smells wrong. Have you got yourself into trouble once again? Did you bring me here to help you?"

"You have never once helped me." Petra's eyes were wide and furious. "I brought you here to give me your technical opinion, and that is it." She turned and handed the driver a leather wallet, the tops of several bills sticking out. "Return in an hour."

The driver nodded, wiped his goggles, and climbed back up to his perch on the carriage.

"Wait, was that actual paper money you gave him? Didn't I teach you to use promissory notes? That's real money. Money that you could use for something else."

Petra gave her brother an icy stare. "You conduct business your way, and I'll do mine my way. Maybe there's a reason one of us keeps being run out of towns." Her teeth ground back and forth as she reconsidered her plan. She didn't want to risk showing anyone else what she'd discovered, in case it was valuable. For all of Oskar's flaws, she understood him well, and in the end, she was certain she could trust him to keep his mouth shut. She'd long abandoned the fantasy that maybe he'd finally act like the man she'd hoped he'd be.

The brisk morning air whipped around them. Petra pulled her long coat closed and started walking.

"Where is your boss?"

"I don't have a boss, Oskar. I have exclusive rights to salvage everything from this palace. Whatever remains of the Pieman presidency that hasn't been stolen or ruined by weather over the past two years is mine. Thankfully, there's a local story about a curse on this place. Otherwise, it would have been a foolish risk to take."

He frowned. "And how did you get this exclusivity? They don't give things like that to people like us."

She looked at him, her face blank. Offering only a shrug, she continued walking.

"I don't believe you. You would have workers here if you did. You can't do everything by yourself."

"I gave them the day off, so we could discuss things in private."

Oskar stared at the back of Petra's head as he followed behind her. They navigated the thin path through the broken marble, shattered columns, and the chunks of wood and plaster. "And I bet you still paid them."

"I would be an idiot not to," Petra answered.

"More money wasted."

"No." She stopped and glared at him. "It buys me their loyalty and their silence. But loyalty would be something you know nothing about." She continued forward.

Oskar grunted. "You know this place …," he noticed the official stamped seal of the Piemans on a piece of a front door. "This really was where Marcus Pieman lived, eh?"

"It's hard to imagine that a man who went from Conventioneer to High Conventioneer, then regent, and then became the elected head of a fledgling parliament would later be taken down by a civil war of the very secret society that he used to solidify his power. I can only imagine what it was like when the Fare smashed this palace, and his legacy, to pieces. And then, the Fare, ruled by the Mad Queen, hauls Pieman off to Belinia for a Trial by Royals, and he turns the tables and fights her to a draw with airships of his own." Petra gazed up at the broken ceiling. "Unbelievable. A friend of mine, a librarian from Kondla, says that history travels in spirals."

"What are these?" Oskar asked, pointing at a stack of wooden crates.

Petra hurried over to them, stepping right in front of her brother. "These are to be shipped out tomorrow." She opened a waterproof bag that was attached to one of the crates and pulled out a roll of paper. "The shipping information looks right. Good." She returned the paper and re-tied the bag. "Let's keep going, it's just a bit further ahead."

They made their way to the grand receiving area, an inner-foyer of sorts. The white plaster walls were stained by rain, and there was a sun-bleached outline of where great paintings had once hung. "Did you know this was the castle of Queen Pastora Willard over two hundred and forty years ago, and Pieman had it restored. Again, history moving in spirals."

She stared up at the grey sky through the massive holes in the cathedral ceiling.

Oskar scratched the back of his neck. "Yes, yes, this place is old and was fancy, I know. I know. But why am I here, Petra? I don't care for antiques. I like new things. I like making things. Besides, I don't appreciate you trying to make yourself sound important. You have the same tiny store as you have had for years, with the same little warehouse attached. That's it."

"Actually, it's three times the size, but I wouldn't expect you to notice. It's not like you've ever come to visit," she said without looking back. They passed a wide set of white marble stairs, covered in debris except for a narrow path.

Oskar stared at a piece of a painting that stuck out from a pile of chunks from the ceiling. He bent down to grab it.

"Don't touch that," Petra shouted. "That's nearly priceless. My team is going to dig it out carefully."

He straightened up and glared at her. "I don't like all this mystery. How did you get all of this?"

"I helped some influential people, people who have since become official king's-men."

"King's-men?" Oskar perked up.

"You know, people of privilege. The highest of the elite in the ladder that ends with the royal family. Title, privilege, and incomes like those of small countries."

Oskar moaned and folded his arms. "No. No, I don't think so, Petra. I think someone was lying to you. I don't believe you could know people like that. You aren't somebody."

Letting out a loud sigh, Petra shook a hand in the air. "I don't care *what* you believe." She continued walking, passing through a large, black stone archway. "I already regret having you here ten times over. Let's not make it eleven."

Oskar pulled his lips tight and hung his head. "I didn't mean to sound …"

"Like Oskar?"

He grimaced. "Unappreciative for you paying to bring me out here. You know I will always help you. Whatever you need."

Petra nodded to herself as they arrived at the sole set of doors that still stood.

"These doors are in great condition. Look at them."

Oskar approached and marveled at the thick, dark, cherry wood. "They are tough, eh? No rain stains. Nothing can hurt them. Tough doors. They should fetch a good price."

His sister pushed the door open. "I didn't have you come to give me your advice on the doors. Anyway, they've already been purchased by the Grand Library in Kondla."

Oskar's eyebrows shot up. "How did you do that?" He shook his head and raised a hand. "Never mind. Sorry."

"Huh. A sorry," Petra remarked as they walked into the room. Its high ceiling was still intact, though the large windows on the north and south side were smashed. In the center was something large hidden under a set of tarps. The tarps were tied to iron spikes lodged into the wood below the smashed marble tile.

"Help me take the tarps off." Petra went to one of the spikes and released the knot.

As the figure underneath was revealed, Petra watched Oskar's disapproving expression give way to wonder. A smile crossed her lips, she hadn't seen him have that look since they were kids.

"What is this?" Oskar asked, the words reluctantly rolling out. "Is this a statue?"

"I don't think so, but that's what you're here to determine for me."

Before them stood a large, shiny black horse, reared

up on its hind legs. Over its head was a cedar helmet and mane.

"Have a look in the holes. My guess is that they are for venting." Petra pointed at one of the shadowy areas that peppered the horse's body.

Oskar peered in, and a nervous laughter escaped. "There are gears." He stuck a finger in. "There's a belt?"

He backed up, another giddy laugh escaping, and then a cloud came over his mood. His head lowered like a turtle's recessing into its shell. Narrowing his eyes, he stared at his sister. "This is a joke, isn't it? No one has gears and belts and things in a statue."

"The rich have strange desires." Petra shrugged. "That said, I believe this isn't what it appears to be."

"And what is that?" Oskar snapped.

Shooting him an icy stare, she waved a hand at the horse. "That is why you are here."

Oskar scratched his face and muttered to himself. "This … can't be real. No, the very idea of a mechanical horse that could work and be ridden, it's a thing for story books."

Walking around the horse, he kept making disapproving noises and shaking his head. "Ah," he snapped his fingers. "The Piemans had airships, yes? Maybe that started with a wooden carving to show the idea and then I would bet they made a prototype. A lot of inventors, they start with this way of building things. Perhaps, Pieman had this made to inspire him. To remind him of that old story of the mechanical horse, but this isn't really one. It's just a … what's the word?"

"Scale model?" Petra proposed.

"Yes. One that was big and lifelike, to feed the imagination. But look at it, it's too artistic to be a prototype or real machine. No one would spend so much time to make something this pretty." He nodded to himself, his arms crossed in what looked like a hug. "I am certain of it."

"My first impression when I found it was along similar lines, but, then something made me change my mind," said Petra, letting her hand run along the smooth body of the horse. "I realized I needed a second opinion, because I don't think an artist would have done this."

"Done what?"

She walked over and picked up a simple, three-step stool, placing it below the head of the horse. Climbing up, she carefully removed the heavy helmet and started to wobble.

"Oskar."

"Huh? Oh," he hurried over and took it from her, placing it on the ground with a brutish thud.

Shaking her head, she forced the stiff, horse's mouth open and squinted inside. Taking a deep breath, she slid her hand into it and took hold of something. "Are you ready?"

"I do not have all day," Oskar said.

"Actually, you do. Stop complaining." Petra pulled, but nothing happened. She frowned and tried again. Still, there was nothing.

Just as Oskar wound up to say something, his face twisting with familiar nastiness, she pulled hard one last time. There was a mechanical clanking and cough from within the chest of the horse that lasted for several seconds.

They stood there in silence, Oskar staring at his sister with big eyes.

"Oskar?" she asked, stepping away from the horse.

He licked his lips and rubbed his hands together, studying the mechanical horse. "I ... I need some time to examine this." His expression shifted from wonder to fear and back. "Maybe this is a strange prototype of some kind? I can only give a rough guess right now. I'd need to have time to examine it, and given that you have me scheduled to return home in a few hours, the best I can tell you is that it isn't simply a statue. It should fetch a good price."

Petra narrowed her eyes at her brother and put her hands behind her back, a glint of steel on her hip evidence of her sidearm. "I'll reschedule your return and have this brought to my warehouse, then. Even if this turns out to only be an exquisite statue, I have someone willing to pay fifty thousand crowns for it."

"Fifty   thousand?"   Oskar   laughed.   "That's too much."

"But if it's a *prototype*, or better yet, if this is a secret creation of the Piemans that works, it could be worth hundreds of thousands."

Oskar burst into laughter. He pointed at his sister expecting her to at least crack a smile, but instead she glared at him. He quieted down. "Who would pay such ridiculous amounts of money?"

"King's-men. Weren't you paying attention?"

"Ha. Now I know you are lying. Even if you knew one, they don't have money like that. Only wealthy royal families and the heads of establishments, like the one that runs the port in Yarbo, have that type of money. Why, when I lived in Yarbo years ago, I watched one of the gangs turn into an establishment, and with that their power and wealth grew. Not even the local government would say a thing."

"So, are you calling me a liar then, Oskar?" Petra asked.

Oskar stroked his chin. His gaze kept shifting between his sister, the horse, and the helmet for the horse. "Maybe not. But if you were looking for a lot of money, I would look to the growing establishments. They are going to replace the royals, you watch. You know, I might be able to make some introductions for you, for a cut."

"For Yarbo?" She scoffed. "No." Petra ran her hand along the body and then stopped abruptly, raising an eyebrow at her brother. "Will you stick this out, actually determine what it is for me? Or are you going to abandon this because it's difficult, running away as you have so many times before."

Oskar drew in a deep breath. "I would need a place to stay."

"Done. Plus meals and a very small amount of spending money. But no gambling," said Petra.

Oskar nodded. "And I will need some tools."

"I already have more than enough tools." She walked over to him. "So, will you figure out what this mechanical horse is for me, Oskar? Show me that you've finally grown up and become the brother I knew you could be?"

Swallowing hard and raising his head up, he nodded. "I will do my best."

"That's all that I can ask."

Oskar laughed. "I cannot imagine, if this is really a machine of some kind, who could have invented it. Wouldn't we know their names?"

7

KEEP'ED WOMAN

As Christina shook awake, her arm twitched and hit an open ink bottle sitting on the edge of her desk. Her eyes zeroed in on it as it teetered on the edge of the desk and she caught it.

Since her dad's funeral a week ago, old nightmares had returned, pushing aside the ones that had haunted her from the fall of Kar'm.

Sitting back in the simple wooden chair, she stared straight ahead at a beautiful charcoal drawing by Mounira.

She thought back to a year ago, when Mounira had forced her to sit down at the workbench in Christophe's room. She had insisted Christina wait there until finally, Christophe noticed and recognized her.

He'd come over and taken her hand. Then they had

started talking in a way they hadn't in years. Christina had battled tears fighting to escape down her face, until the glimmer of brilliant life in Christophe's eyes faded and they seeped out.

His gaze wandered about, his brow furrowed, and his expression on of a man lost. Settling on a pile of papers, he'd sighed and commenced working away, happily mumbling to himself. Christina had left shaken.

A week passed before she'd found the strength to push past her demons and through the forest of emotional scars to return. Every day she came and waited patiently for hours at first, and then days, to have minutes with the man she struggled to understand. All the while, she'd watch, mystified by Mounira's ability to integrate herself into Christophe's broken world, becoming whomever he needed. Despite Mounira's efforts to explain, Christina couldn't understand.

A gentle, late spring breeze flowed in from the open stained glass window beside her, drawing her back to the present. There were the familiar sounds of students sparring coming from two stories below.

For a moment, she thought about going to his room, and then she remembered he was gone. She sniffed and grimaced, refusing to allow sorrow or sadness to take hold.

Staring out the window, grave concern washed over

everything else as she saw only a few Moufan-Men wearing the classic grey cloak. All the others were wearing Rumpere's charcoal black color, with the elites' sashes hanging from their hips like spilt blood. She couldn't ignore the alarm bells at the back of her mind anymore.

Things had changed so fast. The same day as Christophe's funeral, the Moufan had held a snap leadership election, with Rumpere getting the most votes under questionable circumstances. The next day, Christina had been unable to find the former leader or the deputy, whom she'd come to know rather well. Then others started disappearing, and all of Mounira's professors changed. Everyone who replaced them wore black and all had a broken tree tattoo on their forearms.

Christina turned her attention to the packed bags that peeked out from under her bed. In a few hours, they'd be gone, on their way to Augusto to reunite Mounira with her family.

Standing up, Christina rolled her stiff shoulders and cracked her neck. Her reflection in the full-length mirror stuffed into the corner of the small room caught her eye. Her blue eyes were darkly rimmed, and her uneven dark blonde hair reached past her black-horse tattooed shoulders. The thirty-five-year-old, square-jawed face that stared back at her seemed like her own, for the first time in a long time.

Closing the window first, she pulled out a fresh

beige blouse, brown cotton pants, and a vest from the freestanding wardrobe and changed into them. Once dressed, she returned to the wardrobe and pulled off the false back she'd created months ago.

Hanging on a hook was a dirt-brown coat that went down to her knees. Slipping it on, she slid a compressed-air canister into the coat's pouch at the small of her back. Next, she removed a strange-looking pistol from the wardrobe, attached a hose to it, and screwed the other end to the canister. She cinched the pouch closed, then slipped the pistol into the shoulder holster that was part of the coat. Lastly, she took out a three-inch, flat, black knife and slid it into the top of her boot.

Mounira's familiar battle cry came from outside. Christina eagerly went over to the window and pushed it open a bit more. She watched as Mounira stalked her two opponents, a large, chalk circle around them. The other students stood at the edge, restlessly moving back and forth. The instructor had his arms folded and a disapproving frown on his face. Clearly, Mounira was doing well.

Mounira pulled down the hood of her yellow cloak and swayed from side to side, watching the foot movements of her two fellow students in their grey hoods. She was listening carefully for the sounds of anyone jumping in from outside the circle, as had been happening more and more lately.

She'd never felt welcome as a trainee, with few, if any, of her fellow students ever uttering so much as a single, unnecessary word to her. To them, Mounira was an outsider, a foreigner, and one who had not pledged herself to their cause. Mounira hadn't cared. Her tremendously strong sense of family kept her grounded, and she'd adopted the venerable Christophe and Christina as hers.

Every day, between training sessions, she'd spend time with Christophe. When he recognized her, they'd talk about inventions and ideas, and when he didn't, they'd often talk about the garden. His passing had been a painful relief that reminded her of when a grandmother of hers had passed a few years ago.

She ignored most of the heckling by her fellow students and the blind eye turned by the instructors. Her mother had taught her to rise to the challenge and to deliver to such people a steady diet of defeat and humility wrapped in politeness. Most days, she gave the other students their fill.

As the bigger of the two opponents ran at her, she watched the other one anticipate her dodge to the left, ready to grab her. With a cheeky smile, Mounira turned and ran for the wall that led up to Christina's window.

"Ha. Finally, we see she's a coward," shouted out

one of the dozen other students from outside the training square.

As one of her opponents chased after her, she smiled. Planting one foot on the base of the wall and then the other further up, she flipped over her fellow student. Unlike her fellow trainees, Mounira constantly took risks and was willing to endure the bruises.

Her landing was off, costing her a valuable second to steady herself. She kicked at her opponent but missed. As a punch came for her jaw, she narrowly dodged it and kneed the student in the chest, sending him to the ground. Mounira wished her old friends, the Yellow Hoods, could see her fighting like they did.

Out of the corner of her eye, she saw her instructor's face tense. His hands waved angrily at the students.

Mounira tilted her head all the way back and her hood slid off, allowing her to see the other student preparing to deliver a hammer punch to her sternum.

He was two years older than her and easily twice her size. She'd been mentally preparing to face him for weeks, watching his moves, waiting for this moment. The hammer punch was always the one to end fights. It was risky and left him exposed for a few vital seconds.

Mounira let her arm go slack. As she fell, she felt his fist brush against her tunic. A cloud of dust erupted as she landed. Her opponent coughed, and Mounira kicked him hard with both feet in the chest. He stumbled backwards, clutching his chest and gasping for air.

Getting up and dusting herself off, Mounira prepared herself. She knew him well enough to know he had plenty of fight left in him.

"You fight with no respect for the rules," he said between coughs. "I guess that's what *Southerners* do."

Mounira's hand was loose and ready. "You do know my homeland of Augusto is west and slightly north of us on a map, right? Why do so many call people from that area Southerners? Was everyone in Inglea when we had our first geography lesson this season?"

She inched forward while swaying from side to side, studying how her adversary matched her movements and started to anticipate them.

He took a swing at her. "You should shut up."

Mounira slid back and then started her swaying all over again

"Oh, you started it," she replied, pulling the hood over her face so that he couldn't watch her eyes. "And as for rules, you guys have taught me the only rule is don't get caught breaking someone's bones."

"Come on, don't get beaten by a girl," one of the students yelled.

"Have you all been blind to the other fights you've put me through?" asked Mounira.

The guy took another swing and she once again slid

to the side and restarted her swaying, studying his movements each time.

"And girl? Sorry, I'm a woman," said Mounira, lowering her stance and slowing her breathing.

"Says who?" her opponent shot back.

"Other than biology? You in two minutes. Trust me, knowing your friends, it'll be less humiliating to say a woman kicked your butt than to say a one-armed, little girl did."

As he swung again, she ducked down and slid right up to him. A second later, he struck the ground, his chin red. He blinked slowly and repeatedly.

Mounira looked around at her class, breathing heavily. Everyone stood in silence. There was no cheering, no chants of *king of the ring*, nothing. She was used to it.

Shaking out her stinging hand, she turned to the instructor.

He turned his back and started walking. "Let's move on to the front grounds and to the next lesson," he said.

"She must have cheated," one of the trainees added as they followed the pack.

Mounira stared at the big guy lying there on the ground and shook her head. The Moufan-Men hadn't been like this when they'd arrived. They would have at least revived him, but something fundamental had changed.

Frowning, Mounira confirmed all the students had left. There were several adult Moufan-Men about, and while all their faces were covered by their grey or black hoods, she could feel their suspicion.

"Something's definitely changed about this place," she said, bending down beside the big guy.

She tapped his face. "Hey. Hey, wake up."

He groaned, a hand slowly coming up to his red chin.

"No hard feelings." She offered her hand to help him up.

Glancing around first to make sure they were alone, he hesitantly accepted her hand.

"I know you cheated," he said. "I just can't figure out how." He turned and spat out blood. "No one your size can hit like that."

"You're right, I do cheat." Mounira smirked. She caught his eyes go wide and his eyebrows shoot up. "You punch with your arm. I don't."

Mounira came up close to his face. "I use the pain from having been shot in my arm, the pain of having seen my father twisted up as he had to amputate it to save my life, and the pain the stump gives me, each and every day, as my nerves scream at me. When I strike, it's from my soul outwards. I'm pain incarnate when I want to be."

He scoffed but his sarcastic words failed him as she held his gaze with an intensity he didn't recognize.

"You, Moufan have taught me not to hesitate, to draw on everything, and I appreciate that. But Anciano Creangle and Christina, they remind me of the good in people, of the balance I need. You could learn a lot from people like them."

His face twisted into a snarl and his hands clenched into fists.

"Come on," Mounira said. "I think they've gone to the main entrance courtyard for more drills."

As she started to turn, she saw the boy's opposite shoulder pull away. A breath later, his fist scraped across her cheek as she dodged to the side.

Spinning around, she belted one of his shins with her own, dropping him to the ground with a scream. He clutched at his leg and rolled around, cursing.

She looked down at her torn pant leg and the shining metal shin guard underneath. "Maybe now you guys won't mock me for working on my little projects."

The hair on the back of Mounira's neck went up and she gazed about. A dozen adults, all in black hoods, were pointing at her, their burning gazes sending a chill through her.

Pulling her own yellow hood over her face, she let out a steadying sigh and straightened up. She pointed at her fallen opponent. "I'm heading to the courtyard. Come after me again, and I will break your leg at the knee. That's how you Moufan talk now, isn't it?"

She furrowed her brow, irritated at having to stoop to their level. "You can help yourself." She turned and left.

Christina waited until Mounira turned the corner before closing the window. She frowned, wondering if behind the deep brown eyes and generous smile of her protégé, there was pain and frustration, or if somehow it all slid off Mounira.

There was a rapid knocking at the door. Pulling a sheet and blanket over the packed bags and tapping her holster for luck, Christina silently approached the door.

Putting her ear up against it, she heard a hand rubbing back and forth against the door in a familiar pattern. "Two, three," she whispered and then drew her head back. Another two quick knocks came.

She opened the door and stepped back as a grey-hooded figure stepped into the room and pushed the wood and steel door closed.

"They have guards posted on your floor. Outstayed your welcome already?" The woman knocked her hood back and smiled. "It's been too long, Christina."

"Angelina?" She shook her head. "Angelina," she said excitedly and jumping up to hug her, but stopping. Instead, she gave her friend's hand a quick squeeze. "Why are you here? I half-expected it was going to be Sam or someone else from the Tub, given that knock. Maybe even Abeland."

"Abeland, really?" Angelina shook her head. "Anyway, when I didn't get any replies to my letters, I got worried. Then I heard the Moufan were making some interesting moves, and I had to come and check on you. I'm glad I did."

Christina glanced at her dusty, empty letter tray. "I haven't received anything in months."

"And that didn't set off any bells for you?" Angelina pulled the sheet and blanket back. "At least you haven't completely lost your mind. But it's a bit late for all that. We've got to move quickly."

"We've still got a few days at least. The elders—"

"The elders are dead. There were whispers about their bodies being found in a mass grave yesterday afternoon. That's why I'm here. Rumpere's solidified his grasp. He even has someone coming in a horseless carriage from Doyono. I overheard it this morning."

Christina frowned, her rusty instincts kicking in. "That's a lot of coincidence."

"You know how our lives are. It's only coincidence if it isn't useful, otherwise, it's providence." Angelina touched her chin and cheek. "Do you have a plan for where you're going?" she asked as she swung her satchel around to her front and opened it.

"Honestly? Not really," Christina replied.

"I made you something. It's what I was writing to you about in my letters. I know you've been trying to find a way to get Mourina home. Well, I found one." She handed Christina a notebook stuffed with letters and bank notes in different currencies. "There's a safe-enough route all the way back to the city of Catalina. That's where she's from in Augusto, right?"

Christina stared at the notebook and then at Angelina, a soft smile appearing on her face. "Yeah, it is. Um, I don't know what to say."

"Say that after you get her home, you won't wander around lost, and instead you'll come and find me."

Shaking her head, Christina looked up at Angelina. "Pardon?"

Angelina raised her eyebrows and tilted her head.

Christina lowered her eyes, an uneasy laugh escaping her. "Yeah, okay. I'll keep that in mind."

"How is Christophe? Will he be okay to move?" asked Angelina, her words coming out unevenly, her eyes darting away.

"Uh." Christina sucked in a loud breath. "He died a week ago."

"I'm sorry to hear that." Angelina put a hand on Christina's shoulder.

Christina frowned, glancing at the hand and then at Angelina who had turned her attention to the bags under the bed.

"We'll talk more later, but right now we need to get

moving." Angelina reached down and pulled one of the packed bags from under the bed. "You're going to need to pack lighter."

Rubbing her forehead, Christina picked up the charcoal picture, folded it carefully, and placed it into a pocket. "Yeah, okay."

Angelina pulled on a chain that was wrapped around the buttons of her jerkin, and a pocket watch popped out of a pocket. "We need to get moving."

Christina reached out and held Angelina's forearm. "Something's off."

"Christina, your instincts are what's off. At worst, you should have been out of here the day Christophe passed. At best, you should have taken Mounira and Christophe somewhere, anywhere, months ago," Angelina replied.

They stood there, looking at each other.

"If you need, we'll talk about this now, but I don't recommend it."

"Okay, sorry. You're right," Christina said. "I know our time's up here."

"You have no idea. The Moufan have made announcements in every corner of the kingdom of Dery that they exist. This is unprecedented. Did you know that they informed the royal family they will not recognize the monarchy's authority over them or their land?"

Christina ground her teeth. "They what?"

Angelina nodded.

With an inner surge she hadn't felt in a long time, Christina threw a bag onto the bed and pointed at the wardrobe. "I have two backpacks in there. Take one next door and fill it for Mounira. Then find her. We'll meet at the Wobbly Dumpty Tavern and Inn at sundown."

"That's the Christina I know."

Tossing one backpack to Christina and slipping the other over her shoulder, Angelina was about to leave when Christina slipped her hand around the back of her neck and pulled their foreheads together.

"Thank you. For coming, for the notebook, for everything."

Angelina smirked as Christina let go. "I don't know if I can handle this mushy version of you, but you're welcome."

Christina shook her head and started stuffing her backpack, her mind going a mile a minute for the first time in ages.

8

OF MIGHT AND MEN

Oskar threw open the back door of Petra's building and sprang over the threshold into its warehouse, humming to himself. Rubbing his hands together, he danced through the maze of antiques, shooting a glance at the door that led to the front office where Petra spent most of her day.

"Today's the day," Oskar said to himself. "Petra promised the mechanical horse would be here, and if there's anything to say about my sister, she delivers on her promises."

For three nights, Oskar had slept and eaten better than he had in years, and now he was ready to show his sister that her renewed faith in him was well placed.

Breaking into an old folk song from his youth, Oskar spun around the final corner and there before him, where an empty space had been the day before, was the majestic mechanical horse, reared up. It was surrounded by a dozen crank lanterns, all hanging on poles that slotted into holes in the floor. He glanced over at the workbench he'd inspected the day before, every tool acquired and arranged just as he'd asked.

Closing his eyes and imagining himself as a knight in shining armor in a coliseum, gazing at a wounded dragon, he pointed ahead as if a sword were in his hand. "Today, you will tell me your secrets."

"Sir?"

He opened his eyes to see a woman dressed in a beige dress, holding a tray of fine brushes, her brow furrowed.

"Not you." Oskar waved at the woman angrily. "Get out of my arena. I have battle to do with this monster."

Unfazed by his rudeness, the woman pointed at the crank lanterns. "They should be good for a few hours."

"GET OUT!" he screamed, his face going red. His chest heaved back, his hands at his sides in clenched fists. "Out."

The woman looked at him, her face unflinching, and slowly made her way to the door to the front office and showroom, where Petra was dealing with customers.

As the door slammed closed, Oskar glared about. "Where does my sister find you incompetent people?"

he yelled, his head seemingly descending into his body as his shoulders rose up.

He walked over to the work bench and carelessly shoved the tools around, scowling down at them. "These are not what I asked for. And look at these." He picked up a magnifying glass and held it up.

The rim of the glass was shining silver, and he dropped it on the table like it was worthless. "How am I supposed to do anything with these?" Oskar muttered.

Holding on to the edge of the table, he bowed his head. Letting his anger go, he turned around. "You asked Petra for these and for this chance. Don't do this, Oskar. Not this time."

He rubbed his stubbly chin and stared at the horse. Gone was its sense of majesty, and instead, it stood there like an imposing Titan.

"You think you are so magnificent, eh? I will break you. I will show you who is the master here." He picked up the magnifying glass and a wrench. "All of your secrets? I will put them in here." He tapped the wrench on a fresh, leather-bound notebook Petra had provided.

He sauntered up to the mechanical horse, staring up at its head. "And the world, all of the world, will know my name. When I walk down the street, people will say, 'That's Oskar the Great.' And that club? They will beg me to come in, but I will say no. I am too busy."

The horse was unmoved.

The next morning, Oskar threw open the front door of Petra's storefront and stumbled over the threshold. He squinted about, his hand shielding him from the sunlight that streamed through the large windows of the showroom.

"It is too bright. I cannot think," he mumbled, as he made his way to the long, marble-covered counter and rested his head.

Petra forced a smile at the well-dressed gentleman she was with and raised a finger. "If you'll excuse me for a moment. Please, feel free to enjoy the chesterfield or have a look at the rest of the faux-room we've set up for you. And, of course, if you want any fabric changes, I can make arrangements."

He nodded and sat down while Petra hurried over to her drunk brother.

"Oh, you smell. What have you been doing? How could you come in here? It's eleven o'clock. I'm with a customer," Petra whispered loudly into his ear. She then grabbed him by the collar and hauled him around the counter and through the door to the warehouse.

Shoving him to the ground, she glared at him. "Do you have any sense?"

Oskar turned himself around and got up. Wobbling, he hugged a large, blanket-wrapped grandfather clock. "When did you get so strong?" He frowned at her. "You're so small." He waved a hand at her.

Planting her hands on her hips, she shook her head. "I should have known you couldn't do it. That I couldn't trust you to come in on your own, like an adult."

"That thing mocks me," he yelled, shooting out a finger in the direction of the mechanical horse. "It's impossible such a thing is real. It is a puzzle, a riddle made to tease the mind of anyone who doesn't have the wisdom to see it is a joke."

Petra grabbed him by the collar and shoved him, letting him trip over his own feet and fall to the ground. She waved at the horse. "This is real. Even from my limited research, I have learned there are stories about a machine like this. Made by some Conventioneer for a King of Teuton forty years ago. He supposedly rode through the town once. I need to know if this is one of those. It doesn't look like the ones I've seen in pictures, but the gears, the parts ... It's so similar. So, Oskar, is it?"

He rubbed his face and frowned at the horse. Standing there, he ummed and ahhed and scratched his head. "I don't know."

She took several steps away and then spotted something. Her face contorted in anger as she approached one of the horse's legs. "You scratched it? And are these dents?"

"What? No."

"Then what are these?"

"Bah, they are not big." He crawled over to his work bench and dragged himself up.

"Why would you do that? I'll have to pay to have that fixed, and my prospective buyer is coming later today to see if it's truly worth his time, let alone money."

"You want to sell it? Sell it," His bluster evaporated before his sister's red face. He shrugged. "Besides, I know Abeland Pieman. I met him once."

"You have not, you liar. And you must be a complete idiot. This came from his father's palace. Abeland is mortal enemies with the people I'm dealing with."

Oskar threw his hands up. "Then is this a joke? Are you trying to prove you are smarter than me by giving me a puzzle like this? Is this some sick revenge for all the times I hurt you?"

Petra clenched her fists and then relaxed her hands, drew in a deep breath and then came right up to her brother's face. With slow, measured words, she replied. "For the last time, Oskar—and it is honestly the last time—no! This is not a joke. If you damage this again, I will shoot you and stuff you in a couch." She left.

Oskar winced as the office door slammed shut.

He sat on the edge of the workbench, staring at his hands, the memory of past failures swirling around in his mind. After a few minutes, he wiped his face on his sleeve again and stood up. Glancing in the direction of the office door, he let out a pained sigh.

"How can she still want to believe in me, even after everything? It makes no sense." He vigorously rubbed his face with his hands and then slowly made his way over to stand below the head of the horse. "I am not very good when I get upset, and I was rude and arrogant yesterday. So, shall we start again? Will you share your secrets with me? For Petra?"

He patted the horse's face. "Good. Okay, we'll work together then."

Returning to the work bench, he picked up his notebook and flipped it open. There were several pages of angry rants and then a remark about Petra having made it cough. He spun around, his eyebrows up and his eyes big and wonderous. "The thing in your mouth. Yes, that is where I should have started."

9

CREANGLE'S ESCAPE

In the Past
Twenty-Eight Years Ago

T he cell door creaked open, and Christophe squinted at the dim doorway. He was in the corner, leaning against the cold, stone wall.

"Are we to do this again?" he asked, pushing himself up. "After two years of the same games, do you not see how pointless this is?" he grumbled. "Who is the emissary this time? You are all terrible at this. You know that, don't you?"

There was the sound of footsteps heading away. Christophe stared at the dark doorway; it was like staring into the heart of the abyss.

"Where is your chair? Where is the one who thinks

they will break me this time? You are all idiots. I will never help you."

A figure appeared at the doorway.

Christophe leaned back against the wall, his arms at his sides.

A figure stepped into the lone beam of light that shone through the overhead, barred window. It was Marcus Pieman.

"After two years, you finally dare to visit me?" Christophe yelled. "I expected you to be the first to come, to open that door and tell me if I just walk through it, I could have my old life back. But you never came."

Marcus put his black gloved hands together in front of him. "I told the king it would be a waste of time."

"It would have."

"I knew you wouldn't walk through that door with any amount of convincing I had available to me," said Marcus. "There is one thing I'm sure you don't expect."

Christophe scoffed. "And what is that?"

"I have to thank you. Your handiwork has humiliated everyone who spoke against me. They have burned every opportunity they had, and now, I am left, and they have fallen. But that is not why I am here. While I don't have the influence yet to grant you freedom, I want to get you and Nikolas out before things change."

For a moment, Christophe stared blankly at Marcus, his brow wrinkled. "What do you mean?"

"I've been thinking about how we could discuss this, for me to be able to get my point across in the five-minute window I have before I'm discovered. My political strength has grown in recent months but being seen here will undercut all of it."

"Ah, a good ploy," Christophe said with a laugh. "Urgency, risk. All the best elements of any story, except for one problem. I don't believe it." He narrowed his eyes and leaned forward. "No, I see it now. You want Nikolas to go, but he won't leave without me. A true friend to the end, isn't he?"

Reaching into his long coat, Marcus pulled out three sheets of folded paper. "Here are your instructions. In three days, at midnight of the next full moon, your cell will be unlocked."

"Why the next full moon?" Christophe asked.

Marcus glanced behind him. "Because the guards will be looking for dancing lights out of place. I've had the patrols reassigned as much as possible in order to keep this route clear. Stay in the shadows, and you should be fine. But understand, things could change at any moment."

Christophe squinted at the papers, studying them quickly. "Hmm. This leads me to the north side of the castle and Nikolas to the east."

"I'll have a King's-Horse waiting for each of you there." Marcus scratched his nose.

Christophe looked up in shock. "The Conventioneers were able to rebuild them? The Conventioneers managed to build new ones?"

"No." Marcus laughed. "But you didn't build just four, did you? I have to admit, your resourcefulness and sneakiness are certainly paying dividends."

"The king has all of them?"

"No, I do."

Christophe stared at Marcus silently. His expression then twisted to anger, and he threw the papers aside. "Nikolas told you, didn't he? You tricked him with this talk about escaping."

"Be ready. There will not be a second opportunity," Marcus said, leaving the small cell and closing its door.

"What did you tell him, Kolas?" Christophe rubbed his face vigorously. "And what do you know? I can't imagine I slipped up, that I shared anything that could let you accidentally harm the both of us."

He crouched down in the corner and ran his finger along the scratched shape of a horse. "And did you know of the one I've kept secret, even from you?"

The click of the cell door's lock woke Christophe from his shivering slumber on the stone floor. Feeling the light of the moon on his face, he pushed the thin, wool blanket away. It was time to see if Marcus was playing him or was going to go through with any part of the escape ruse.

The icy floor bit at his feet as he stood and made his way over to the silhouette of the wood and metal door.

His lips curled in tightly, and he reached out with a trembling hand. To his surprise, the door moved.

Its loud creak tore apart the silence of the night and made the hair on Christophe's arms and neck stand up. Stepping out of the room, he kicked something. Reaching down, he found a pair of boots and slipped them on.

Continuing down the corridor, he stopped every few seconds and listened intently. There was nothing but the sound of his heart pounding in his chest.

Opening his eyes, he squinted at the crank lanterns that had been turned down to give little more than a nudge of guidance. Thinking of the map he'd memorized, he made his way to the stairs. There he found the iron gate that had stopped many a prisoner's escape sitting ajar.

Could this be real? he wondered. The image of his young daughter and her valiant smile popped into his mind. His eyes welled up. Suddenly his mood flipped, and he growled in anger at the gate.

Did Nikolas know about Christina? Was he trying to hint at that over our last dinner? Pulling at his long, white beard, he took a step in one direction, then the opposite, then the first again.

Did Marcus know? Was this all a trap to lead them to her so that they could use her to blackmail him into doing their bidding? He scratched his head vigorously with both hands.

"Enough, Christo. You'll drive yourself mad," he blurted out, then leaped back, expecting guards to appear.

Putting a hand on the iron gate, Christophe wondered if it was wiser to return to his cell and wait for the morning, rather than risk playing the fool and being caught for trying to escape. Still, he had a duty to Nikolas. If he could help get his friend to freedom, he had to do it. And if he could see Christina again ...

Pulling the gate open, he made his way up the stairs.

Christophe lay on the ground against the wall, hidden completely from the light of the oil lanterns in the secret tunnel of the castle. *Where are you Kolas? You must be late. Or am I in the wrong place?*

His hands shook and beaded with sweat. *Did I forget a turn?* He scratched at his forehead feverishly.

The sound of shoes scuffing along the stone floor

drew Christophe's attention. Looking up, a sense of relief came over him.

"Kolas, over here," he whispered in their native Brunne. He got up, dusted his hands off, and stepped into the meager light. "It is good to see you my friend."

Nikolas grabbed Christophe and gave him a quick hug. "It is good to see you. I was worried."

They pulled back and looked at each other. They were like mirror images of one another. While both of them had slim faces and cheekbones showing, one had brown with white in his beard, the other had white with brown. One always looked on the positive side, the other had a darker tilt.

"Why aren't you dressed?" Nikolas asked, pointing at Christophe's prison clothes.

With a frown, he pulled back and gave Nikolas a good look. He was dressed like a simple villager, with a tunic and jacket, pants and decent shoes.

Christophe clenched his jaw as a sense of icy dread started to spread through his soul. "I was so excited, I missed the turn to go get it. I'm glad you didn't," he said, patting Nikolas on the shoulder. "I would forget my head were it not attached."

"Now, come," Christophe continued. "The secret passage to your King's-Horse is that way. We should get you going."

As Christophe went to move, Nikolas held his forearm. "Not yet, Isabella isn't here yet."

"Isabella?" Christophe shook his head.

"Yes, she's coming with me. She's escaping with us. Marcus did tell you, yes?"

Christophe gritted his teeth. "Yes, of course. My mistake."

On cue, the sound of scuffing boots came from a passageway. Nikolas' face lit up as his fiancé stepped into the light.

As the two embraced, Christophe backed up and looked away, his arms folded across his chest. His shoulders were up, as if protecting his neck. Closing his eyes, he thought of the maps Marcus had provided and tried to remember what other passages and corridors existed.

"Christo?" Isabella gently took his hand.

Christophe glanced at Nikolas, a nervous happiness on his face that seemed alien to Christophe.

He'd been certain Isabella was a plant by Marcus, meant to watch or twist his friend, but she always seemed to genuinely put what was best for Nikolas first. Still, Christophe had his suspicions, but Nikolas' happiness kept Christophe's concerns at bay. The dice had been thrown, now it was a matter of playing as much of the game as possible before the results were revealed.

"Let's get you two safely to where you need to be," said Christophe.

"What? No, you need to go." Nikolas nodded affirmatively.

Christophe drew Nikolas in close. "I will forever owe you a debt, my friend, but I cannot repay any of it if I do not make sure, with my own eyes, that you got out." He glanced at Isabella, surprised to see the genuine fear in her eyes.

Nikolas was about to rebut, but Christophe glared at him. After a silent moment, the two nodded at each other.

The three of them headed out until they came to a single crank lantern that was turned all the way up. A figure was standing there, a black hood over its head.

"Nikolas, good," the figure said, pulling his hood back. "We don't have much time. There are guards already circulating about."

As Nikolas and Isabella went up to stand with Marcus, Christophe stayed behind in the shadows, watching.

Quickly and carefully, he reached out to the crank lanterns on either side of him and turned them off, leaving him in complete darkness.

Marcus pushed on a perfectly round stone in a wall of oddly shaped ones, and a small doorway opened outwards. The sweet smell of the outdoors wafted in.

"Come now, both of you. The King's-Horse is just at those trees," Marcus said, letting the couple out and then stepping out with them.

The edge of Christophe's mouth turned down as his spirits rose and fell. "I wish you all the speed and fortune. Live well, my friend," he whispered.

As Marcus returned and closed the secret door, urgent footfalls and clanking armor approached from the other end of the corridor. Christophe glanced about; he was trapped in the middle. He gasped for air and kept shifting his gaze back and forth between the danger at one end and the danger at the other.

His back against the wall, he slid down, his heart feeling like it was about to leap out of his chest.

A solider rushed passed Christophe. "Lord Pieman."

Marcus glared at the soldier, immediately putting him on his heels. "How did you know to look for me here?"

"Conventioneer Stimple thought you might be around here," he replied. "Sorry, my lord, but there are two Conventioneers missing and it is past curfew."

Christophe's eyes went wide. *Stimple? What does that ambitious rat have to do with any of this? Just looking for another way to bite Pieman for having taken him into his house and given him shelter? Ingrate,* he thought.

Marcus put his hand to his forehead. "Oh, that is of concern," he said, his voice distant and somber. "Who are they?" They started walking toward Christophe.

"Nikolas Klaus and Christophe Creangle. Stimple did the inspection himself."

"Hmm." Marcus stopped a few feet from Christophe. "I'm afraid Conventioneer Klaus has drowned. I saw the body myself only a few minutes ago. I will tend to it, but Creangle …," he rubbed his clean-shaven chin in thought.

Christophe's chest tightened as the moment of truth arrived.

"Check outside the northern castle wall. If I was Creangle, that's how I'd try to escape. He'll likely be heading eastwards."

Bastard! Christophe's fists shook. He bit his lip until it bled to make sure he stayed hidden.

The soldier stood there.

"Get me Creangle, unharmed," Marcus commanded. "If you need me, I'll be having a word with Conventioneer Stimple."

Marcus turned to the crank lanterns above Christophe. "Those shouldn't be out. One more thing. Have someone tend to these. They must be broken, as they don't just go out on their own."

"Yes, sir."

After Marcus and the soldier had left, Christophe stood up, his breathing fast. He went over to the stone he'd seen Marcus push and opened the secret door. Once outside, he searched about for a way to close it, but there was none. Abandoning it, he went to double-check that Nikolas had left.

Crouching down, he found the torn-up soil. "So,

there was one of our King's-Horses for him. Good. I wish you well, my brother."

He gazed about in the full moonlight, a plan unfolding in his mind. Once it was ready, he struck off into the wilderness.

10

NOOSE TIGHTENS

In the Present

As Mounira rounded the corner to the inner courtyard, she saw her instructor finishing up a talk with a black-cloaked Moufan. With irritation, and a hint of confusion on his face, the instructor waved at the trainees to turn around and head back the way they'd come.

Skidding to a stop, Mounira noticed there were dozens of Moufan elite all over the courtyard and on the parapets. Darting over to an old, broken column, she scaled it, perching herself on top.

"What's Rumpere doing here?" she whispered to herself, the red stripe on his black hood unmistakable.

As the great, iron gate creaked open, everyone

straightened up and took notice. A thunderous rumbling flooded into the courtyard.

"Mounira, come," her instructor yelled.

She clung to the column, leaning forward eagerly. As the sound grew louder, there were distinctive clanks and clinks. Then a smoke-belching, horseless carriage roared in and screeched to a halt, sliding and kicking up a cloud of dust.

"What is that?" Mounira leaned even further forward, precariously balancing herself on the edge of the column.

"Come, Mounira. Come." Her instructor started marching over to her. "You cannot be here."

The carriage was one-and-a-half-times the length of a normal horse-drawn carriage. It had a variety of gears and belts on the back, surrounding a black steel encased engine. Two stove pipes rose out from the engine, the inky-black smoke streaming out of them.

Mounira pulled her hood back and stared in wonder as the driver shoved a lever forward and the engine's noise dropped notably. He sat on a bench bolted to the forward fringe of the carriage, an array of gauges before him like strange, brass flowers on metallic stems and levers to his right. He had an excited smile that stretched from ear to ear—the work clearly agreed with him.

He studied the shining array of gauges that stood

before him and pulled another of the several levers beside him.

Rumpere and his deputy stepped forward, ready to greet their guest.

The driver climbed down the ladder affixed to the side of the carriage and knocked on the cabin door. "We're all good," he shouted extraordinarily loudly. "Is it okay if I shut her down for a bit, let her cool down and check for any cracks?"

"Yes, by all means," said a man's voice from inside.

As the driver went to the back of the carriage, a man opened the cabin door.

He stomped his foot and a set of stairs unfurled themselves to the ground.

As Mounira's instructor went to grab her, she leapt from her perch and headed into the crowd, toward the carriage. With a frustrated grunt, he waved dismissively at her and returned to the departing trainees. "It's your death."

As she slipped through the crowd, a shiver ran down Mounira's spine as more and more Moufan hoods turned to face her. *They must be under strict orders not to move. I've never heard of this.* Arriving near the front, she looked at the mystery guest from behind Rumpere.

Those purple spectacles are hiding his eyes, but there's something familiar about that face.

Stomping on the last step of the carriage and

hopping to the ground, the man smiled and then kicked a pedal. The stairs rolled back up into the carriage. Closing the door with his cane, he peered about and then nodded at his host.

He touched his purple-lensed spectacles and gazed about. "What an impressive display. I assume your hold is complete and your plans are unfolding as you'd mentioned in your letter. Congratulations, Rumpere."

"Thank you, Doctor Stein." Rumpere offered a shallow nod and bow.

Mounira froze, her eyes going wide. *Stein?* She looked at the carriage again, this time noticing the mechanisms that reminded her of the mechanical arm she'd lost at Kar'm. *You took it. I knew it!*

"What's she doing here?" a female Moufan-Man said from behind Mounira.

Without looking back, Mounira bolted straight for Stein.

Rumpere turned, seeing the yellow blur, and with a single barked word, the Moufan-Men came to life.

Stein recoiled, banging into the carriage, as the yellow streak rolled over one Moufan-Man and dove between the legs of another.

Just as Mounira prepared to spring at him, Rumpere grabbed her by the neck and threw her to the ground.

Looming over her, he put his foot on her chest and glared at his men. "How dare you embarrass the

Moufan like this." He looked at his troops. "Can someone explain how a child, a Xenia Southerner of all things, got to the first guest of our new era?" His words silenced the courtyard, echoing off the fortifications.

Rumpere turned his furious gaze on his deputy. "An explanation for our guest?"

The deputy swallowed hard and stared at the ground. "Our apologies, Doctor Stein, this lapse in our security practices will not go unpunished."

"No, it won't," Rumpere said, seething. He held on to Mounira's cloak tightly, making her cough in protest. "As we come out of the shadows, to be a force unafraid of the light, we cannot have this happen again."

"It won't." The Deputy stared at the ground.

"You'd be surprised what I've run into in my travels," Stein replied, planting his cane and offering a brave smile. "Things are a lot more relaxed and enjoyable when my wife's with me for some reason, I must say. I think of this as nothing more than being in the wrong place at the wrong time."

"Indeed." Rumpere glared at Mounira. "And as for you, you rodent." He pulled her close, his beady eyes staring deeply into her. "I should thank you, for now even those who might have resisted taking action against you and Xenia Creangle will now fall in line.

You attacked a guest of the Moufan, on our sacred grounds."

"We are guests," Mounira coughed out, her hands holding the cloak from her neck.

"You are refugees. Why do you think we call you Xenia?" He pointed at Stein. "He is a dignitary." Rumpere shoved Mounira into the hands of two muscular Moufan-Men. He smoothed his mustache and sighed.

Mounira twisted and swung a leg out, striking Rumpere in the shin. While he stood there, she cried out and clutched her leg.

"Do you truly believe I wouldn't be prepared for any of your little antics?" said Rumpere, reaching down, under his high socks. He removed a wooden shin guard covered in small spikes. "Your pathetic little protection was defeated by the preparation of a superior mind."

Dusting off his hands, Rumpere turned to his guest. "Let's return to our business. You are safe here, Doctor Stein."

Stein wiped his forehead with a cloth and then stuffed it in his pants pocket. His eyes narrowed. "I would hope so, but if I may, I'd like to examine her cloak. I'd always wanted to, back at Kar'm."

Rumpere frowned. "I do not recommend it."

"Indulge me, please." Stein's fingers twitched in anticipation.

With a nod from Rumpere, the two guards brought Mounira forth and pinned her to the ground with their hands on her shoulders. She reached out with her one arm, only to have one of the guards put his knee on her hand.

Stein crouched down and glanced into Mounira's eyes. "It's been a while Mounira. I see you've very much followed in the steps of your compatriots, the Yellow Hoods." He felt the cloak.

He pulled out a jeweler's lens from his pocket and examined the fabric.

"Hmm, this is most astounding. I haven't seen such fine, woven metal links as these before. I think Jacqueline may be correct, that some of the secret societies had a light, bullet-proof fabric." He stood up. "May I examine yours?"

Rumpere frowned and then held out the edge of his cloak.

"Thank you." Stein examined it and then nodded to himself. "Definitely what one would expect."

He let the lens fall and then popped it into his pocket. "May I take it? The cloak I mean, not the girl."

"Why?" Rumpere asked.

"Well, assuming she's been here since Kar'm, that would say to me you haven't noticed what she's been wearing. Now, if I take it to my lab, between my wife and I, I do believe that we could come up with some form of light, bullet-resistant cloaks or clothing for you.

This could be essential as you expand your reign of control. The Moufan will make new enemies, and it's guns, not swords and bows, that are the weapon de jour. Interested?"

Rumpere nodded. "Give him the cloak."

"No," yelled Mounira as one guard grabbed her around the neck and the other removed the cloak.

Folding it first, the Moufan-Man then handed it to Stein, who put it in the cabin of his carriage.

"Jacqueline will be quite pleased with that find."

"You are a coward," Mounira said, her face red and eyes bulging.

"And you are a one-armed little girl, lost in a cruel world. We all have to change to adapt to it. If we're lucky, we'll find our place, our missing half." Stein looked at Rumpere. "I'm done. Shall we get to Creangle's effects?"

"Yes." Rumpere gave the guards a sharp nod, and they hauled Mounira away.

As Mounira was dragged through the compound by the two large guards, she kept her eyes low, avoiding the disdainful glares of the Moufan. Her cheeks were red and her body slick in sweat from the dozen times she'd already tried to break free. She was working on the strength for the thirteenth. Her mother's words about mythical heroes only succeeding the thousandth time rang in her ears.

Looking up, she saw two guards up ahead, posted beside the door that led to a dungeon. She wondered if that's where the old, grey-hooded leaders had been taken and likely killed.

Mounira clenched her fist and was ready to plant her feet again when she noticed a Moufan-Man approaching from the distance, blond hair peeking out from her hood. *There aren't any blond Moufan.* She thought of Christina. *I need to warn her. They're going to go after her.*

Staring at the door ahead, Mounira's pulse sped up as panic ripped through her. *What if no one's coming?* she wondered.

"Finally, someone's doing the spring cleaning," said a large man from over on the left. He laughed, his face hidden beneath his black hood. "You should have had the wisdom to never come or the sense to have left early."

Mounira didn't recognize the symbols on his cloak's trim, but she knew the voice of the history and traditions teacher that had taken over for her favorite professor.

"You ruined so many of my classes." He pulled up his sleeve, revealing a split-tree tattoo.

"I can't allow you to do that," said one of the guards.

The Moufan-Man with the blond hair peeking out was rushing toward them.

Mounira clenched her jaw and narrowed her eyes. "I am a *Titan*," she yelled. "I am a *Titan* and my wrath shall be your end."

"Titan?" said the teacher with a scowl, tugging on his grey sash. "Are you quoting that Augustan garbage? You are nothing. No, less. You are three quarters of a nothing." He swatted at her missing arm. "I hope you rot in the dungeon. I shall sleep well knowing that our new leader removed the stain from our home. I hope Creangle resists and dies. Enjoy your fate."

As he went to leave, Mounira pushed off the ground so hard that it caught the guards by surprise and forced them to follow her into the teacher's path.

"I will take the fear you have given me and forge it into a sword, laced with my conviction, with which I will earn my victory." Mounira's eyes were on the blond stranger, whom she could now see was a woman.

"What garbage scripture." The teacher shook his hands angrily.

"Exactly." Mounira grabbed a firm hold of the cloak on one of the guards and pulled on it while throwing her leg up.

Striking the teacher in the face, she then threw her

head back, hitting the guard just right to knock the wind out of him.

Just then, the blond stranger leapt forward, drawing a foot-long silver rod out from her sleeve and striking the second guard with it. As arcs of crackling blue lightning shot out of the device, the man flailed and then dropped to the ground unconscious.

As Mounira struck a knock-out blow against the teacher, the stranger shocked the remaining guard.

"Who are you?" Mounira asked, trying to catch her breath. "And do you have another shock-stick? I haven't had a working one in ages."

The rod clattered on the ground as the stranger let it go and swooped in close to Mounira. "We've got eyes on us. We need to get moving before this gets wildly out of control."

Mounira's eyebrows went up. "Angelina?"

"You've got a good memory, kid." Angelina tapped her on the shoulder. "Walk quickly."

"What about the shock-stick?"

"There's no easy way to recharge that one."

Mounira pointed with her chin. "The guards by the dungeon door, they know something's up."

Angelina glanced over her shoulder at the prison door guards who were cautiously approaching. Putting three fingers up, Angelina then turned her hand ninety degrees and made a fist.

The guards stopped and made a similar gesture.

Angelina confirmed with an open palm, and they nodded, returning to their post.

"Where'd you learn their signals?" Mounira asked. "And what are you doing here?"

"I see your questioning old self is still in there. Now shh, we need to get moving before someone points out I stole this cloak."

They walked briskly past the dungeon door and into a tower of the keep.

Entering the empty lobby of the tower, Angelina closed the door and leaned against it. "I have to say, that was impressive to see firsthand. Nice to see that sharp tongue of yours has some sharp skills to go with it," said Angelina, wiping the sweat from her forehead. "You've grown a lot too."

"If you try to pinch my cheeks, I'll break your hand," Mounira replied.

Angelina chuckled. "Can we get to the old servant tunnels from here? I stashed a backpack with your clothes and drawings."

"How do you know about the tunnels? Or the hand gestures?"

"They're already hunting for us. We need to get out of here and into town." Angelina's hands slid to her belt, hidden underneath her cloak. "And we need to do it with the least mess possible." She shot Mounira a look. "Christina's going to be fine. She told me where to meet her. We need to get out of here now."

Mounira held her gaze for a moment. There was something in Angelina's look she couldn't place, something she'd never seen at Kar'm. "The old tunnels are this way."

Christina pushed open the door to Mounira's bedroom. It was a mess. There were clothes on the floor, drawers half-open, and the wardrobe doors still swung gently.

"Angelina's effective, I'll give her that."

Dropping her backpack, she quickly ran a hand under the bed and then under and behind the dresser.

Satisfied that she hadn't missed any secrets Mounira might have been hiding, Christina stripped the bed sheets and tied them together. Opening the window, she then secured the sheet-rope around the bed frame and left the rope in a curl on the bed.

"Always best to prepare an emergency exit, just in case." Picking up her backpack, she closed the door and headed down the hallway, one hand running along the wall.

At the sound of voices approaching from around the corner, she froze, looking back the way she'd come. There were a dozen dormitory doors between her and Mounira's room.

Thinking about it, going down the sheets to get outside

would be risky in broad daylight. I should have thought of that earlier. I need a better plan.

She glanced at the doorknobs of the other dorm rooms in the corridor. *I don't have time to go room to room hoping to find an open one. And if someone's in there? Too risky.*

Clenching her teeth, she remembered the grey-hooded cloak she kept hidden under her bed, a present given to her by the former deputy leader. *How can you be so rusty at this stuff? There's no time to go back for it now. And if the Moufan see you running, they'll know something's up. Think, and later, I need to get back to being the squirrel: always prepared and paranoid.*

She closed her eyes and listened to what the approaching Moufan-Men were discussing. A smile crossed her lips as she figured out the context. Reaffirming her grip on the backpack, she lifted her head high and moved with purpose around the corner.

"You're on the wrong floor," she said, pointing at one of the two women in grey robes, their hoods back.

"Pardon?" the shorter of the two replied.

"They moved the wine room up a floor after one of Rumpere's lieutenants almost found it." Christina stopped and frowned at them as they stared at her completely confused. "That is what you're looking for, isn't it? You're just done with a fighting test, right?"

The Moufan women glanced down at themselves. "How did you know?" asked the shorter one.

Christina pointed. "Blood stains and you've got a fat lip. You're missing your sashes, but there are still a lot of red fibers from your practice ones."

"Oh."

"You've earned the break, so I just assumed you were going to indulge in a little contraband like the others."

The other woman glanced at her friend and then at Christina. "How do you know about all of this? Moufan aren't allowed to drink alcohol."

"Why have a xenia at the compound if not to get it? The term means foreign friend for a reason." Christina subtly bit her lip. *I can't believe I just said that. Still, it's better than having to fight them. That could go either way.*

Christina bowed her head, a sheepish smile on her face. She noticed the shorter one narrowing her eyes, picking up something out of place.

"Are you supposed to be here?" asked the shorter one.

"I thought Rumpere said there were no more foreigners allowed. He called you all xenos, not xenia."

"Ah." Scratching the side of her cheek, Christina looked at the stone floor, her eyes darting about. She peeked up at the women. "You guys would make good embeddeds. You sound like I did years ago."

"Embedded?"

"Moufan spies who hide amongst our enemies, trusted by them as friends. You should know this by now." She shook her head and looked over her shoulder. "I shouldn't be saying anything. They'll tell you when they think you're ready. Let's just say that elites aren't the true top of the heap for the Moufan. And there *might* have been embeddeds fueling the civil war within the Fare, bringing about the fall of Marcus Pieman and flushing the Mad Queen out into the open. But I never said anything." She stepped around the women. "I have to go."

"And that alcohol? If we change our minds?" asked the taller woman.

"Third floor, seventh door on the right from the end. Double knock, scratch twice, single knock." As Christina walked away, a modest smile broke out. *Not that rusty.*

Christina hiked up two floors. Leaning against the stairwell wall, she peered around the corner. There was only one door at the far end, thirty feet away, and it was open. A Moufan-Man elite was posted outside of it, his red sash blowing gently in the breeze from the open door behind him.

They said I was the only one with a key to the room. And what are they doing here?

Just then, a figure stepped out of the room. Without thinking, she sprang out into the open corridor.

What's he doing here? "Rumpere!"

11

FLIGHT OF THE CREANGLES

In the Past

Hidden among bushes and shrubs, Christophe peered down at the half-dozen soldiers waiting for him further down the hill. Their rifles and medals shining in the moonlight.

At the bottom of the hill was the clearing Marcus had marked on the original map. Standing in the middle of it was a horse-like form.

Christophe wiped the sweat from around his mouth. "That cannot be a King's-Horse. No, it must be a trick." He rocked back and forth, bowing his head as his inner voice screamed at him to run. "But what if it is the King's-Horse? I cannot leave it here to be used for evil," he said to himself.

He ran a hand through his sweaty hair.

"Marcus has baited this trap well. He knows you. He knows that you cannot stand leaving any of your ideas or machines to be used by dishonorable men."

Glaring at the horse in the moon's spotlight, he shook his head. "No, you are wood. Marcus would never dare risk me destroying a prize of his. Fortunately, Marcus, I have my own escape. Now where is the point?" He searched the landscape until he found the haunting glow of a snow-topped mountain. "That means," he turned about, "I must head this way."

Stumbling over rocks and roots, Christophe scrambled through the forest like a man possessed. Finally arriving at a small clearing, he counted the trees and smiled. "Five. She's this way."

Christophe wiped the blood from the scratches on his hands and face and walked up to the largest of the trees. There was a blanket of darkness behind it.

Reaching out with his hands, he felt them hit fabric and took hold of the camouflage tarp. Pulling it away, he smiled like a joyous child at the ebony head of a mechanical horse.

It was larger than any other and shone proudly in the moonlight.

"Ah, there you are, my Black Beauty."

A twig snapped in the background and Christophe spun around. His eyes darted about.

"Who's there?" he called out, his arms outstretched, his pulse racing.

As the forest only offered the distant sounds of owls and other nightlife, Christophe sighed and turned back to his creation. "You are the king of the horses, the true King's Horse." He patted the horse's face.

He bowed his head, heart feeling heavy. "You have no idea how many times I wanted to tell Kolas about you. How guilty I feel for deceiving him, but he couldn't know. He couldn't. He would have been so excited, so overjoyed that he would have told Marcus. He is too trusting, and too generous, and kind enough for the both of us." He sniffed and rubbed his face on his sleeve. "And I lied to him about so many things." He looked at the belly of Black Beauty.

A hoot made him jump and look up at the waning night. "I must get going."

He inspected the body of the mechanical horse as he removed the rest of the tarp, then folded the tarp up and put it in one of the two saddlebags. "Two years and five months you have stood here, and you look as good as the day I hid you here."

Bending down, he pulled out a leather sack that was hidden under the body of the horse. Christophe ran his hands along the edges and bottom. "Ah, dry. Perfect. You have done well, my Beauty." He patted the horse's black steel chest. Putting two fingers into hard-to-see slots on the underside, he pulled, and a large panel opened, revealing a storage space filled with bundled papers and letters. "All of the designs, letters for Christina, everything is here. Good." He reached up into the belly and drew out a pair of goggles, then closed it up.

Putting the goggles on, he returned to the head of the horse. Christophe opened Black Beauty's mouth and reached inside. Giving a firm tug, he broke into laughter as there was a warm and even revving of the engine in its chest.

"Tonight, we start our new life with Christina. And no more stories about the Black Beauty of the forest, tonight she sees I was always sharing my life with her."

A shiver ran through him. "Is there someone there?" He rubbed his throat and peered into the darkness.

Again, the forest offered nothing in return.

With a furrowed brow, he shook off the moment and mounted Black Beauty. Christophe put his feet on the pedals and pushed down. The horse's engine roared loudly.

After he tugged on the reins to release the brake, Black Beauty trotted forward, legs decisively striking the ground, her head up high and eyes alight.

"Hmm," Christophe tugged at his beard. "I'll need to hide you somewhere close to town so I can get

Christina and leave quickly. I cannot afford anyone seeing you."

Closing his eyes, he thought of the town and the area around it. "Yes, there's that area of forest. My Meeshich is big now, she will make it." He revved the engine one more time. "And then, we leave for a new future in Freland. Maybe soon she can meet Kolas." A smile crossed his lips. "Yes, that would be nice."

Christophe looked up at the sky. "Ah, the black has lost its conviction, the sun will be coming soon. Now, to unlock a whole new future," he yelled. As he pushed the pedals, Black Beauty rocketed off.

"You have no idea," said a man in the darkness as Christophe rode past. A minute later, another King's-Horse revved up and followed suit.

Pressed up against the side of a stable on the edge of town, Christophe stared down the deserted cobblestone street and caught his breath.

Tridecto was a small town twenty miles north of the Teuton's capital city, Teutork. The town was often thought of more as an extension of the palace than anything else.

The halo from the pole-mounted gas lanterns had drawn him like a moth to a flame. He huffed and puffed as he stared up at them, a reluctant smile on his face. "So, this is what you did with my work? Kolas was right. They look good." He wiped his sweaty hair back and looked at the streets. "Every citizen can walk safely, like he argued." Scratching the back of his neck, he sighed. "No, it's good. But, tonight, it only makes things more difficult."

He continued running in the dwindling shadows, glancing about nervously every few yards. Then as he was about to cross a street, he noticed a merchant and his helpers loading a cart.

"It's not worth it," the head helper hollered.

Christophe froze and looked at him. The man was looking in a different direction and was pointing at a broken barrel.

"Just get another one," finished the man.

Standing there, his heart pounding, Christophe glanced about. *Is this worth it? Surely, Christina's been well taken care of. Is this worth the risk? Objectively. You are a man of science, think objectively. You have a solemn duty to protect society. If they find Black Beauty, they will have a powerful tool. But if they catch you with Christina, they will turn you into a battery of weapons, used to threaten and break countless others.*

Christophe swallowed hard. He paced back and forth, pulling at the skin on his throat to soothe himself. "But I am her father. I promised her," he whispered.

He darted into an alley as a horse-drawn cart came by.

It will take at least half an hour to get Christina and get back to Black Beauty, if not more. You know even if Marcus has not betrayed you, you are now a hunted man. You could get maybe a hundred miles away before they sound the general alarm. Look now, look at the light that's waiting to dawn.

Christophe looked up at the dark crimson sky. "I have a duty to her, as well."

She will be strong. You can reunite with her later or send money. Will you jeopardize everything for her?

He hit the sides of his head with his palms. "I have to. I have to!" Christophe stumbled about, landing on all fours. "It can't be the wrong thing. I can't believe Fate would be so cruel."

With a deep breath to clear his mind, he got up and dusted off his hands. He then headed down the streets, hiding in doorways as morning patrols passed by and dedicated drinkers staggered out of closing taverns.

Stopping at a bakery, Christophe turned around, his hands in his hair. "Wasn't it here? How could so much have changed in the past few years?"

"Sir, are you okay?" a firm and crisp voice asked. It was a constable, his arms behind his back and an eager-to-please smile on his face.

"I'm …," Christophe backed up, his fingers fluttered back and forth.

"You seem a bit lost, sir." He adjusted his cap and approached with an arm outstretched. "Do you need a doctor? Or is there an address I can help return you to, perhaps?"

"Yes, I ..." Christophe smoothed his beard. "Do you know where the inn is? I've been away for a few years. I thought it was here."

"Which inn, sir? Do you mean the Daventry? It was two streets south of here and then there's another one."

"Ah, it's more south," Christophe said, cutting the constable off. "Of course, I forgot to account for the edges of town having grown, in addition to the densification of the core downtown, and then the Conventioneers' urban planning committee's idea to redevelop the west side." He laughed and shook his head, his eyes closed tightly. "Ah, what I fool I am."

"Did you say Conventioneer?" the constable asked, stiffening.

"Hmm? No. Did you say south?"

He looked Christophe over and then nodded. "I did."

"Thank you." Christophe rushed off. A few minutes later, standing in the middle of another quiet street, his ears picked up a medley of laughter, music, and cheering. "At this time?" He looked up at the sky, where the blackness had surrendered, replaced by a bold crimson with a tinge of orange.

Following the noise, he found himself in front of a

two-story building with a familiar upper floor, but a startlingly different main floor. Once an inn, the new two-floor tavern had an open ground level, with a huge terrace extending over where a neighboring building had once been. The place was packed with lively people, and glancing up and down the street, Christophe could see as many coming as going.

The perimeter was outlined in wooden poles, all connected by ropes. On the ropes hung crank lanterns of various sizes and shapes, each one offering an individual amount of light.

"Clumsy, no consistency." He approached one and flicked at it. "Second hand parts, inefficient. Functional, but they look so cheap. They look like the work of a child."

Taking a good, long look at the place, his stomach twisted and turned. He didn't recognize any of the staff, and studying the second floor again, he saw that the windows had been changed. He wanted to believe it wasn't the same building, but he knew it was. He swallowed hard as the obvious question manifested into a chilling thought: *Is she still here? Or have I lost?*

A man tapped Christophe on the shoulder. "Excuse me, you're blocking my view of the band," said a man with a mug full of ale.

"Oh." Getting out of the way, Christophe turned to see a pair of musicians playing inside the tavern. A large wooden placard stood beside them. "Hazel Grey?"

"They're great. You should sit and listen. I love Paper Thin Kingdoms," said a stranger. "It's better out here on the terrace. Too loud inside."

Christophe listened for a moment and nodded. "Yes, very good."

Entering the tavern, his hands clenched into fists and his eyes searched for something or someone familiar. There were at least a dozen servers going every which way, skillfully carving paths through the bustle of patrons.

His heart leaped as he saw a child asleep at a table by the bar, but as he rushed forward a man leaned over and shook the child gently, then picked the boy up.

You have wasted enough time, said the voice in his head.

A woman appeared out of nowhere with a tray of ales and plates of mutton. "Sit where you can find a seat. We stop serving at five, so you better get your order in quickly. Or wait until we reopen for breakfast at six."

Christophe raised a hand. "Wait. I'm looking for … never mind."

The woman was gone.

He searched the walls for a clock, finding one behind the bar. There was something about it that drew him. At first, he thought it was the time running out, but that wasn't it. There was something familiar about it.

Shoving the other patrons aside, he planted his elbows on the bar and stuck his head as far over the bar as he could.

"The second hand. It's going backwards. Backwards!" He looked one way down the bar and then the other. "Hey," he called out to the bartender. "Hey."

"I'll get to you in a minute," the bartender replied.

Christophe stared at the clock, a nervous smile on his face. "She said she was going to do that. She was going to build a clock with a hand that ran backwards." He laughed and rubbed his trembling hands together.

Frowning and handing a patron a glass first, the bartender came over. "What is it? You'll have to speak up." He tapped his ear.

"That clock," Christophe said, his mouth suddenly going dry.

"Sorry, it's not for sale." The bartender shook his head. "Belongs to the owner. Did you want a drink?"

"The owner? But two sisters owned this place."

The bartender shook his head again. "Sorry, the owner doesn't come down until lunch time. She's pretty old."

Christophe threw two fingers up. "There were two sisters."

"Two?" The bartender glanced upward in thought for a moment. "Oh, yeah." He leaned beside Christophe's ear. "There's a plaque in the garden out back with the name of the owner's sister on it. So yeah, there was two of them. That was before my time though."

"Out back? Of course." Christophe pushed off the bar and ignored the person he bumped into. "I can probably still get up to her room." He laughed as he headed for the kitchen, and the door he remembered that led to the backyard. "How could I forget such a thing? I must be losing my mind."

The bartender glared at two large women standing at the edge of the bar and then nodded at Christophe.

Immediately they grabbed him and hauled him out the front and threw him to the ground. Several patrons stopped what they were doing and stared at him but quickly lost interest.

Christophe dusted himself off and looked at the terrace and then at the buildings on the other side. "The back is easy enough to get to. All I ask, Fate, is that Christina is still here."

Christophe crashed into a set of empty crates in the thin back alley that led to the tavern's backyard. Scrambling back to his feet, he crouched down, peering over the short, weather-beaten fence. Hurriedly making his way to the gate, he opened it and entered the ten-by-ten-foot yard.

Stepping in, his feet sank an inch. "Must be new," he said staring down at his muddy shoes in the sunken sod. Lifting his gaze, he saw an old familiar bench and flowers. Then in the corner, he saw something that made his heart soar. There was a pile of old, rusty lantern parts and a set of small-sized tools.

Crouching down, tears in his eyes, Christophe picked up a half-sized wrench and smiled at how worn it was. "She's a smart girl." He kissed the wrench and put it back down.

The back of the building had a door to the kitchen, which was closed, and a vine-covered trellis that brought another smile to his face. "You're still here. Of course, because Fate is with me," he shouted and then covered his mouth with a laugh.

Grabbing hold of the old trellis as he had years ago, he took a deep breath and started hauling himself up. It creaked and moaned horribly under his weight.

Arriving at the second-floor window, the reflection of the dawning sun forced Christophe to squint.

He rubbed his sleeve on the dirty window to find there was a wall of books lined on the sill. "She's reading? Of course. She's so smart."

It's not her room, whispered the dark voice inside

him. The tide of fear threatened to submerge the small island of confidence that he had left.

Christophe's hands went slick and his heart raced even faster. "No. No, it has to be." He rapped his knuckles on the window.

The trellis creaking grew as Christophe started swaying left and right. He banged on the window desperately. "Please be here. Please."

A shadow appeared at the window followed by a rapid-fire set of snapping sounds, and Christophe plummeted to the ground.

As he fell, the thought of villages burning with soldiers riding in on hundreds of Black Beauties filled his mind. Then a single sound washed it all away and returned him to the present.

"Papa?" a sweet, soft voice asked. "Papa?"

Christophe's eyes shot open. He stared up at an open window, but there was no one there.

Slowly, he pulled his aching body out of the impression he'd left in the new grass. "I heard someone. I know I did." Putting a hand over his eyes to shade them from the early morning light, he stared back up at the window. It was indeed open.

He turned around, shaking his head, gazing about the small yard.

Then suddenly he was struck from behind as the tavern's backdoor opened, sending him sprawling forward.

As he stumbled about, someone grabbed him and tackled him to the ground.

"Papa! Papa!"

He peered down at the head of long, dark blond hair. He'd never felt such a mighty grip in all his life.

"I knew you would come. I knew it. I missed you so much."

Tears streaming, his throat and chest tight, Christophe gazed down upon the image of hope and faith itself. "You are so big, and I am so sorry."

"I'm six now, and I don't care that you are very late." She gave him an extra squeeze, making him cough.

"I need to get up," he grunted, peeling her off and standing back. He cleared his throat and dusted his hands, as he stared at her.

Her eyes had rivers of tears that ran into the edges of her immense smile.

Stepping forward, Christophe groaned from the rising pain of the fall. He took her hands and ran his thumbs over their tops. "They are pretty rough for a little girl."

He nodded at the pile of lanterns. "Did you make all of them around this place?"

"Yes. And I fixed the stove. Twice." She bounced with pride.

"That is amazing. A-mazing." Christophe stared at the tools.

"Where were you?" she asked, her question cutting right through him.

His shoulders sank, and he bowed his head. "I was arrested, Meeshich."

Christina's eyebrows shot up. "Why?"

"Because I wouldn't do bad things. The King of Teuton is not a good man."

Do the right thing, Christophe. She deserves a good life, a better life than you can give her.

"But they let you go?"

Christophe grimaced and shook his head. "No, I escaped." He licked his lips and sighed heavily. "And I've come to say …," his throat tightened, and his words disappeared as he stared into Christina's eyes. Into her innocent little eyes, darting back and forth almost imperceptibly, trying to predict what he was about to say so as to insulate herself from the pain. It was the same look he'd had time and again growing up as Fate tested his resolve.

He cleared his throat and stared at the ground. "And I came to tell you that I will—"

"Take me with you." Christina's voice was firm and decisive. She reached out for him and he unconsciously recoiled.

"No, I was …," Christophe glanced up at her. He stepped forward and put his thumb on her chin. It looked like an angelic button placed on her perfect square jaw. Closing his eyes, he pulled her to him and hugged her, kissing the top of her head. "Yes, if you want."

"Let's go right now."

"We will need to tell your aunt and then go right away."

Christina sprang back and pointed at the window. "She already has my note. I left it by her bed."

"What?" Christophe frowned. "How?"

"I wrote a note that said Gone with Papa a year ago and told Auntie all about it. She knows that if she ever sees it, that you came back and I'm with you."

Christophe's chin quivered, and he looked away, wiping his eyes on his sleeve.

"We have to go before the bad men come." She furrowed her brow and he laughed.

"Yes, yes, we do, Meeshich," he said, pinching her cheek. "And we will need to be quiet."

Christina hunched over. "It's okay, because I am quiet and fast." She straightened up and looked at him.

"What is it?" he asked, his fragile confidence feeling threatened again.

She should stay, and she knows it, said the inner voice. *Don't do this.*

"Is Black Beauty waiting for us?"

He smiled from ear to ear. "Let's go see."

12

LAIR OF A GIANT

In the Present

Francis Stein finished climbing the stairs and noted the Moufan-Man elite at the end of the corridor at the lone door. Without his host, Rumpere saying a word, Stein knew it had to be the room of legendary inventor Christophe Creangle, one of his wife's all-time heroes.

Surely there will be some precious invention here that will convince the Queen of Dery to finally make me a king's-man. We desperately need that promised income, thought Stein. *Please, have something to turn this dream-become-nightmare opportunity around.*

The door was made of wood and steel, with a padlocked latch keeping it secure from the world.

Stein removed his spectacles and rubbed his face with a worn-leather gloved hand.

He thought back to the initial letter from the Queen's council that had dangled the opportunity for riches and fortune before Stein and his wife, Jacqueline. It seemed like the world was finally taking notice of the work they were doing and offering them a golden opportunity.

Throwing his usual cautiousness to the wind, Stein signed the lease for a Baron's Manor and surprised Jacqueline over a romantic dinner. Gone would be the days of their small apartment with the leaky sink, and instead, the life they'd dreamed of would start immediately. The letter virtually guaranteed that their monthly stipend as king's-men would start as soon as a few more details, all of them declared formalities, were ironed out.

Then a letter had come asking for money to pay for an arbitration fee and then another asking for them to surrender the rights to an *invention of note* in order to prove their worthiness over other potential candidates. Stein had shielded Jacqueline from it and their mounting debt. He would get them out of the hole he'd created for them.

Weeks ago, when he'd received a letter and noted that Jacqueline's name had been dropped from it, he found himself staring at the one thing that inspired Jacqueline every day, the Creangle mechanical arm. He was tempted to take it and send it in, certain it would clinch the king's-manship, but he couldn't do that to her. That was when an idea came to him, and he reached out to old Kar'm contacts of his.

He'd discovered that Christophe Creangle was still alive, though in poor health. A bit of investigation revealed Christophe to be at the Doyono compound of the Moufan and at death's door. Desperate, Stein sent off a letter to the usually reclusive Moufan with a proposal: money for the final effects of the once great inventor. A few weeks later, a reasonable counteroffer had arrived, signed by the Moufan's new leader.

"Doctor Stein?" Rumpere asked. "You don't look well."

Stein stared at his host and then straightened up. "I am fine. Top form. Just a few rogue thoughts fighting for attention." He took a deep breath and forced all the bubbling guilt for his secret deeds back into its emotional bottle. He was going to solve it, here and now. It was as simple as that.

"I do believe this is what you've been waiting for." Rumpere shoved the creaky door open. "Welcome to the final home of the late, great Christophe Creangle."

Stein took off his hat and entered the room, a draft immediately whipping around his legs. The room was round, set in one of the keep's towers. There were two large windows high up on the back wall.

"With the stone walls, floor, and ceiling, it's almost

like living in a cave." Stein frowned. "Hard to imagine such genius being able to flourish in a place like this."

Rumpere gave him a sideways glance. "He had nothing left but madness in the end. Xenio Creangle didn't recognize his own daughter or even his own name."

Stein pointed at the only two pieces of furniture in the room. "Is there just the stripped bed and the worktable?"

"The entire room was covered in papers and undesirables. After we purged everything of no value, we cleaned the floor and walls with bleach and left those windows open for a week." Rumpere stood by the door, his hands together in front of him.

Sniffing the air, Stein nodded. "It seems to be fine now." He walked over to the metal-framed bed that was in the middle of the room. Bending down, he pressed a hand on the naked mattress and stared at the large divot in the middle.

"I have to say," Stein continued, "I didn't think much of Christophe back at Kar'm, but then, I didn't really know his history. It was my wife, Jacqueline, who told me of his accomplishments and the stories surrounding him. For a man who seemed unable to tolerate people, there are many tales of him helping those in desperate need with small favors and gifts as he ran from the clutches of one person bent on controlling his genius to another."

Making his way over to the workbench, Stein's frown grew. All that remained of the once legendary genius were two one-inch-high piles of neatly stacked paper. He picked up one of the stacks and flipped through it, shaking his head. "Is there anything else other than this?"

"No," Rumpere replied.

"Nothing at all?" Stein felt hot and tugged at his shirt collar. Gripping the edge of the table, his heart pounding in his ears, Stein stared down at the papers. *They want a kingly sum for this? This? I was hoping to sell off some of the trinkets to cover the promissory note I have on me, but for these scribbles of a madman? I can't do anything with this. I spent the last of our funds getting here. I've ruined us.*

"I sense your disappointment." Rumpere folded his arms.

Stein turned around and leaned against the table. He folded his arms as well. "I was rather explicit in my letter about wanting any pieces of machines, half-built devices, and whatnot. I didn't come all this way for just a stack of papers. They aren't even written in a sensical language."

"They are written as Creangle wrote them." Rumpere walked over and tapped a stack of papers. "They are in his own cryptic language, but I'm sure a worldly man such as yourself knows that all great inventors do that."

"This wasn't our deal." Stein shaking angrily. He put his hat back on and gave Rumpere an icy stare.

Rumpere wandered away, unfazed. "If you look at the terms of our agreement, you'll find it is the deal we made." He looked over at Stein. "I am certain there is more value there than you can imagine. The only reason we are selling them is to recoup our expenses for having housed Creangle, his daughter, and the feral girl that attacked you."

Stein lowered his gaze, the sound of his own heart distracting him. "Expenses, ah, I see your game." Raising a finger, he nodded to himself. "Yes, you are trying to drive a harder bargain. There *were* other items, weren't there? How much for everything? All of it."

Rumpere stared at Stein for a while before shaking his head. "The other items are not for sale. I have a plan for the Moufan, and we need a few things for ourselves. That said, we have no interest in flying machines and carriages that are not pulled. These drawings and plans and rantings, they can either be yours or they can go to someone else who sees the tremendous deal I'm offering."

"Tremendous deal?" Stein grabbed the papers and marched over to Rumpere. "These? You do realize that you have implied that either you can't make sense of them and therefore they have no value, or you do understand them and know they have no value. No deal."

Rumpere straightened, his piercing glare pushing Stein back. "I have something I offered you, that I know has value. And you have offered something to me, which will have value."

Thinking for a moment, it hit Stein. "The armor based on Mounira's cloak."

"Yes."

"Ah." Stein relaxed and nodded. "That's a secondary deal that would have significant value."

"Yes, it would. We would be able to pay for such innovation in kind or with funds. Whatever would be your need."

Stein stared at the wall, mulling over his options. The Moufan-Men were going to be a formidable force going forward, and Stein relished the idea of being of value to them. Still, it all felt like another form of what had been happening with the Queen of Dery.

"Those papers are the seeds of greatness, Stein. You and Benstock can grow an empire from them. Do not waste this opportunity to be the first ally of the new Moufan."

Stein looked desperately at the papers in his hands, his mental wheels turning. "I can only offer half of the agreed-to-amount."

"Ah, so finally we've come to this." Rumpere stroked his mustache.

"I had stated in my letter that my price assumed papers, devices, tools, and more," continued Stein. "All you have for me are papers. Papers are filled with hypotheses, ideas, designs, but nothing in them can speak to whether or not any of them work or are even possible."

Stein swallowed and thought of Jacqueline, steeling himself. "Do we have a new deal?"

Rumpere shook his head. "No, you see, I know a few things about you, Stein. For one, I know that you are not yet a king's-man, despite what you had implied in your letters. I also know that you need me more than I need you."

"The date was simply moved back for my confirmation," Stein quickly replied.

Rumpere scoffed. "Are you trying to lie to a spy master, or are you so easily deceived as to not see the obvious?" He let his words hang there, eating away at Stein's confidence. "I will accept the full payment, but as a show of good faith, I will not redeem the promissory note for the money you've committed to for two months."

Stein's face went pale and he tugged on his lower lip.

"I am certain that Professor Benstock will have been able to turn those seeds of greatness into a small fortune, at least, by then. She's very resourceful. And as for the payment," Rumpere laughed, "make sure you have the funds for when that promissory note is redeemed. Looking over one's shoulder for assassins, every minute of every day for the rest of your life, can cause terrible cramps in the neck."

Clearing his throat, Stein looked at the papers he had wrung in his hands. "Seeds of greatness?"

Rumpere shrugged. "Nothing is certain in this world, but I believe this will lead you and the professor to your true destiny. But my opinion doesn't matter. What do you say, Doctor Stein?" He put his hand out.

Chewing on his cheek for a moment, Stein shook Rumpere's hand. "We have a deal."

With a devilish smile, Rumpere ended the shake and turned his hand to accept something.

Stein reached into his coat and took hold of the envelope with the promissory note in it. With his fate literally in hand, he hesitated, glancing about the room. Swallowing hard, he plucked the envelope out and handed it to Rumpere.

Rumpere quickly checked the details and then tucked it away. "Very good. I will send word to you by Neumatic tube the week before we hand this over to our bankers in Plance."

"How do you know I have a Neumatic tube machine? We just had it installed."

"Do you need to know your wife's favorite color?" Rumpere went to the doorway. "When you deal with

—" Recognizing the figure at the end of the corridor, he retreated.

Stein frowned. "What's going on?"

"We have an untimely wrinkle."

Peeking through the doorway, Stein's eyes went wide. "Christina Creangle? She seems quite angry."

"Rumpere." Christina kept one hand on her pistol as she raced toward the doorway that Rumpere had just disappeared back into. She slowed as the door to her father's room closed and the black-hooded guard stepped forward.

"Halt," he said, reaching under his cloak. "You are not permitted to come any closer."

"Like yigging hell, I'm not," Christina replied, her free hand slipping down to the small of her back. Flipping a switch on the canister, little puffs and clinks announced the compressed air getting ready for use. "You're the one who's not supposed to be here."

The Moufan-Man pulled out a two-foot-long metal staff and shook it, extending it another foot in each direction. One end was wrapped in wire, while the other was covered in a black rubbery substance.

"A bit primitive, isn't it? You guys could at least have stolen a recent design for a shock-staff. I don't want to hurt you. My issue is with Rumpere, not you."

The guard lowered his stance. "Then it's with me."

The guard double-tapped the bottom of the staff sending sparks of electricity about. "Surrender."

"Please, that's far from impressive. I built stuff like that when I was twelve."

As the guard went to strike, she ducked and plucked the wire out from where it connected to the second segment. He then swung, and she caught the staff.

"I'm sure Mounira would say something plucky but that's not my style." She pulled out her pistol and pointed it at his head.

The guard stared at his staff, confused.

"You just need to put that wire back in to bring it to life," she said, letting the staff go and pointing with her free hand. "But I recommend you just walk away while you can."

The guard shoved her back with a foot to the waist. As Christina regained her balance, he grabbed the wire and stared at where she'd pointed.

"Now, you're not going to walk away." Christina pointed the pistol at his foot. A powerful whoosh of air was immediately followed by the sound of bones cracking.

As the guard fell against the wall, clutching his foot, Christina plucked the staff from his hand and slipped her pistol back into its holster. "I'm surprised you kept that scream in. Big guys like you, they usually have the highest screams, in my experience."

The guard swung at her with one hand, nearly teetering over. She easily stepped out of the way. "You'll rot in the dungeon like your whelp."

"Is that where she is? Thanks, I'll head there next." Christina squinted at the wiring. "Fitting this back in is a bit tricky but let me do that for you as repayment. There." She banged the staff on the ground, making arcs of electricity come out the other end. "Here you go." She dropped it on the guard's other foot.

Sparks flew, and the guard flailed for a few seconds before dropping to the ground, unconscious.

Searching him, she found the padlock in one of his gigantic pockets. Examining it, she frowned in confusion. "These are the clumsiest and strangest lock-picking scratches I've ever seen." She looked over at the door. There were more scratches all around the door handle, where the padlock had been, and even randomly on the door. "How haven't I noticed those before?"

She rubbed her forehead. *Rumpere must have a key. That means things really were going missing from Papa's room.*

Tossing the lock aside, she stood up and gave the door a shove, the discharged staff in hand. "Rumpere!" A second shove swung it open.

Inside, the Moufan-Man leader was standing to her

left, while a man in modern dress was over to the right. She looked at the stranger and was taken aback. "Stein? What are you doing here?"

Stein put his hands behind his back. "Ah." He bowed his head. "I had no idea you were here. Perhaps it is best that I be going."

"Not so fast." Christina pointed the staff at him. She then shifted her attention to Rumpere. "What are you doing in here?" Her gut twisted and she glanced about the room. "Where are all my father's things? And where's Mounira?"

"So many questions." Rumpere put his hands behind his back, his shoulders and face relaxed, and a hint of smugness sat coyly on his face. "But, I'm afraid," he said, scratching his cheek and moving forward, "that I have to ask you to leave immediately unless you want to be arrested like that young vermin pet you've had."

Christina's nostrils flared, and her eyes went wide. "What did you do?"

Rumpere shrugged. "Mounira attempted to assassinate our honored guest. You should be thankful that I didn't behead her on the spot for such a crime. But I thought our guest might find it barbaric." He waved at Stein. "As for you, you are no longer welcome and in accordance with our laws regarding Xenias, you must remove yourself immediately."

Christina shifted her burning gaze to Stein who

stood his ground, his expression telling her that Rumpere's story was at least partially true.

He didn't mention Angelina, that's good. She'll get Mounira; I just need to focus on the here and now.

The staff emitted a high-pitched whine, indicating that it was ready for use. A wicked grin crossed Christina's lips.

"We had an agreement," she said to Rumpere. "No one was allowed in here. There was to be no key, other than mine."

Stein went for the door and Christina glared at him, waving the staff at him again. He retreated.

"All agreements with you, Xenia Creangle, ended with Christophe's death." Rumpere tugged on his cloak. "Every day since, every meal, every training session the little free-loading Southerner attended, has been because I allowed it. And today, that has ended."

He leaned to the side and pointed. "I would recommend running along now before I verify that you have indeed killed my guard. That would undoubtedly make you an official enemy of the Moufan, and we have a long, long memory."

"He's unconscious," snapped Christina.

"A matter for a Moufan tribunal to determine, a tribunal that as leader I would undoubtedly head. Now run along." He waved his hands at her. "Shoo."

Just then, Stein made a break for the door and managed to get past Christina. As she turned to try and grab him, Rumpere pounced and struck her in the back of the head, knocking her to the ground.

"I believe this is our property," he said, snatching the staff. As he went to tap her with it, she managed to grab the wire, but not before getting a nasty shock that made her world spin.

As Christina pushed herself up from the ground, Rumpere smiled at her from the other side of the doorway.

"I've changed my mind. Please, stay as long as you like. And I do find some irony in locking another Creangle in this room. Don't you?" He pulled the door tightly closed.

Staggering to the door, Christina heard the muffled sound of the padlock being fitted into place.

She sank down to the ground. Reaching the bottom, she banged her head several times against the door.

"That could have gone better. Now how the yig am I going to get out of this?"

13

CLUTCHES OF THE MOUFAN

"At least there's some light from those overhead grids, or we'd be in pitch black. Mind you, I also wish one of them would move and let us find another way out of the Moufan compound." Angelina leaned against the slimy, brick wall of the old aqueduct tunnel. Resting her hands on her soaked knees, she stared at her shadowy reflection in the water. Half of her stolen cloak floated beside her.

"That's the spirit," Mounira said. "I knew you could find something positive to say." She continued sloshing through the thigh-high water.

"Are you always this positive? Did your brain adapt to your arm pain and make you perky?" asked Angelina, pushing off the wall and following. She looked at her hands in disgust and wiped them on the cloak.

"My mother says despair corrodes the spirit and then dooms the soul," said Mounira. "Which way do you think we should go? The water seems to be flowing from both directions."

"I don't know, let's take a second. It's been a busy day," Angelina said.

Mounira examined the brickwork around her. It was falling apart, with the mortar worn away so much it wasn't clear how the bricks in the arched ceiling of the tunnel were staying in place. "This place certainly has been here a long time. You'd think they'd take better care of it."

"You'd be surprised how many cities build something vital like this, forget all about it, then can't afford to fix it." Angelina went several yards down one of the two tunnels ahead of them. "Hmm." She then went down the other one. "I think the light at the end of this one's brighter. What do you think?"

"It does seem a bit brighter. Also, there's something different about it. Is it more blue?"

Angelina nodded. "Most probably daylight. You said that there's a lake on the west side of the Moufan compound where they likely get their drinking water, right?"

"I think so. No one ever gave me an answer. I think many of them don't know."

"You didn't get an answer?"

"I ask a lot of questions. I only get a few real answers," Mounira said with a shrug.

"Fair enough." Angelina turned her head about. "I can't get my bearings; we've done too many twists and turns." She checked her pockets again. "That compass I brought hasn't reappeared either. Anyway, I think this way is west." Angelina pushed forward. "Please be west, I hate being soaked."

"Be positive," Mounira said, following.

"Be less annoying."

They soldiered on for several minutes, finally arriving at the mouth of the tunnel. Stepping out onto a plateau, they each took a deep breath and sighed.

"That smells a lot better." Angelina gazed at the tall trees and greenery. "They must have quite the pump system to get water up from that lake down there."

"That's one of the seven lakes."

Angelina raised an eyebrow. "Don't you mean five lakes?"

Mounira didn't say a word.

"Your expression. Are you practicing lying?" Angelina asked.

This time it was Mounira who raised an eyebrow. "How did you know?"

"Firstly, because you just told me. Secondly, because you looked like you wondered if I would buy it. A good liar always convinces themselves that what they're about to say is the truth. That way, their face doesn't react like that."

"Oh," Mounira replied, with a firm nod. "Well, there are four lakes."

"Next time, tell yourself that there are five lakes first. You might need that skill someday."

Angelina pointed to the right. "It looks like there's a path this way. Come on." She pulled the hood of her cloak up and motioned for Mounira to stay behind her.

They came to a clearing with a thick ceramic pipe. It had a leak right before the pipe disappeared under water and joined the others in the tunnel. From the leak shot a fountain of water high into the air.

There was a bent over woman in a ratty, old, grey cloak standing in the spray of water, two buckets beside her. Off to the side was a mule, loaded with saddle bags, tied to a tree.

"I think we should go around, avoid—" Angelina was surprised to see Mounira dart past her toward the stranger. "Mounira."

The old woman turned, a look of shock on her face. "Mounira?"

"Professor, I've missed you," Mounira shouted, throwing her arm around the woman, who immediately hugged her back. "You were the best history and languages teacher. The guy who replaced you was just evil, definitely one of Rumpere's guys."

"What are you doing here?" the professor asked as Mounira let her go.

"I was going to ask you the same thing," Mounira said. "Why aren't you in the compound?"

"Ah …"

"And your face. You've lost too much weight."

The woman frowned.

"Sorry. But you have, though I know I shouldn't have said anything. Augustan habit. But why are you …?"

Unable to help herself, the woman laughed.

Angelina cautiously approached.

"She a friend of yours?" the professor asked, pointing.

Mounira glanced back at Angelina. "Her? Yes. She kind of helped me with having been arrested and then escaping. It's why we're here. We're sort of escaping."

"And Xenia Creangle? Is she all right?" the professor asked.

Mounira looked up as she realized she was being rained down on from the pipe. "Yes. She'll be joining us soon."

"Good, I liked her. Troubled soul but good woman." The woman bent down to check the levels of her buckets. "Oh, I forgot the lids."

"Are they with your mule?" Angelina asked.

The professor nodded.

"I'll fetch them for you. Happy to help a friend of Mounira's."

"Why are you here, Professor?" Mounira asked, looking straight at her.

The woman bowed her head. "Life has been harder these past few months. The last of us were cast out, excommunicated by Rumpere."

"How are they allowed to do that? The rules of the Moufan state are clear."

"The rules of the Moufan," the professor tapped Mounira's cheek, "only work if everyone abides by them. Rumpere is reshaping what it means to be Moufan; changing the rules, supported by those of his inner circle, and they are surrounded by a vocal and violent group who wish they could be him."

Mounira furrowed her brow. "We must do something."

Angelina pulled her hood forward and handed the professor her lids. "We're kind of escaping at the moment, Mounira."

"But we can't just allow this injustice to stand," Mounira said.

"You didn't mention exactly what are you escaping from?"

Mounira looked at the professor and offered an awkward smile. "I might have taken a run at Rumpere's guest?"

"Mounira, I warned you."

"But," Mounira raised a finger in protest. "it wasn't until *after* Anciano Creangle passed away. So technically, I kept my promise to you."

"You're claiming you stuck to the letter of the law but not the spirit?" asked the professor. "And how many times throughout my classes did we see that work out well in history?"

"Rumpere's used it, so I'd say pretty well," Angelina said, throwing cold water on the conversation. "We have to get going."

"Maybe she can help us. Can you, professor?" Mounira asked.

"I can't. While the rules don't apply to Rumpere, they do apply to those of us that remain living outside of the compound. If I'm seen helping you, I'll be beaten and left to die." She pulled on her hole-riddled, mud-caked cloak.

Mounira closed her eyes. "The rules of exile," she muttered to herself. "There's got to be something."

"Nice meeting you, but we need to get going," Angelina said.

"What I can say is that you won't likely get far, I'm afraid." The professor glanced about. "I'm guessing you caught Rumpere by surprise, which is why you've gotten this far. He doesn't do well thinking on his feet, but some of his advisors do. You're heading to Doyono, aren't you?"

"I figure it's the best way to get out of Dery," Angelina answered.

"It is, but sadly, he knows that. Searching a city that size would take too long, so he'll have the paths guarded."

Angelina scoffed. "I thought you said you couldn't help us."

"Trust me, this isn't any help. It's just fact," the professor said, putting the lid on one of her buckets.

"Ah, I've got it." Mounira opened her eyes and scanned about. " I need something. That will do." She snatched a two-foot-long stick with a sharp edge and pointed at the professor.

"Mounira, what are you doing?" the professor asked.

"By the code of conduct for exile, you are allowed to take actions for self-preservation. I'm taking you hostage."

The professor frowned, then smiled. "It does state that, yes, but I don't see how that changes anything. I know you, as do all the Moufan here. They also know that you would never harm me, and therefore, I would be accused of being complicit in helping you."

Angelina grabbed the stick out of Mounira's hands. "But you don't know me." She poked the woman in the arm.

"Ow." The professor rubbed her forearm.

"Now we've established that I'm willing to hurt you." Angelina gave Mounira an evil smile. "So, is there a way you can get us into Doyono without being noticed by the Moufan or tipping off anyone who's going to be trouble?"

The professor thought for a moment and then nodded. "You're kidnapping Mounira, I assume."

"Of course," replied Angelina. "I'm planning on selling her to the slavers in Kaban. It's a bit of a hike, but I like the exercise."

Mounira went to protest but Angelina clamped a hand on her mouth. "Shh."

The professor put the lid on the second bucket. "I can get you there safely. What about my water and mule?"

"We might need supplies," said Angelina with a smirk. "Best to bring them in case we need them. Mounira, would you mind getting the buckets tied to the mule?" She removed her hand and Mounira glared at her. "Well?"

"Sure." Mounira picked up the first of the buckets and headed for the mule.

The professor looked at Mounira, shaking her head. "She's smart, that one."

Angelina laughed. "She is, and a good fighter, but a bit too trusting for her own good."

"That'll change," said the professor, giving Angelina a sideways glance.

Christina rubbed her forehead thoughtfully. "Well, screwing up like that is one way to get the mental rust out." She gazed about the locked room that had been home to her father for two years. "How am I going to get out of here before they show up with a small army? Because there's no chance Rumpere's just going to leave me in here to die, he's too impatient."

Slowly getting herself up, she double-checked that the door was indeed padlocked, and all the hinges were strong.

Standing there, she couldn't help but notice Christophe's nail marks on the door and its frame. A shiver went through her as she recalled her father's muffled cries and screams at her locking him in.

Turning away, her hand over her quivering chin, Christina remembered only two weeks ago as he beat his hands against the door until he fell over. She'd found him asleep an hour later, on the floor.

Prior to locking him in every night, her father had taken to wandering the halls in the dark. Confused and disoriented, he'd fallen down stairs and badly injured himself several times. Once, she found him unconscious in the main courtyard.

Stroking her forehead like her Auntie used to, Christina reminded herself that she'd done the right thing. His dementia had grown to consume him, and her actions had been out of caring and a sense of duty, not out of malice or a desire for any form of revenge for breaking her heart time and again when she was young. He had even been the one to suggest it, in a rare moment of clarity.

Christina stepped into the sunbeam from one of the windows and closed her eyes. The warmth was welcome and calming, and her thoughts turned to Mounira. The guilt of having kept Christophe's imprisonment from her surfaced and melted away in the sun.

Opening her eyes, she sighed and gazed about the room with a foreign sense of calm. The windows were too high up for her to use the bed as a ladder or hook, and the workbench was too solid for her to take apart, so she was going to need to innovate if she was going to get out.

Turning to the windows again, she shook her head. "Even if I can get up there, the rocks are too smooth to scale, never mind being an easy target for the Moufan as I climb down three stories." She glanced at the door. "That's going to be the only way out."

Taking the canister off her back, she played with it in her hands and approached the workbench.

It had once held a mountain of mutant and misfit technological contraptions of all sizes and a blanket of papers. The floor had been a sea of drawings of landscapes, horses, and her at various ages.

Drawings, thought Christina, her focus suddenly polluted with the taint of sorrow. She reached into a pocket and pulled out a piece of folded paper.

Opening it up, she studied Mounira's charcoal drawing of Christophe. It was him laughing, with a spark of life she'd only ever gotten to catch glimpses of.

The edge of her lips turned up tenderly as she stroked the side of the paper with her thumb. She chuckled and rubbed her nose. "That girl. One day she's eleven years old and helping me build a rocketing flying machine to save our friends, and now she can catch a lifetime in a single image." Christina carefully folded the paper back up. "I'd be a kite lost in the wind without her."

She casually glanced downward at another piece of paper. Reluctantly, she crouched down and stared at it. "I should leave you here," she said, gently picking it up.

It was an inch-and-a-half-square in size. Its corners were rounded with age, and its folding lines nearly completely torn through.

Christina let out a heavy, uneven sigh as she ran a finger along its tear-stained top, hints of the black ink inside having soaked through over the decades. Even though every time she looked in the mirror she saw its image decorating her shoulders, she'd been unable to let the paper itself go. Despite its tiny size, her shoulders slumped, and she felt like the demons of her past were climbing out of the shadows on top of her.

She dropped herself onto the bed, which squeaked oddly and loudly in protest. Lying there, she flexed her tingling fingers and fought for breath. Glancing about, she tried to tell herself that the rising tide of sorrows wasn't real, just the result of a childhood nightmare, but her body didn't seem to care.

After slipping the paper back into a pocket, Christina grabbed the edge of the bed hard. Gritting her teeth, she imagined herself grabbing the embodiment of her past. Pulling herself up, she felt the sorrow once again transform, as it had many times in the past, into an inferno of anger.

Finally, able to draw a full breath, she found herself staring at the ground, blood dripping from one hand. Christina examined her wound, a light scratch from a sharp piece of metal sticking out oddly from the wooden frame of the bed.

Christina pulled her shirt back and forth, cooling down. She was soaked in sweat.

The last attack, the first in years, had been hours after Christophe's funeral where she hadn't allowed a single tear to betray her steely veneer.

Standing up, she walked over to stand in the sunbeam from one of the windows, her arms folded. Closing her eyes, she relished the warmth of it, the glow beneath her eyelids. After a minute, she opened her eyes and looked at the room again, calm and focused.

Christina stared at the bed, scratching the back of her head. *Why are you calling to me?*

She walked over and sat on it. It squeaked again. Unhooking her air canister, she placed it and her air gun on the ground and lay down in the bed, her hands on her chest.

Ignore whose bed this is. Ignore where you are. Just focus on something else.

A bird chirped outside the open windows, and a faint smile crossed her lips. "Someone was listening."

Christina let her hands wander along the edge of the bed frame, and then a thought hit her, and she sat up. "This bed's wooden. There's not supposed to be any metal." She looked at her hand. "A cut and squeaking? There's something going on here."

She bounced and heard it squeak again, this time noting it wasn't coming from the middle of the bed but rather specifically from the right side.

Flipping the bed on its side, she studied its underbody. "These wooden slats aren't original, or necessary. Who has two layers of slats?" She got up close and examined the edges of the slats. "The craftsmanship ... he did all of this himself. But why?"

She leaned back, furrowing her brow. "Because he was hiding something. So, what were you hiding?" She flipped the bed completely over.

With a grunt, she yanked out one of the slats and then another. "There's something here, what is it?" With a valiant tug, she pulled out another slat and something caught her eye. "What's that shadow?"

Reaching into a groove, she gently removed a long, rectangular metal box that ran the length of the bed. Inside it was a thin, five-elbowed mechanical arm with a pincer at one end and a set of rings at the other.

Christina stood up and held the apparatus out in front of her. The pieces flopped about. "This doesn't look like it's all of something, just part of it. What's missing?" She stared at it, her mind running through dozens of possibilities. "The rings, they're supposed to have some kind of wire. It should run through here, over to these. That's how I would have built it. So, is that what he did?" She placed it on the floor in the window's sunbeam and tore the bed apart. Eventually, she found a false panel in the headboard of the bed, revealing a set of small mirrors and steel strings.

She brought the new pieces over and assembled the arm. "The one he made for Mounira was controlled by her neck and her stump and required a backpack-sized mechanism to control it. This is much simpler, but what is it? It's definitely not for her."

Slipping her hand into a mechanism at one end, she manipulated the arm with incredible precision, moving each of the elbows and controlling the pincer unlike anything she'd ever seen. "Why would you have made this?" She stared at the door and it clicked in her mind. "That's what those scratches on the outside were." She put the arm down and dashed back over to the bed. "There's got to be something else here somewhere."

Inside one of the discarded slats, she discovered a slot where lo and behold, she found a crude lock pick.

Placing the pick in the end of the apparatus, she went over to the stonework surrounding the door and felt around until a stone eventually gave up its secret and moved out of the way.

Staring through to the corridor, she bowed her head and swallowed. *He got out whenever he wanted, whenever he was coherent. He really did appreciate being locked in.* Her eyes stung with tears. "Thanks, Papa."

14

FATE OF THE CREANGLES

In the Past

As his six-year-old daughter tripped over a root, Christophe grabbed her tight. Falling to the ground, he smacked his head against the base of a tree.

Groaning as he let her go, little Christina put her little hands on his bearded face. "Papa, are you alright?"

He smiled at her. "I'm okay. This head of mine is made of wood." He gave himself a knock with his knuckles and she smiled. Getting back to his feet, he dusted himself off.

Looking at the sky, the sun was not offering him any reprieve. The morning was coming, fast and furiously, bringing with it a haunting sense of despair for Christophe.

Christina tugged on his hand. "Papa, you said we have to keep moving." She frowned and puffed out her lips. Then in a silly, deeper voice, she said, "No looking at the birds, Christina, we must go."

He ran a finger down her cheek. "You are very right, Meeshich." His eyes darted about at his suddenly unfamiliar surroundings. "Where was I going?" He put a hand to his forehead.

"We were going that way." Christina pointed. "Were you testing me?"

He patted her hand as he recognized where they were. "Yes, of course. Good girl. Now remember, the early morning light can play tricks on you. Some roots and rocks are hiding in shadows, waiting for feet to come by. Don't let them grab you."

"Okay."

"Good, let's go."

As they headed off, Christophe heard another wet cough come from Christina, and his pace slowed. They'd started shortly after leaving the inn, and despite her not complaining, he'd spent too much time with some of the medically-trained Conventioneers to know that it wasn't nothing.

She needs medical attention, you know that. How are you going to provide that on the run, with no money? He rubbed his face. "No."

"Ah, the clearing, we are here," said Christophe, a

smile showing his hope reigniting. "She's right over there. Can you see her?"

"Where Papa? I don't see Black Beauty." Christina stood there, shaking her head. "Is this a trick?"

"What do you mean? I can see her." He pointed at the bushes between two trees. "Do you see her?"

Christina shook her head, her ponytail flapping.

He walked over and took hold of the camouflage tarp. With a smile and a showman's flourish, he pulled away the tarp and waved at the horse. "How about now?"

With a chirp of excitement, Christina clapped and danced about before running over to join him. "She's real. She's real!"

"And we are going to ride her to a new home."

Christophe watched as his daughter's gaze darted about, and every thought that tried to make it to her lips was pre-empted by another cough and then another.

He picked her up and gave her a tight hug. "I have wanted to show you her for a long, long time."

"Does she work like my lanterns?" she asked, her arms still around him.

"She does, just more complex."

"Like the lanterns are harder than the clock?"

"Exactly," he said, tapping her nose as he let go of her. "I need to check the saddle is secure and then we go. It can loosen with you."

"I know," she said, staring at her reflection in the side of the shining horse.

He took out his goggles from one of the saddlebags and checked the saddle straps. "How do you know such things?" he asked playfully.

"I read." She turned and looked up at the sun, closing her eyes. "I read lots of things."

Christophe stopped and stared at his little girl, the morning light kissing her innocent face. "You ...," he abandoned the banter and looked at the sun dancing on her dark blond hair.

A lump formed in his throat and he folded his arms, a hand on his chin. *Am I being selfish?*

He glanced at the belly of Black Beauty, and the tendrils of guilt reached out from the darkness and touched his soul, sending a sharp chill through him, making him shiver violently.

Stepping forward he put a hand on her back. "Time for you to go up."

She opened her eyes and smiled at him, which only seemed to intensify the chill that lingered inside.

He lifted Christina into the saddle. "You in front and Papa behind. Hold those reins, we don't want her running away."

"Okay." Christina held them tightly in her hands, a pretend scowl of concentration on her face.

"Hold on," he said as he went to the head of the horse. "She's about to wake up."

Reaching into the mouth, he brought the King's-Horse to life. Christina yipped loudly in excitement.

Christophe put on the goggles and got into the saddle, placing his feet on the pedals.

"The wind will be fierce. You may need to close your eyes," Christophe said, putting a hand around her waist. "But don't worry, Papa has you." He eased the pedals downward, and Black Beauty took a few slow steps forward, then a few more a bit faster.

"Go, Papa. Go," cheered Christina, leaning her tearing face into the wind as Black Beauty rose to a gallop.

Black Beauty roared out of the forest and on to the road.

Christophe adjusted his goggles with a hand. He could see the edge of Christina's smile.

"Soon everything will be per—" His words fell away as he spotted mounted figures in the distance. Christophe slowed Black Beauty down. The figures were racing toward them.

"Why are we stopping?" Christina asked.

"We have to find another way," he said, turning them around.

Christina raised a fist. "Let's zoom past them. Nothing's as fast as us."

"Maybe, but I fear they have guns," said Christophe, the worry in his voice making his daughter turn to look at him. "I will not risk you getting hurt. Nothing is worth that, not even my soul."

He slammed the pedals down, making Black Beauty's engine roar and she leapt forward.

Two minutes later, Christophe cursed loudly. "No. More soldiers ahead." He pulled on the reins hard, making Black Beauty brake and nearly sending father and daughter to the ground. "There must be a dozen mounted soldiers." His body stiffened as he saw two small shining lights, and immediately recognized them as those of a King's-Horse.

"Papa?" She tapped his face. "What do we do, Papa?"

Avoiding gazing into her terrified eyes, Christophe turned to the nearby forest. *I memorized all of the roads. I was ready for anything. How can this be happening?* Holding his breath, he kicked the pedals down and headed into the forest.

As they dodged trees and bushes, Christophe felt a horrible chill growing inside him. He had no idea what he was doing, and his enemy was more prepared than he was.

"Papa, they're behind us," Christina yelled, squinting behind them. "They're close."

They popped out of the forest and onto a road. Bringing Black Beauty to a stop, they looked both ways. There were soldiers on horseback waiting for them in both directions.

"Which one do you think we can race past?" he asked.

Christina looked at him, her cheeks red and her eyes big and fearful. "I thought you said it was too dangerous. They have guns."

"If we do not try, then we will never get to see each other again. Not like this," said Christophe.

"Those ones," Christina said, pointing.

And with that Christophe catapulted them ahead, grabbing Christina as she nearly slipped off.

The soldiers raised their weapons, their cavalry swords and rifles shining in the morning light.

His heart pounding in his ears, Christophe made Black Beauty zigzag sharply back and forth as they charged the soldiers at an incredible speed.

The soldiers fired into the air as they broke their line and charged forward.

You cannot scare this horse, you should know that. So, this tells me you have orders not to kill me, thought Christophe. *So now, I will use your weakness against you.*

Black Beauty dodged to the left, then to the right, outmaneuvering the soldiers. Christophe laughed as they approached the final soldier. His horse snorted a small cloud in the chilly air.

As the soldier swung his sword, Christophe pulled Black Beauty hard to one side and slammed the pedals, making Black Beauty roar like a lion and shoot forward.

Christophe watched in soul-crushing horror as his six-year-old fell to the cobblestone road screaming.

His mind and heart racing, he brought his mechanical horse to a stop several yards away and dashed to her side.

She was clutching her bleeding arm. Her face was red and her jaw clenched, her eyes were bulging, but not a tear had yet streaked her face. "I'm sorry, Papa. I didn't mean to fall."

"No. No, no, no." He scooped up his baby girl into his arms and stood there as the soldiers surrounded them. "I … I can't let them do this."

Christophe gazed up at the soldiers, their faces all in shadow. "You cannot do this. You cannot use her against me. You cannot use my ideas. I will not allow it. Let us go, please," he sobbed.

As the lights of the other King's-Horse approached, he felt the icy chill that had been growing inside him extinguish the last of his hope.

I have ruined everything, he thought, his body shaking. He stared at the terrified, injured girl in his arms, almost surprised to find her there. There was something about her, and he felt his chest tighten and an anger swell up in him.

The other King's-Horse stopped, and a man got off it and approached. Recognizing the man, Christophe walked over and forced the girl into his arms and then turned to walk away.

15

WOBBLY STEPS

In the Present

Angelina peeked around the corner of a building on the very edge of town. The road was rather busy, even for late afternoon. "Doyono's nice and everything, but give me Palais or a city on the Frelish coast any time," she said. "Okay, I think the Professor's gone, we can head out. Let's go this way."

"Why did you want to watch her leave?" Mounira asked. "She was helping us."

Raising an eyebrow, Angelina stared at Mounira and waited.

"Does this have something to do with why you had her drop us on the west side of Doyono instead of on the city's south side?"

"I made her take us to where she wasn't expecting. Less likely that there would be an ambush waiting for us." Angelina smiled. "And?"

"And you wanted to make sure that she wasn't going to signal or talk to anybody on the way out."

Angelina's smile grew. "Look at you, learning spy stuff and everything."

She put her arm around Mounira and they started walking. "There's a lot of reasons, but that's the main one, yes. We need to stay sharp and keep an eye out for anyone watching or following us. And by the way, I hope you're not too attached to that hair."

"Got it. Wait, what?" Mounira said, stopping.

Angelina frowned. "The Moufan are going to be looking for you. The more we change, the better chance you have of slipping out of here and to somewhere safer. There's a place I know here where we can get your hair cut and your clothes changed without any questions asked. Christina's going to do the same thing before we go. After that, we have to stop at the NTO. I've got to send a message."

"NTO?"

"Neumatic Tubes Office," Angelina answered. "You know, sending messages by tube."

"I guess a few things changed while we were with the Moufan."

They walked a bit more until Mounira stopped and shook her head. "Aren't the Moufan just going to leave us alone? I mean, we didn't kill anyone, and I didn't even touch Anciano Stein. Why come after us? We're nobodies."

"Ha, you know, it's cute that you still use that honorable term for Stein after what he did to you at Kar'm. It's even more cute that you think someone like Rumpere's going to let anything go. That man doesn't leave witnesses or opposition around."

"You're serious?"

Angelina scanned the passersby in the busy street. "No one strikes me as one of Rumpere's Moufan."

"How would you know?" Mounira glanced at the people around her. Most of them were well dressed, in well-made dresses and suits, everyone moving with purpose and some weight on their shoulders. She noted a beggar sitting on a street corner, his face wrinkled and leathery from the sun, a few coins and paper money in a bag in his lap.

"Other than trying to spot the tattoo on their forearm? I'm just looking for anyone watching people whose face reads as angry or driven. None so far." She tapped Mounira. "This is a shortcut to the haircut place." They headed into a back alley.

Angelina noticed the distress on Mounira's face. "Never had someone hunting for you before? It's unnerving, I know."

"Why is Rumpere so extreme?"

"Relative to whom? If you're comparing him to the

Piemans, then yes. Marcus, his son Abeland, and his granddaughter Richelle, have had their reins on power for a long time, and even though they suffered a setback, they're rebuilding piece by piece. Marcus always wanted a better life for his people, and that's why he took so long to secure his hold on power."

Putting up a hand, Angelina had them stop outside a restaurant's back door, by their cans filled with garbage and flies. Her eyes were on a silhouette at the mouth of an alley that connected to theirs. When the figure left, they continued through the labyrinth of alleyways.

"The Mad Queen, as she's nicknamed these days, came to power faster and has a firmer grip on it than Rumpere. She's also interested in some social benefit, some improvement for the everyday person, but not a lot. Now Rumpere? He's been in power for about fifteen minutes, and one of the most public things that happened was a teenage girl with one arm not only embarrassed him but then escaped."

"And if I could do that to him, then what's to stop anyone from challenging him directly?" Mounira pushed her hair over her ears.

"It'll entirely depend on his Deputy and Lieutenants. If he's turned them into devout believers, then his grasp on the Moufan will hold." Angelina put her arm around Mounira again. "But, and this is important, you are one kick-butt teen who is not someone to be messed with. Plus, you have friends who know a thing or two." Angelina rapped on a back door, one of a dozen in the narrow alleyway they were in. "This is the one we've been looking for."

The door was wooden, with a rusty metal frame, and had a faded rainbow painted on it.

"That doesn't seem very subtle, a rainbow."

Angelina scoffed. "It doesn't need to be subtle, it just needs to be part of the landscape such that you don't think twice about it. If I hadn't stopped, would you have noticed we were walking past it?"

Mounira thought about it and looked at the other doors in the area. All of them were painted with different images, all in a similar state. "I guess not."

"You'd be surprised what can hide in plain sight." Angelina knocked on the door again. "Come on."

"Hey, I have a question." Mounira stared at the door, pushing her hair over her ears again. "What have you been doing since Kar'm? I don't remember you knowing about any of this stuff back then."

Angelina tried the door, but it was locked. There was a new figure at the end of the alley. She straightened up as the figure started heading their way.

"I was going to ask earlier, but I didn't think it was a good time."

The door opened inward.

Pulling a flintlock pistol from somewhere under

her cloak, Angelina fired a shot. The target ran off. "That won't keep them at bay for long." She shoved Mounira into the building. "It's not a good time now, either."

Stein stared out the dusty window of his horseless carriage, his mind a million miles away from the streets of Doyono they were driving through. He'd asked the driver to go through the city, rather than take the direct route home. He wasn't ready to face Jacqueline yet. Instead of returning home victorious, hoping to have his sins washed away by the prize he was bringing home, he had another secret failure in too long a line of them. It was time to come clean and tell her, once he gathered his strength.

Glaring at the bundled Creangle papers on the cracked-leather bench opposite him, his stomach turned violently. He snatched one of the few remaining clean kerchiefs from the stash under his seat and held it to his sweaty mouth.

Every time the tide of guilt had risen too high, he'd urged the driver to stop the carriage and rushed outside to be sick.

"It was utter lunacy paying for those—those nonsensical scribblings of a mind long lost," he said to himself, waving a hand at the papers without looking at them. "Why didn't I just walk out? What would they have done?"

He reached for a small cabinet, threw the safety latch, and opened it. There was a lone bottle of scotch inside with a single swallow left.

Sighing heavily, he picked up the bottle and stared at it in his hands. "Best I save you for when the carriage stops and I make the steps to the house." He put it back and closed the cabinet.

"There's no avoiding it, no final chance to double or nothing my way out of this. I need to confess everything to Jacqueline, how I'm a mockery of the man she thought I was, that I accumulated a mountain of debt in both of our names, and that I spent the last of our funds to buy Rumpere's *seeds of opportunity*."

He closed his eyes and leaned back against the wall of the carriage's cabin. "I feel like the boy tricked into selling the family cow for hope and dreams. How easily a fool and his riches are parted."

Stein rubbed his throat, trying to soothe himself. Opening his eyes, he saw the name of a college in gold lettering, and his stomach turned again. "Oh, by the way, Jacqueline, love of my life, most brilliant person I've ever known, the Queen's committee dropped you from consideration for a king's-manship with no rhyme or reason." He wiped his face with the kerchief. "Despite her strong exterior, I'm certain that will crush her, it would me."

He leaned forward, his head in his hands. "The Creangle papers, the fake Pieman airship plans before them, and the revolutionary horseless carriage design … utter wastes of time and money."

Stein reached into his coat and pulled out his wallet, which was terrifyingly thin. "All our dreams and hopes, boiled down to the price of a moderate lunch for two. I guess it's good that I have no appetite."

He shifted in his seat. With a shaking hand, he reached up and pulled the black cord to summon the driver. Holding on to the foot-long railing bar attached to the roof, he leaned forward and brought his mouth up to the green-tarnished speaking horn.

"I need …," he sat back on the seat, his face blank. "What do I need?"

The carriage came to a gradual stop, the rumbling of the engine at the back filling the air with its own music.

As the door creaked open, the driver took off his grimy goggles. "Sorry, Doctor Stein, I couldn't make out what you were saying. I'll make sure to give the horns a good cleaning when we're back at the manor. Is there something I can help you with?"

Stein stared at the driver, part of him wanting to apologize for making him stop, but he dared not show any sign of weakness to anyone, least of all himself.

Instead, he waved him out of the way. "I need some air." He climbed out.

Standing on the busy sidewalk, Stein looked at the metal sign embedded in the brickwork of the building in front of him. It was for a financial barrister. Beside it was a bank. "We're in Doyono's financial district, good."

He straightened the cuffs of his shirt and smoothed his jacket. People streamed around him, paying him little-to-no attention. His attire blended right in, down to the top hat he'd instinctively taken with him out of the carriage.

"Shall I shut her down?" the driver yelled, wiping his goggles with a rag from his belt. "We don't want to waste fuel. We have enough to make it home but not much else."

"No, we certainly do not want to waste a drop," said Stein. "Keep her running, I only need a moment."

The driver nodded. "I'll make sure the engine's not running too hot. Let me know when you want to depart or shut her down."

Stein flashed a half-hearted fake smile and stood there, looking at all the people with important places to go and people to see.

A constable approached, baton in hand, his grey cap and uniform shining in the sunlight. "Afternoon, sir." He pointed the baton at the carriage. "I'm going to have to ask you to move that. You're not allowed to park on this road, not even for a moment."

Stein looked up. "Oh, sorry." Stein put his hat on. "New driver. She was nervous about the engine overheating."

"Hmm." The constable looked at the horseless carriage, black smoke pumping into the air from its stovepipes. "I don't like those things. What's wrong with a good horse or two? I guess there's one good thing to come from them, coach companies are offering great prices these days. I went to Plance for half of what it used to cost." The constable put his baton into a belt loop. "Just move along in the next few minutes, if you please. If I see you again, I'll need to fine you, and I can promise you it will be a meaty one."

"Understood, thank you, constable."

Stein waited for the officer to disappear into the crowd before taking his hat off. He stared at it. The felt was so thoroughly worn it had barely any shine left to it. Examining the edge, he shook his head as it looked like one more bow would make it fall entirely apart.

"What do I do?" he said, looking up at the cloudy sky. He bowed his head, shaking it. "I know, how sad indeed. A man of science, reduced to superstition in a time of weakness. But there must be something I can do. Jacqueline's genius deserves a chance to shine, and I've done the very opposite. I've created a shadow that will loom over us for years. She's as good as those master inventors, those giants as she calls them. She just needs the right inspirational moment."

The sounds of the city melted away as he thought of his father, a strongly religious man. They'd always fought, with Stein's mother forever locked in the role of mediator between them. But now, in this moment, he felt he had a glimmer into the man's soul.

He rubbed his nose and let out a heavy sigh. He frowned as a woman crossing the street a dozen or more yards away caught his attention. "I believe I know you but from where?" Folding his arms, he stared at her intensely. "And that girl beside her, she's got only one arm."

Stein's eyes went wide as the woman looked in his direction. He threw open the carriage door and dove in. Popping his head back out, he yelled at the driver, "Take me home. Now!" He then slammed the door closed and slid down so that he could barely see over the sill of the window.

A minute later, the carriage started moving.

"The one time I break and ask for a bloody sign, and you give me Angelina and Mounira? What's next, Christina Creangle banging on the door?" He paused, his pulse racing, and stared at the papers on the bench in front of him. "If she saw those, she'd be furious. She'd do anything to get them."

He let a big breath out, his gaze still on them, and then slowly took hold of the Creangle papers like they were worth what he'd paid for them. "Maybe they'll mean something to Jacqueline. Maybe enough to even forgive me."

As Mounira and Angelina exited into the back alley, Angelina handed Mounira a backpack. "These new clothes should fit. And I like the cut. The chin-length hair reminds me of what you used to look like."

"What happened to my backpack?" Mounira asked.

Angelina shook her head. "I know, Christina mentioned it. I put one together so that if she checked, she'd see I'd done what she asked, but once we got to the sewers, I dumped it. I don't want people recognizing you, so we're changing your appearance. First your hair and now your clothes. This way, it'll take some time for the Moufan to get their facts straight and know who they're looking for."

"They're looking for a one-armed girl."

"That's harder to pick out in a crowd than you might think. And fortunately, there's a lot of people with the same skin tone you have, so you don't stick out like you would in Inglea," Angelina said. "So get changed."

"Here?"

Angelina glanced about. "There's no one looking. This way, even the people in the hair salon won't know what you were wearing. Come on, don't be shy. Just get it done."

After taking a moment to determine if Angelina was serious, Mounira quickly changed her shirt and pants.

"Good." Angelina led the way out of the alley, through several others, and then onto a main road. "This is the financial district. We'll cross here and then continue down that road. It's the start of the pedestrian-only market district of town."

As they crossed, Angelina noticed a smoke-belching carriage but ignored it. They hurried until they entered the loud and lively beginning of a grand bazaar. The smell of spices filled their noses and spectacles by performers caught their eyes.

"I feel like I'm back home in Catalina. We have a place like this in the downtown." Mounira had a huge smile.

The streets were lined with crafts and food vendors, from scarves to fine, flaky pastries. Mounira walked up to a bead merchant's stand and examined her wares.

"We're not shopping, so get moving," said Angelina.

Mounira didn't budge. "If we're trying to blend in, then we browse."

"Ah, that's a good point." Angelina laughed. "But that said, I need to get us to the city's fountain, which is in the middle of the merchant district. From there, it's only about ten minutes to the NTO."

As they walked through the bazaar, Mounira checked out a handful of displays, thanking each of the merchants for letting her look. Along with the bounce in her step, came the first real feelings of homesickness in a long, long time.

"What if Christina doesn't get out of *there* quietly?" she asked Angelina. "Do you think that Rumpere would send an army into town to get us?"

Angelina scratched the back of her neck. "Honestly? If she's not back by midnight, I'm putting you on a coach and sending you all the way home back to your parents. Don't think I missed that look on your face. You've done more than your fair share of helping out the Creangles and everyone else. It's time we took care of you."

Mounira went to say something and Angelina cut her off with a raised finger.

"No arguments, Mounira. Christina's dealing with her own problems, and you don't need to babysit her until those are done."

Lowering her gaze and narrowing her eyes, Mounira watched Angelina out of the corner of her eye. She'd almost bought into what Angelina had said, except there was something that didn't quite fit. Something in the wording about her parents, but

Mounira hadn't paid enough attention to catch it. She stared at the slick cobblestone street, thinking.

"Hey, I didn't mean it like that," Angelina said. "Christina would never forgive me if I let you go after her."

"I think you're wrong. She knows she's the only family I have, the only family that I know is alive." Mounira glared at Angelina. "She would expect me to be there, because she knows that I will not stop at anything to help."

Angelina was knocked back on her heels by the comment, her mouth open but the words lost.

"Why did you think I spent so much time with Anciano Creangle? Because I'm a stupid little kid? It's because they mean the world to me, and I tried my best to give her a little bit of what my father gave me. I always felt wanted, I always felt like the most important thing, in his words." Mounira sniffed and rubbed her nose. "And there's nothing you or anyone else can do that will stop me from going and finding her."

Angelina stared quietly at Mounira for several seconds and then, without a word, turned to the marble fountain they'd arrived at. It was large, about twenty feet in diameter, and made of grey and black marble. In the center was a raised platform with fat wooden ducks on it, all lined up wing to wing. The water came up to the brim and sparkled in the sunlight.

Mounira leaned against the six-inch-thick rim of the fountain and dropped her backpack to the ground. "Is there a new yellow cloak in it at least?"

Angelina shook her head as she studied the fountain's ducks. "No cloaks, no hoods. Your time with the Yellow Hoods has been over for two years, and more importantly, all the kingdoms have revoked the protections they gave the Tub and the Fare. People are no longer taught to ignore colored cloaks, and law enforcement now picks up red, yellow, and the other secret society colors immediately. You're going to have to let the yellow hood go."

Mounira turned and stared at the water. The new world was going to take some getting used to. "Those aren't regular ducks, are they? They'd normally be bill to tail, but those are beside each other."

"Those are dub-dubs," Angelina said. "Many people believe that if you rub one, it'll give you luck. You know that old rhyme, rub a dub-dub?"

Mounira shook her head.

"Huh. I think it was a Frelish children's rhyme." Angelina looked up at the sun as she walked around the fountain. Then, glancing at the ducks and then at the sun again, she sat down and plunged her hand into the water.

Biting her tongue, Mounira watched, confused by

what Angelina was doing in broad daylight. Several people had taken notice but didn't care enough to break their stride or say anything.

Shaking her wet arm, Angelina dumped something in front of her. Mounira got up, picked up her backpack, and went to join her.

"Did you hide that there?" Mounira asked.

"No, someone else did." Angelina opened the wet leather sack. "The dub-dubs, and the markings along the edge of that wooden circle that they're on, mean it was created by the Tub a long time ago and used to exchange information or special items between agents, or even with select members of the Fare who shared a common cause with them."

"But the Tub and the Fare are gone," Mounira said.

Angelina winked at her. "Some of us still use these. And it's a good thing too, I was light on funds." She flashed some paper money from the bag and stuffed it into a pocket.

"And no one notices? You did that in the middle of broad daylight, with people around."

"People do strange things at fountains all the time. I've even seen someone strip naked and try to have a bath. That got some looks, let me tell you." Angelina pulled out two wax-sealed letters from the bag and then put it back into the fountain where she'd found it. "It's amazing how much people will accept if you just behave like you're supposed to be doing it."

"I suppose there were consequences for people stealing from it."

"There were. These days, it's a bit more risky, but the system still works." Angelina stood up and shook out her soaked arm.

Mounira frowned. "Huh."

"Next we head to the NTO and then to the Wobbly Dumpty."

"What's a Neumatic Tube Office exactly? You mentioned it earlier, but I've never heard of it before."

"Oh. Well, it turns out that Marcus Pieman built a large series of tubes that ran between cities. They were invented by a man named Tulu Neuma. Marcus revealed to the world not only that these things existed but also shared how they could add on to them. Every king and parliament has gone crazy expanding that network. Every place a message can go to has a unique address, which is written on the shipping label."

"Wow. That's incredible." Mounira stiffened. "Have you heard from my parents?"

"There's no connection to Augusto yet. There's a lot of mountains and hills there, but one day. For now, wherever the tubes don't go, good old couriers pick up the message at an NTO and then ride to wherever it needs to go."

"Unbelievable."

"The funny thing is," Angelina said, "some believe

that the Piemans have a secret way of reading messages or sending them, but it's impossible."

"People will believe anything, I guess," said Mounira, and then she paused. She noticed that Angelina's mouth was smiling, but her eyes weren't. Her eyes looked like she was concentrating. "You've changed since Kar'm."

"Me? I'm the same." Angelina scratched the side of her nose and looked away. "Back then, we expected the enemy was on the outside, and my job was to keep our people safe and lead whenever Christina went off gallivanting about. Now, my life is different. Plus, I don't think you and I ever had a real conversation, just the two of us."

"True."

Angelina gently shook Mounira's shoulder. "I'm still the same person you trusted back then. Now, the sooner we get to the Wobbly, the sooner we eat."

Just then, a roaring horseless carriage came tearing up a side street, nearly running them over.

Mounira sprang forward to chase it, but Angelina grabbed her by the hand.

"What do you think you're doing?"

"I'm going after it," said Mounira. "I think that's Stein."

Angelina frowned, her grip like iron. "There was no black smoke, for starters. It was just a horseless carriage. There are dozens zooming about every day, in every major city. Different colors, different designs. But what if it was the Steins? What would you have done?"

"I don't know." Mounira relaxed and Angelina let her go.

"You need to think first. Getting killed isn't as much fun as it might sound. Let's get moving." Angelina started walking.

Mounira followed, her mind haunted by one thought: *She said Steins, as in more than one, didn't she?*

16

ROADS TO REDEMPTION

Christina rushed down the last stairwell and arrived at the archway doors that led to the garden with the gazebo frequently visited by Mounira and her father. Instead of bursting through the doors to the outside, she stopped and let her backpack fall to the floor.

She paced back and forth anxiously. Looking at her freshly-bloodied knuckles, she thought of the two Moufan she'd tangled with only minutes before. She turned and put her back to the door, wondering if they'd truly been knocked out or if they were going to be showing up for a second round.

Christina tugged down on the hood of her stolen black cloak, covering her face better. "The big question is, is this the best door to go out?" She put her hands on her hips, breathing heavily. *I should have explored the tunnels with Mounira like she wanted me to instead of wallowing. But there's nothing to do about it now.*

She went to open the door and stopped, letting go of the handle. *I need to clear my head first, make sure I'm not running around without a plan. They're going to catch me if I don't.*

Christina crouched down and leaned against the double doors. Watching the stairs and listening carefully, she let her mind wander. She thought of the gazebo, and the courtyard, and then of the gardens.

She shifted, grimacing as she realized something was sticking into her ribs. Fumbling about in a pocket, she pulled out the lock pick from her father's apparatus which she'd taken before leaving his room.

Staring at the pick in her hands, she thought of his invention and then his all-encompassing sense of civic duty, and it hit her. "There wasn't just whatever Stein took, was there?" She ran a finger along the pick. "Rumpere took everything else, so where is it?"

She turned about, thinking. Then she remembered all the suspicious activity around the old tomb in the great eastern garden.

But if I go, I might not make it back to Mounira, she thought and then a chill ran through her, stabbing her soul. *Duty or the kid— that was your struggle that night that you came to get me when I was six, wasn't it, Papa?*

A sorrowful smile appeared at the corner of her quivering lips. "Of course it was." She ran her hand through her hair. "When I found you lost and confused, homeless and being fed by the kindness of strangers, I brought you to Kar'm. I did everything I could to overcome our past, but I had so much anger, and I couldn't understand why you did what you did."

She held the lock pick out in front of her. "But I think now I understand a little. You really believed, through and through, that we have a sacred duty to protect society from the evil we can be responsible for."

Lifting her head and shaking off the threat of tears, she stood up. "Protect me while I go up against Rumpere here, so that I can get to Mounira, and then I will hunt down whatever else of your legacy remains. I promise." A tear rolled down her check, and she quickly brushed it away.

Picking up her backpack, she pushed the exterior doors open. She winced and looked down as the harsh, bright light of the outside hit her.

She noticed the feet of two Moufan-Men turn toward her. *They must have been guarding the exit. Okay, think quickly.* Christina glanced about quickly, making sure to keep her face covered by the hood. "Did she come through here?"

"Who?" one of the female guards asked.

"Xenia Creangle," Christina replied. "I was chasing her." She showed her bloody knuckles. "I got a piece of her too, but not enough."

The guards looked at each other and shrugged. "No

one's come through there," the other female
guard said.

*Rumpere must be keeping things quiet. Maybe he's afraid
it'll cast doubt on his leadership.*

"She must have double backed to the north side of
the building," Christina said. "I doubt anyone's
claimed Rumpere's reward for her yet. It's probably
worth still hunting for her." She stepped back into the
building and closed the door.

After a minute of standing there, Christina pushed
it open and the duo were gone. Glancing over her
shoulder back at the stairs, she saw her backpack and
tossed it inside the building. *I'm lucky those guards
didn't ask why I was carrying that thing.*

Christina walked over to the empty wrought iron
gazebo. There were a dozen or so Moufan going about
their usual business, but there were two who had
stopped and were looking in her direction.

*Best to take a second and see if those onlookers leave or if
the trouble's already started.*

Christina felt the urge to tell Mounira and her
father to come inside for dinner. Letting her gaze
wander about the metallic construct, she couldn't help
but see it as a large, pretty, metallic cage, with
wonderful views, and one that Mounira had helped fill
with laughter. Giving it a pat and letting go of a deep
sigh, Christina turned and headed for the old tomb.

There were dozens of Moufan milling about.

Nothing seemingly out of the ordinary, other than every hood and robe was black. Here and there, she spotted the bright red sashes of elites posted on the ramparts and the glints of arrowheads from windows. They were watching like hawks for anything out of place. Christina pulled her hood forward.

The great garden was a natural amphitheater, with a large, stone tomb at the bottom of its bowl-like shape. There were concentric gravel paths decorated with old statues, wooden benches, shady trees, and brilliantly colored flower beds. There were about a dozen Moufan men and women enjoying the garden, a little less than she was used to.

Stopping at a statue of one of the founders, she pretended to read its plaque and instead gazed about, studying her surroundings better without moving her black hood. A nearby flower bed had fresh, bright flowers in it, and a small sack of fertilizer waiting to be taken away. There were several oil lamps beside it.

I always thought it odd how much the Moufan liked gardening in the evening. What was it Mounira said? Something in one of her classes about the Moufan believing that plants preferred to be transplanted when they are sleeping.

She kneeled down as if she was going to do gardening and felt the soil. *I know that particular fertilizer. It's the one that some of the trainees used to create the dirt-bomb they tried to blow up Mounira with last month.*

Christina checked out the lamps for fuel. *Half full.* She gave it a sniff. *It's oil alright. I guess I should be thankful Rumpere hates crank lanterns, because this will burn well.* She surreptitiously emptied out a sack of fertilizer into a flower bed until it was the size of two loaves of bread, and then subtly poured all the oil into it.

This thing's pretty heavy. Now, I just need something to light it when the time comes. Out of the corner of her eye, she noticed something moving and looked over. An elite was heading her way.

Her fingers tapped against her thigh as she looked at the tomb and then at the people around. *All of these Moufan could just be pretending to enjoy the gardens, but instead be guarding the tomb. Perhaps Rumpere's smarter and more paranoid than he looks.*

Narrowing her eyes to focus on a woman reading nearby, her heart skipped a beat when she realized the title of the book was upside down.

I could still be wrong. That tomb could be nothing more than a hangout for Rumpere and his inner circle to meet. I could still make it back to Mounira.

As if an invisible signal went out, all but five Moufan got up and left at once. Two elites lingered near the tomb's elaborately carved stone door, two more were sitting on benches on opposing sides of the amphitheater, and one was coming straight for her. Though she couldn't see their faces, Christina could feel the intensity of their glares.

There goes any question about there being something precious inside the tomb. She stood up, sack in hand, and started walking southward toward the tomb. The approaching Moufan was coming from the west.

Fighting your way into that place and trying to blow it up with a little bag of crap? This is a terrible plan. A smile crossed her lips. *I haven't enjoyed a bad plan in a long time.*

Then Christina bolted for the tomb, and the five Moufan jolted in surprise. *Moufan don't run inside the compound. Surprise, surprise, girls and boys, I'm not one of you.*

Shifting the sack to her off-hand, Christina reached behind her and flipped the switch on the air canister sitting at the small of her back. As it started powering up, she drew her air pistol. The only sound she could hear was her heart beating.

As the first Moufan elite came up behind her, she spun around and whacked him in the knees with the sack, toppling him to the ground. Next, one of the Moufan from the side ran up. She threw the sack to him, which he caught, his fiendish smile showing, and Christina shot him in the foot and bowled him over.

Rolling over him and picking up her bag of fertilizer, Christina continued on.

You guys are rookies, aren't you? I bet you're just brutes who are friends of Rumpere's inner circle. Real Moufan elites wouldn't have shown the surprise you all just did.

Christina slowed as she saw the Moufan from the other side running along the path toward her. The glint of a blade from under his cloak gave her an idea.

Slipping her pistol back in its holster, she pulled at the knot of her black, hooded cloak, making it come loose.

As the Moufan drew his sword out and stepped onto a bench to pounce, Christina skidded to a stop on the gravel path and whipped her cloak around in front of her.

The curved blade sliced through the mid-section of the cloak and as the assailant landed, he found his legs swept out from under him. As he scrambled to get up, Christina let the sack drop on his head, knocking him out.

Three down, two to go. A younger me would be getting cocky about now, she thought, her face lighting up with enjoyment. *There's no rust left in these bones.*

Picking up the sack, she bolted for the tomb, the two remaining Moufan-Men charging forward, curved sabers in hand.

Christina drew her pistol again and rolled its barrel on her other arm. "Perfect," she said, glancing down. Heaving the sack into the air, she slid and pulled the trigger. The blast of air brought her to a stop and pushed the sack hurtling into the face of one of the two guards, knocking the woman clean off her feet. Her head struck the ground with a dull thud.

As the other guard turned to look at her partner, Christina let go of her pistol and grabbed the final opponent by the wrists. Then with a firm downwards stomp, she flipped her over and with a swift kick knocked her out.

Christina put her hands on her knees, sweat dripping from her nose, breathing heavily. "Don't feel bad," she said to the unconscious guards, huffing and puffing. "That was a lot harder than it used to be." She stood up, her hands on the small of her back. "I swear I pulled something."

Looking up at the ridge of the amphitheater, she could see people peeking down at her. *They're going to bring more guards once their curiosity is sated.*

Picking up the sack of oiled fertilizer, she staggered over to the tomb's door and found it ajar. Pushing it open, she was immediately greeted with a pungent breeze and the sounds of two voices somewhere inside.

Christina entered the tomb, glancing at the oil lamps mounted on the walls and lining the staircase down.

That's Rumpere's voice.

Looking down she noticed her pistol dangling from its connecting tube. Rolling the barrel to the minimum setting along her leg, she held it against her other hand

and tapped the trigger. *It's almost out. This isn't going to do me any good.*

She returned the pistol to its holster and stared at one of the oil lamps. *They're just sitting in holders. How considerate.* Putting the sack on one shoulder, she then plucked a lit oil lamp from its holder.

Cautiously and quietly, Christina descended the stairs, until she finally arrived at the bottom and turned the shadowy corner to gaze into the connecting chamber.

Rumpere and his Deputy were standing in the middle of the long, wide room, surrounded by papers and contraptions of all sorts. The back appeared to be a floor to ceiling wall of metal canisters with some wording painted on them that she couldn't make out in the poor lighting.

On one wall was a large geographical map showing from Laros to Tangears, to the east sides of Teuton and Dery. There were dozens of pins, each with a small slip of paper on them. The opposite wall was covered in drawings and notes that immediately made Christina's blood boil.

Those are Papa's. And here I thought that he'd somehow lost those. You've been stealing from him for months.

Then one in particular got her attention, making her face twitch and jaw clench. *That one went the second week we arrived. They haven't been stealing from us for months, it's been for years. Since before Rumpere's climb to power.*

Without another thought, Christina stepped into full view. "How could you steal from him? He only wanted to help the world. We trusted you."

"What?" The Deputy turned to stare at her, confused. "Who are you?"

Rumpere's eyes opened wide in surprise. "Creangle. It's the infection, she's here." Rumpere struck his Deputy in the chest with his fist, stirring the man to action.

At that moment, Christina understood the word written on the metal canisters at the other end: kerosene. Her eyes then lowered to a large puddle. Lighting the sack, she then charged forward, knocking the men out of the way. Throwing the flaming sack of oiled fertilizer at the pool of kerosene, she turned to face her two adversaries.

Rumpere took a swing at her, hitting her in the chest. The Deputy then gave her a hard shove backwards against a wall, unintentionally rebalancing her.

In a blink, Christina pulled her air pistol out and put it right to Rumpere's temple. Everyone froze.

What are you doing? You wouldn't kill him even if you had the air for it, would you?

"How could you do this to us?" Christina's eyes welled up, the sack's flames shining in her eyes.

"How could you be so naive?" Rumpere asked.

"Sir, the kerosene!" The Deputy pointed. "We have to get out of here."

"No, put it out. We cannot afford to lose all of this. It'll set us back months, if not years!" Rumpere reached for a large blanket.

A glint of steel caught Christina's eye as the Deputy rushed forward. She shot him in the shoulder, with just enough force to make him wince and drop his sword.

Letting go of her pistol, Christina kicked at one of his legs, dropping him to the ground.

With a whoosh, the blanket that Rumpere was using erupted in flames, and flames leapt around the room. The map ignited, along with several wooden boxes that had been hiding in the shadows. Glancing at them, Christina somehow knew they were filled to the brim with Christophe's papers, and her shoulders lifted as they burst into flames.

The Deputy kicked back at one of Christina's legs, and Rumpere took advantage of the moment to wrap his hands around her neck.

"Put the fire out," he screamed at his Deputy. "And as for you, now I will finally cleanse this place of your vile presence."

"I was thinking the same thing," she croaked as her fingers pulled a three-inch, flat, black knife from the top of her boot. "I was saving this for a special occasion." She thrust it forward. As Rumpere let go, she pushed him aside and scrambled toward the stairs.

Seconds later, the room violently exploded, blowing the tomb to pieces in a spectacular, fiery display that would become legend among the Moufan for centuries.

"Why does Petra have so many things from Yarbo?" Oskar slapped a blanket-wrapped, antique, Frelish desk, shaking his head at the hand-written shipping receipt that was pinned to it. He walked down another aisle of Petra's small warehouse, flicking at the shipping labels. "Half of all these things are from Yarbo or are going to Yarbo. Who does she know in Yarbo? She's probably just trying to look important to anyone who comes back here."

Oskar continued walking about, grumbling, until a chill ran through him. "I'm not ready for you yet." There was no need to look, he knew the mechanical horse was behind him. He moaned like a displeased child and turned about sharply, his arms folded in tightly, his head down.

Giving a flick to another shipping receipt, he nodded. "I remember now. Petra had a client in here the other day. They said how impressed they were with her stock and how much she exports." He nodded, satisfied with himself. "I see it now. Smart girl, she has a good con going on here. But she shouldn't try to con me and pretend this isn't what I know it is. I can see the truth."

He shot a dirty glare at the mechanical horse. "You've eaten days, Black Demon. Days. And you've offered nothing," he said, his fist outstretched toward the horse. "Two days, and all I know is how to make you make that noise, that infernal belly noise that does nothing else!"

"And the thing, the panel at your heart, it turns, but so what? And your mouth, it opens, but so what? If I pull your ratty reins tightly, there's a click, and on your sides, it looks like things screwed in, but what? Pedals? Wings? I don't know." He growled and ran his hands through his unkempt hair. Tell me something." His hands were at his sides like claws, and he stood hunched over. He looked like a bear ready to attack.

Seething, he stalked back and forth, glaring at the black horse. "Petra will be here soon, and she will say I am out of time, that she must make a decision." He choked up. "And I cannot take the look of failure and disappointment that will be in her eyes. Not again." His arms drooped to his sides. "Not again."

Wandering over to his work table, he swatted at the notebook full of nonsense and pushed all the tools to the floor with a scream. Oskar hung his head and gripped the edge of the table. "Are you cursed, Black Demon? Is that it? Did your inventor go mad?" He looked up at the ceiling. "All I know is there are indents on your belly, but for what?"

Oskar tugged at his sweat-stained, sleeveless undershirt. He hadn't had a shirt on in two days, and he couldn't remember when he last showered. "It's too hot in here. There must be something wrong with those lanterns, letting off too much heat." He looked at the crank lanterns that encircled the mechanical horse.

"Maybe this is a sick joke, but it's a joke on Petra and me. Some twisted payback for something Petra did." He rubbed his face and leaned against the work table. "But I am her big brother, and I will not let whoever it is, a king's-man or whomever, make a fool of Petra."

He turned around and picked up an eighteen-inch-long wrench. "No, you will not do this," he said, walking right in front of the horse's head. Holding out the wrench ready to strike it, he laughed. "Are you afraid? I think maybe I should break you apart and see the candy inside. I don't care what Petra has said about scratching you, I know you have secrets."

With narrow eyes and a vicious scowl, he marched over to the horse's belly. "And what's this? Eh? What is it? Just something else to screw with me?" He put his fingers into a slot and yanked hard. To his surprise there was a sharp squeak like a metal door opening.

He sprang backwards, falling to the floor and the

wrench clattering off to the side. "What was that?" He stared at the horse, nothing seemed different, or did it?

"Oskar?" Petra asked from behind him, startling a surprised scream out of her brother.

He put a hand against the horse, the other on his chest. "Sorry. Yes, what is it?" Oskar raised his head and smiled.

"I hope in the unexpected extra days you've had since we last spoke, that you've come up with something." She looked him over, frowning at his appearance.

"Well, yes." He slowly got up off the floor. "I like your dress, blue and grey are very good colors for you. And the jacket, very stylish. You know—"

"Oskar."

"Ah, yes. I have been working, don't worry. I made good use of the extra time you gave me, while you were with your very important customers."

"I was thankful enough that you didn't come into the front drunk again." She folded her arms and widened her stance. "What can you tell me about the Black Demon, as I heard you calling it?"

He scratched the back of his neck. "You heard that?"

She raised an eyebrow at him.

"Of course, of course, tell you about the horse. Ah, I know that this is definitely a machine of some kind." He moved to the head. "The mechanism here that makes the sound in the belly, it reminds me of the sounds of a horseless carriage."

"Reminds you?" Petra asked. "What are you talking about?"

"This morning, when I was at the bakery getting my breakfast, there was one that had broken down outside. I listened, and I noticed the sound. The pitches." His fingers danced in the air. "Ah ..." His eyes darted about, his mouth going dry. "Oh, and I know that the metal, it is not just very good, but it is the best. Very strong and light, and the lack of seams in how it was put together, this tells me that it was an expert forger. But one, I would say, that worked with the inventor of this thing. This was someone's labor of love. I know this for certain."

Petra tilted her head skeptically to the side. "So, you're certain this isn't just a statue? Then why don't the Piemans have an army of these?"

Oskar shrugged as he walked around the mechanical horse. "I don't know, maybe it's inefficient, maybe he couldn't unlock the secrets," he closed his eyes and tapped his forehead. "Or maybe he just didn't want to use it for some personal reason."

Petra leaned against a wardrobe that was protectively wrapped in blankets and tied with specialized belts, a scowl on her face. "That doesn't really help me, Oskar. It's interesting, but you should have been able to tell me that after a day. The one curious buyer I had has moved on, and you've given me nothing more to work with. What does it do? What is it worth? Who would buy it? You still can't help me answer these basic questions." She sighed and looked down at the ground, her head shaking slowly back and forth.

Oskar's heart fell as her expression transformed into the all too familiar look of bitter disappointment.

Not again, no. I have to think of something. I can do this, I just need more time. If I don't act now, I will lose her forever.

He flicked at a shipping receipt and then as it bounced back, he read it and sparked a desperate idea.

As Petra opened her mouth to speak, Oskar coughed and stepped forward. "There's one important thing I forgot to say. A very important thing."

Her eyebrows arched up. "Oh?"

Oskar noticed a long-sleeved shirt on the floor, peeking out from under the work table. "Ah, there it is." He bent down and picked it up. Slipping it on, he started doing up the buttons. "There's a man I know who can answer a number of my questions." He spotted his notebook on the floor, beside the tools he'd knocked to the ground. He picked it up.

"And where is this man?" Petra asked, her brow furrowing.

"He is in Yarbo."

"Yarbo? What's his name? I do a lot of business in Yarbo. I might know him."

Oskar swallowed hard and lowered his gaze. Taking a step away from Petra, he put his arms behind his back. "No, no. I met him years ago when I lived in Yarbo. He is a friend of a friend, tied to an establishment. You know, what some would consider a criminal organization. He's a very dangerous man to know, but he likes me." Licking his lips, Oskar was unable to stop himself from pushing the lie further. "He owes me a few favors, for helping him with some things. He will make time for me."

"Huh." Petra studied Oskar, making him recoil several steps.

"What?" Oskar barked, leaping forward a step, almost like he was trying to scare off a wild beast.

Petra didn't move or blink. "I'll go with you. I have business to tend to there."

"No, absolutely not." Oskar shook his head violently from side to side. "He will only make time for me. You must remember, Petra, I am your older brother. I will tend to these important matters."

The look in her eyes cut his surge of classic behavior off at the knees.

"You are telling me," Petra rubbed her temple, "that you haven't seen this man in years, and he will make time for you but won't see you if I'm there? I don't care if he's involved with an establishment, Yarbo is run by establishments. The Laros government is on the verge of collapse because of them."

Oskar swallowed hard and glanced about the room. "You have a lot of respectable clients, and that will draw some attention we do not want. You have some Laros government clients, don't you?" Sweat beaded on his forehead as he awaited her answer.

"I do."

"That would not work, then. If you hadn't, then I was thinking maybe, but since you do, no. It won't work. If I go by myself, he won't feel threatened." He bent down to pick up some of his tools, which stopped him from saying any more.

Glancing up, he saw Petra chewing on her lip.

Oskar put a few tools on the work table and then stood up. "He is very good with machines, and I have what he needs in here." He patted the notebook.

"How do you know if he's still there?"

"Didn't I mention we've been writing letters for years?" Oskar put his notebook under an arm and clapped his hands together. "You know, about a year ago, he wrote to me." Predictably, Petra put her hand up, and he stopped.

"He will know what this is, I am sure. The things I discovered today," he scratched his cheek furiously, "he will know immediately."

"Is he a master inventor?"

Oskar laughed. "Master? He's the best. Super

master inventor. *And*, he will know the types of people who would buy it for more than your king's-men." He ran a hand over his greasy hair, slicking it down.

Petra's eyes narrowed. "If this is a trick, or if you abandon me again, I will pay a visit to a bounty hunter I know. Best you tell me the truth, Oskar. Come clean and tell me, right now, or accept that we are done now and forever. My gut is screaming at me, and there must be a reason."

"Ah …" Oskar stared down at his buttoned up, wrinkled shirt. *There must be someone in Yarbo who can do this. Someone I know must still be with an establishment, maybe Matthew? He would certainly know someone.* "I will not fail you this time, Petra." He put his shaking hands behind him.

She rubbed her temples. "Oskar, I swear."

The edge of his lips curled into a snarl and he started to clench a fist. *Stop, don't. You can't afford to.* He closed his eyes for a moment and took a steadying breath. "No, Petra, I know I have wronged you many times, but this time, this time I will do it."

Glaring at him, she shook her head. "If this was a deal, I'd be walking away. The coach takes two days to get to Yarbo. You have two days there. If you haven't returned by the seventh day, then I swear, I will unleash a wrath upon you."

"You won't have to." Oskar darted forward, his hands up. "You won't," he repeated gently.

"Okay." Petra nodded and headed for the front office. She opened the squeaky front door. "My assistant will have an envelope with the money for a basic room and food and the coach tickets. Don't disappoint me, Oskar. Not this time."

The door closed, and Oskar let out a sigh from the center of his soul. "I hope not, too."

17

MADNESS OF THE GILDED CAGE

In the Past
Twenty-Seven Years Ago

Christophe glared at the guard at the far end of the room, both of them waiting for Marcus Pieman to arrive. The guard was dressed in the fashion demanded by the new king: a frilly kilt, metal forearm and leg armor, and a pointed helmet. At his hip was a pistol, tied with a bright white string to his belt, and a baton in a loop on the other side.

As Christophe shifted in the high-backed, luxurious leather armchair, the guard's gaze immediately snapped to him.

"My left buttock has fallen asleep, is that a crime?" Christophe snapped. "Idiot. You've been a guard here since Marcus first had me dragged in here a year ago, and still you don't understand a thing." The guard looked away, and Christophe waved dismissively at him.

Leaning on one of the chair's wide arms, Christophe tapped his forehead. He'd already tried to escape twice in the hour he'd been waiting, and the guard had made it clear the last time that the third time would involve breaking a leg. Still, Christophe couldn't help but look around the room for ideas of how to get away. It had been his obsession for the past six months.

Christophe turned his scornful gaze on the dark oak coffee table and then at the red velvet chair opposite him. Lining the walls of the room were towering bookcases, and anchoring the room were two shiny, new globes with updated maps of the world. An oversized mahogany desk with all the papers and writing implements neatly arranged sat at one end. Beside the desk were a pair of closed, mostly-glass balcony doors. Even from his seat, Christophe could see the colorful, well-manicured private garden a story below.

"Finally." Christophe grumbled as the decisive, authoritative pattern of Marcus Pieman's boots striking the marble floor came from the guarded open doorway. Pushing himself back in the seat, Christophe gripped the arms of the chair tightly and clenched his jaw.

Marcus entered the room with a female guard

dressed in the older style directly behind him. As he crossed the room to the balcony doors, she took up position at the opposite end of the room from the first guard.

Christophe scoffed and shook his head, staring down. "Your own personal guard, dressed the way you want? Why am I not surprised that this new king has applied rules to everyone except the Pieman? What a weak fool. He'll have you standing over his cold corpse as thanks soon."

"Good afternoon to you, too, Christophe. You know, I had thought, hoped," Marcus said, "that we had an understanding after our last uncomfortable conversation. Yet, you've persisted with this dangerous behavior of trying to abandon your position." He opened the doors and let the fresh air and the floral smells of spring waft in. "Clearly, I am in grave error."

"My position? I don't want the job. I don't understand why you have me in the Conventioneer's villas instead of the dungeon." Christophe forced a laugh. "And a man who cannot go where he wills is a prisoner. I'm sure that definition's in one of these fancy, gold-trimmed books you've had ripped from the dead hands of the original owners."

Marcus leaned back against his desk, a pained grimace on his face. "Do you know what a friend is, Christophe? It's someone who doesn't let another charge on to a battlefield unarmored and unprepared.

It's someone who takes their friend's daughter and puts her not in a dungeon but in their own home, tended to by servants and given the best education her brilliant mind can handle." He pushed off and glared at Christophe, his voice raising in volume. "It's someone who's willing to tell you that there's something damn wrong with you, and you need to stop this madness because the number of political arrows I can take for you, without jeopardizing my own family and well-being, is quickly running out!"

Christophe bobbed his head up and down. "I like that," he said, with a dark chuckle and pointing a finger at Marcus. "Friends? It's funny. It is. And all of this from a man who wants nothing more than all of the pawns to behave so that he can win the game and rule the world."

Pulling himself to the edge of the seat, his hands so tightly gripping the arm rests that it looked like he was strangling them. "I have no interest in this conversation," he whispered. "This charade? I don't want it. If you won't let me go, then put me in the dungeon." His eyes went wide. "Do you need someone else broken out of prison? Maybe someone else I can be a distraction for, like you had me be for Nikolas. It worked well for his escape."

Marcus stared at his desk and played with a long writing quill. He grimaced and shook his head. "I don't even know where to begin with that delusion."

"How about with admitting it's true," Christophe said, spit flying as the words shot out. He slammed his hands on the arm rests. "Lie to whomever you want, Marcus. Lie to the king, to your Conventioneers, to yourself, but don't lie to me. I know you never intended for me to go free. I heard you."

Tilting his head at Christophe, Marcus offered a pained smile. "Do you? You know this?" He folded his arms. "How do you know this? Were you there when I discovered that Simon St. Malo had gone directly to the king? Or do you know this like I know that you haven't visited your daughter, not for a minute, since you put her in my arms? Hmm?"

Christophe pushed himself back and hunched over. He flicked the fingers of a hand at Marcus and averted his gaze.

Marcus wiped his face with both hands and sighed heavily. His expression one of pure exasperation, he moved to stand behind the second plush chair. Gripping it with both hands, he sighed again. "Were you listening the other times we've been here? Did you hear me when I told you that the sole reason you are alive, that you have not been hanged with a swath of other Conventioneers that the new king seemed to pick at random, is because I managed to construct a dozen primitive, rickety, King's-Horses to celebrate the new king's inauguration? Have you heard this tale?"

Christophe crossed his legs and twisted to put more

of his back to Marcus. "You made pretty looking garbage, and you dared to say I helped you make them."

"That's the point, Christophe. I put my reputation on the line for you. You are alive because they believed you were involved. And these pieces of garbage were designed to burn out quickly. Eight of them have been ridden once and are already scrap. Why? Because the new king knows you are the only one who knows their secrets. I told him that you needed your daughter to be taken care of in the manner that I'm providing, so that you would work on better ones."

Stroking his beard, Christophe shrugged, his gaze landing on the open balcony doors. "And how am I responsible for the lies of the Pieman?"

"You are eating the court's patience for breakfast, lunch, and dinner with this lunatic behavior of yours. Every open window, every minute that you are not locked up or chained, you flee like a stray dog wanting to return to the wild. You need to do the basic Conventioneer duties I assign to you, otherwise, this house of cards falls apart."

Christophe smiled at Marcus. "If it means your demise, then I volunteer my full support. My duty is to help and protect society, not you. You are just another ambitious confidence man, eager to build himself an empire. I know even the most innocent of work for you will have a twisted path to harming the innocent."

Marcus sat down in the chair opposite Christophe and leaned forward, his elbows on his knees. The silver was showing in his dark hair, emphasized by his clean-shaven face. Christophe, by contrast, was entirely white, with a wild and bushy beard.

Scratching his eyebrow, Marcus looked up at Christophe. "Most men would have been grateful beyond measure for what you got."

"Most men are simpletons. Kolas and I are not most men. You banished him from the world of men and malice by sending him to the smallest of remote villages on the other side of the continent. But me? You want me to dance like a monkey. Where is my escape?"

"I offered it to you, and you—"

Christophe went right up to Marcus' face "Lies," he yelled. "I never asked you for anything. There was no devil's bargain. You did these things because you wanted to, and I care not for any of them. You want to educate the girl, then do it. You want to feed and clothe her, then do it. You don't want to, then don't do it. She'll be better off."

"I don't understand how a man can be so dead inside. When I think of my sons, of my wife, they are the center of my world. I would do anything for them."

"We are not the same, you and I." Christophe tapped his chest. "My brain hurts from all the ideas in it, and the things it wants me to build. And my soul, it aches when I have to stop myself from writing them down or creating them, because I know that if they are found, men like you will use them to do unspeakable horrors."

Christophe laughed. "And my reward? I live in this cage." He waved at the balcony doors. "You tell me I should be thankful that the bars are gold, but they are still bars and my soul cares nothing for what metal they are made of."

Marcus looked at the guard in the corner. After a moment, he pointed over to his desk. "I have a ledger there of the inventions of influence that have shown up in the wild, as I like to call it. Several of them are attributed to you, did you know? There's a metallurgist in town for whom you apparently made a splendid knife sharpener. Able to make a blade so fine that it could cut bone with a swift swipe. He murdered his family. Is that an invention in the wrong hands? Or the right ones? Tell me, Christophe. Did you hear about the gas lamp design you gave some down-on-his-luck inventor? They used it to create the first ever gas bomb and blew up a patent office. People died because of the things you created, Christophe. You. I took the old gas lamp design *we*— you, me, and Nikolas— improved, added several safety features, and it has gone on to change the world."

Christophe's gaze fell to the floor. He folded his arms tightly.

Standing up and pulling down on his thigh-length

jacket, Marcus glared down at the smaller man. "I am no tyrant, nor am I a coward in the face of history. I want this world to have educated people running their countries and making a place for everyone. But that takes vision, persistence, planning, and time."

Christophe glared up at Marcus. "Feed your lies to someone else. You are no more noble than the huckster dealing cards on a city corner. You speak so well and engage people with your passion, but I know it's so that no one sees you pocket the real card and rig the game."

"Unbelievable." Marcus scoffed and got up, walking over to stand behind his desk.

"I've been going about this all wrong." He tapped at a neat stack of papers on the desk, staring at his finger. "Can you answer for me why you've not even asked to see your daughter in months?"

Christophe said nothing.

Marcus pointed at the guarded doorway. "She's fifty yards from here, down the hall and up a staircase. I could have her here in minutes. Would you like to see her? No strings attached."

Christophe snarled and curled up in the chair. "If you want gratitude, you'll get none."

Marcus stroked his chin. "I've been accused of being soft on you, of being too much of an idealist and intellectual. There are voices in the court that say torturing your daughter would be the most efficient path to making you compliant."

"All that would do," Christophe said, clasping his hands together, "would be to show how much of a monster you truly are."

"What happened to you, Christophe? I can't believe that you were always like this. You risked getting her, and now look at you." Marcus was at a loss for words.

Christophe bowed his head and gripped the sides of the chair viciously. "At the end of the day, Marcus, I will not do anything for you."

Marcus walked over to one of the guards. He whispered to her. The guard nodded, waved to the other, and they left.

"You know, I had hoped by showing you generosity, by trying to talk to you as a father, that we could find a new way to engage, but we haven't. I've only got one thing left to try."

"What, has the great and mighty Pieman been forced to consider torture?" Christophe stood up, his gaze shifting from Marcus to the balcony and back. "You spin a tale of your family being massacred because your father was a naive idealist of a king's-man, a baby saved by his nanny. I've even heard fabricated tales of how you were hunted on the streets as an abominator, before you found opportunity and rose through the ranks." He shook his head. "You have no idea what it was to be hunted on the streets, to have people try to extort you for favors or they'd turn you in. These were real elements of my life, king's-man. Your family's wealth and privilege were what allowed you to survive, nothing else. If you'd had my life, you'd understand all of this." He waved about the office. "And as to the girl—" his voice broke and he looked away, abandoning what he was going to say.

Marcus stared at the man silently.

"I was a fool to let my guard down and get into a drunken stupor of creativity with Kolas," Christophe said, swatting at the air. "I should have never created those King's-Horses. Don't you see, these things, they only create misery."

Walking over to the empty doorway, Marcus waved at Christophe. "We are at a dangerous crossroads, Christophe. But, perhaps, something I have in mind can bring us into alignment." His tone was soft and soothing.

"I care nothing for your threats. I will not review a design, nor fix a seized gear, nor do anything to feed you—,"

Marcus waved at him, cutting him off, and then continued. "Come with me to my private study. It's just down the hall from here. Let us be two men of different philosophies, trying to understand an opportunity in the world. Hmm?"

Christophe folded his arms and glared at Marcus. "And why would I do that?"

"Because it's related to the seven King's-Horses that you and Nikolas made."

Christophe's face went white and he backed up, stumbling into the chair. "Seven?"

"Wasn't it seven?" Marcus looked up at the ceiling, his fingers moving before him. "Let me think. The four destroyed in the hands of the former king, the one that Nikolas used, the one I left for you but you never showed up at, and the one left hidden in an abandoned building in town. That one was tricky to find."

Swallowing, Christophe drew in a deep breath of spring.

"It was a shame that the one you had that fateful night was destroyed by the soldiers. That old king was a tyrant, and he did loath your creations. That said, I think you might find what I have to show you very interesting."

Christophe's heart skipped a beat and he broke out into a cold sweat. He tugged at his beard, his eyes glued to the open balcony.

"It's this way." Marcus waved for Christophe to follow.

After a moment, Christophe walked over and proceeded to accompany Marcus to a closed pair of large, alabaster, sliding doors. "I am less interested in the specifics of what I'm about to share, and more interested in where it could allow us to go. Let us have no more secrets, instead let us be two men of honesty and intellect."

As Marcus pushed the doors back, Christophe squinted and put a hand up to shield his eyes from the bright sunlight streaming through the skylights high overhead, as well as from the grand windows to the right. In the middle of the room was a curtain hanging from white ropes dangling from pulleys in the ceiling.

"This is what we are here to discuss," said Marcus, moving to a rope tied to a hook. "I apologize for the drama, but it's not every day that we get to inaugurate a new era of understanding." He then untied the rope and let it loose.

As the curtain came down, Christophe gasped in horror, words stuck in his throat.

"How is it possible that I have your black King's-Horse from that night? The King may have given his orders, but each one of the soldiers out that night was loyal to me. They destroyed one of the others."

"My Black Beauty," the words painfully fell out of Christophe.

"That is a wonderful name. I have to say, I was disappointed that she didn't work like the others. She's been a statue since you left her. Anyway, that doesn't matter. It's not why we're here. Not exactly, anyway."

Christophe stared at Marcus, his hand over his mouth, his eyes frozen in unending inner terror as his mind accepted that his worst fear had been realized.

"I've been able to deduce that she came after the others, and it has none of Nikolas' hallmarks. This is pure, unbridled Creangle. Judging by the speed and agility with which you had her moving that night, I know she has marvelous secrets inside of her. And while I could have her carved in half to see how she works, there's only one thing about her that I'm interested in, the engine. I have my own plans, and while I'm investing in those working on steam engines, I believe what you and Kolas created, and what I suspect you improved significantly here, is the key for a big plan I have."

"Why would you ever think I would help you," Christophe said, his voice was shaky, his hands trembling.

"Because I will allow you and your daughter to work here, together, on the engine. An engine is not a weapon and offers no malice to anyone. You can ignore the world, the Conventioneers, the king, everything. I will make you disappear, as I did Nikolas. But I know you, Christophe, I know you would not be able to distract yourself with a family and a new life. You need to let those ideas come out, or the madness will build inside. I've seen it happen to others. Here, you can work with your daughter, and all that I ask is that you show me the progress that you make, and when the time comes, you work with me to bring it to the world. I will not take it from you."

Christophe slumped to the ground. "How can this be happening?"

"Because this is what was meant to happen. Fate is a story already written. Funny thought, for as a man of science, I never thought much of Fate. But here we are, with a most interesting set of events having created this very moment." Marcus looked down at the broken man at his feet.

Rubbing his chin, Marcus put on a friendly smile and crushed down. "By the way, I've fed Christina a steady diet of excuses regarding your behavior. She knows nothing of your escape attempts or lack of interest in seeing her."

He put a hand on Christophe's shoulder. "As a man, I'm telling you to take this opportunity. She will quickly forget that her father was too overworked by the king, and instead, the two of you can make history together."

Christophe pushed his head back, his mouth agape.

Marcus turned and waved at the room. "Imagine this as your office, every day. The far wall is a towering bookcase of the best knowledge the world has to offer, wonderful for a hungry mind like Christina's, and much needed for research and reference for you." He frowned when he saw Christophe's expression hadn't changed.

"A cage is a cage is a cage," Christophe muttered.

Clenching his jaw, Marcus stood as a guard

approached and whispered to him. "It seems Fate has bought you a few minutes of reflection. I'll be back shortly. Consider your future carefully."

With his eyes closed, Christophe listened as Marcus' footfalls became more and more faint.

After a few seconds of silence, he opened his eyes and rushed over to Black Beauty. Opening its mouth, he reached inside and took hold of the second of two ringed controls.

"I am sorry, my Beauty. But I cannot allow my failure to be complete. If they had you as you are, you would bring about the nightmare I have every night." He pulled them for all he was worth. A sharp set of twangs from the mechanical horse's belly.

Sweaty and shaking, he dusted his hands. He peered down the corridor. Marcus was at the far end, barely visible, talking with a small group. "As to my future, Marcus? I will be beholden to no one."

Hurrying back into the office where they'd been earlier, Christophe rushed on to the balcony, the sound of footsteps coming from behind.

Christophe stared at the bushes and flower beds a floor below. Standing on the ledge, he leapt into a flower bed and sprang up.

A young, female voice called out to him, but he ignored it. His eyes were fixed on the forest hundreds of yards away, his mind thinking of nothing other than disappearing into the leafy, green freedom.

A hand touched him, and he glanced over his shoulder. There was a small girl running beside him, yelling at him. Returning his focus to the edge of the forest, he bolted like a man outrunning death.

"Papa!" the seven-year-old Christina screamed, the sound of her soul withering woven around the words. "Papa, I want to come with you! Papa."

As her little voice faded into the background, Christophe felt little pieces of his soul breaking off. His heart felt like it was going to burst from his chest, but no matter what, he kept telling himself he had to flee. Only then could he stop doing harm.

18

OUT OF FAILURE, IT COMES

In the Present

Stein stood in the courtyard of his and Jacqueline's country estate. When he'd first seen the property, in the spring of the previous year, the beautiful acreage had represented their blooming future. Now, in the frigid rain and darkness of night, the very sight of the front door of the main house paralyzed him with fear.

Every silver lining he'd thought up on the ride home had tarnished. The only thing that existed was the cold, hard truth that he had destroyed the life of the most important person in his world.

Without turning his head, he looked over at the carriage house. Though the large doors were closed, there were still plumes of steam seeping out between them, hinting at the horseless carriage hidden inside which was in need of fuel and repair.

He gazed at the silent, dark, servant apartment windows on the second floor of the carriage house. Swallowing hard, he thought of their amazing staff, whom he had also failed with this trip. Maybe if he woke them now and sent them to the neighbors or into town, they'd be able to find jobs, before the stench and stigma of being associated with his pending downfall took hold.

Rain rivered off the end of his nose, and his hair pasted like paint to his head. The flagstone path to the front door was lined with crank lanterns, but only three were working, offering a solemn, gloomy path to his doom.

He could imagine a weaker man turning and running, hoping to protect those he cared for by abandoning them, but he knew that would be folly. Despite being utterly terrified and wishing that somehow he could be mercifully struck down, he was going to face the consequences of his actions.

Stein tried to curl his fingers, but they felt stiff and uninterested. He couldn't feel the icy cold anymore, and he ignored the scientist in him and his warnings.

The door opened, and bright, warm light streamed out.

"Francis? Oh, my goodness, you are there," said Jacqueline, running out, an umbrella in one hand, her nightgown held up in the other. "I thought maybe you'd stayed in town or something. As you always say to me when I'm lost in my own little world, this way my love, this way."

He went to protest, wanting her to go back inside and leave him be, but by the time the words were available to him, she had shepherded him inside.

Closing the door, she then dropped the umbrella in the bronze holder to keep its two dry siblings company. "You are positively soaked to the bone," she said, taking hold of his hand.

He gazed at her, his numb face slack. "I love you, Jacqueline Benstock." The center of his soul warmed as he shied away from his duty as the harbinger of doom.

She raised an eyebrow and smiled glowingly. "Well of course you do, my silly man. Of course you do." She stripped his soaked jacket off him and then his shirt.

"I was in your study when the horseless drove in," she continued. "I was jotting some notes down about— well, we'll talk about it later. Anyway, I happened to notice the headlamps weren't particularly bright. How did the new batteries fare on your trip?"

Stein furrowed his brow as he stepped out of his drenched pants. "Um, not exemplary to be honest. We had to buy more fuel than planned, and the carriage as a whole seems to be in need of another overhaul."

"I swear on my mother's grave, that thing is the closest thing to a tantruming child that we will ever have. Maybe it's a fortunate thing that nature made me the way she did." She shrugged. "I assume you made notes?"

"I did, detailed ones when I could." He accepted a blanket from her and she rubbed his arms vigorously.

"Excellent, then maybe tomorrow in the early afternoon we'll sit and discuss." She smiled at him, rubbing a thumb on his icy cheek.

Stein turned his head away, his joy evaporating.

"I suppose those batteries served their purpose though. They lasted, which is better than the last edition, and we can't all be giants like Creangles, Klauses, and Neumas, now can we? You know, I appreciate being able to hide away in my laboratory while you handle all the peopling. It's just not my cup of tea, but when one is on the verge of becoming kingsmen, as we are, one must invent and engage." She pulled his blanket tight and pulled him close. "And we are such a wonderful team, aren't we?"

She planted a kiss on him and he flinched. "Francis?"

"Um." He drew in a sharp breath, looking at the hardwood floor. "It's that …"

She touched his forehead. "You're positively feverish. What am I doing keeping you in the foyer?"

"No, it's not that." Stein put a hand on the side of

her face and stared into her brilliant, warm eyes. "It's just … it's that you are every bit of a genius as those you admire."

"Ha, feverish indeed," she said, swatting him with a playful smile. "When an invention of mine changes the world, then maybe. Speaking of geniuses, the workmen finally completed installing the Neumatic Tube contraption today. What an ordeal that was, a month of digging up the grounds and the mess. The large tube for sending and receiving the cylinder messages is in your study. Honestly, I still think it's a monstrous thing, but I have come around to your opinion that it might be necessary." She took him by the arm. "By the way, there's a fire waiting to put some heat in your bones."

He scoffed. "My study? You spend half your time there. I swear you have more things in it than I do."

She placed her head on his naked shoulder. "I am there, you silly, to keep you company."

"You get lonely, admit it," Stein said.

"Oh, I would, were I capable, but sadly, I am simply devoid of admitting such things." She pushed him into one of the two high-backed, cushioned chairs and put another blanket on him.

"Here's the important looking new correspondence that arrived for you over the past few weeks." She put letters on the side table. "I know how you like to go through them as soon as you return. So, while you do that, I'll fetch us some tea and sandwiches."

Tapping her chin, she looked at the far wall and the Creangle mechanical arm that Stein had taken from Mounira. It was mounted on the wall. "There was something else, but it's slipped my mind."

Stein's throat tightened, and his eyes welled up, as he recognized the seal on the top envelope. It was from the Queen's king's-men council. He shifted in his seat as a spark of hope lit inside. Perhaps it was a response to his request to have Jacqueline restored to the list of king's-man candidates.

She snapped her fingers and shook her head. "How absentminded of me? I asked about the batteries, but I didn't ask how your trip was." Jacqueline bent down beside him. "So how was it, my love?"

He looked at the crackling fire. "It was vexing in some regards. But," he glanced at the letters and then at his wife. "I did manage to find you something. It's not much, but I hoped maybe it would be of some interest."

With an excited smile, she tilted her head to the side. "What did you get me, Francis? I told you not to get me things."

"Should I dispense of the Creangle papers that I got then? I left them in the carriage."

Jacqueline bounced up to her feet and clapped. "Oh, there were actual papers?" She grabbed the arm of the chair, her eyes open wide and shining. "Actually written by him?" Then with a frown and leaning back, she continued. "Or are we talking about fantastic claims of interviews written up by morons who don't know their *they're* from *there*?"

Stein smiled and raised an eyebrow. "They were the last things he ever wrote."

"Don't toy with me, Francis." She covered her mouth with her hands.

"No, genuinely. But I'm afraid they look like garbled nonsense."

She laughed like a child at her own surprise party. "Of course they are. They're encrypted. Every one of the master inventors has their own language. Oh, these are happy days," she cheered, making fists and shaking them excitedly. "No sleep for Jacky tonight. I wonder if I can make a codec by morning? You know that it was one of my specialties at the university?"

Stein basked in her enthusiastic glow. "I had no idea."

"Yes, well. You tend to those letters, stay warm, and I shall return with tea and nibbles." She stopped and plucked a small, ornamental dagger from the desk. "Your opener."

He stretched out and caught her hand. "I'm sorry to report there were no devices or contraptions of any sort. I'd hoped for more."

She shrugged, her mood unscathed. "Oh, all the

better. No spoiling where those treasure maps will lead. Anyway, let me fetch the tea."

"You don't have to make any," he said. "I'm quite okay, honestly."

"No tea? That fever has absolutely ravaged your sense, hasn't it? But honestly, do you think I'd be allowed to make such a thing with Charis in our employ?" She giggled and rubbed his head. "That woman won't let me do a thing, I love it."

Stein stared at his lap, his face long and drawn. He was thankful that her ability to read people was like a machine. If it wasn't intentionally on, she'd often miss the most obvious things until reflecting on them later.

"Anyway, fear not. Charis made a fresh pot and some sandwiches before she retired for the night. One moment, I'm sitting in the kitchen, scratching out ideas and intending to return to the study. Then the next, I find I've had plates of food and tea served to me, and she's off for the night. I'll be back in a blink."

As Jacqueline left the room humming joyfully to herself, all the warmth seemed to follow her.

Holding his breath, Stein reached out and took the top letter, slicing through its wax seal.

With a trembling hand, he opened it.

To Doctor Francis Stein,

Congratulations on completing the eighth stage of review for your king's-manship. It is a great honor to have made it thus far, and we would like to inform you of some changes Her Majesty has approved.

Firstly, the Royal Council of King's-Men and Her Majesty have approved several process changes to stages nine and ten. This extends the review period to ensure proper time and analysis can be performed, given the quantity and caliber of candidates being considered. Secondly, two additional stages have been added, bringing the total to twelve. More details will be made available regarding these should you reach those levels.

In order to properly support shepherding your candidacy through the new edition of stage nine, an additional sum of fifty-thousand crowns will be needed promptly, or your candidacy will be retired.

As you are well aware, being a king's-man comes with outstanding privilege and opportunity, but it can only be given to those who properly demonstrate worthiness with significant inventions, businesses of considerable size, or other notable accomplishments held in high regard.

Best regards,

The Dery Royal Council of King's-men

PS: In regards to your recent request, the council deemed it most inappropriate for you to raise the issue of Jacqueline Benstock's candidacy and has decided to fine you one hundred crowns. Fortunately, your own candidacy was not forfeited as a result of this behavior.

The letter slipped out of his trembling hands. As it hit his lap, Stein felt himself implode with shame as his shoulders folded in and his head dropped. Slumped in his chair, he stared fearfully down at the letter, its gold-tipped corners sparkling in the light of the fire.

"How could I have been so blind? So easily played the fool?" He glanced at the dagger and then at the other two letters.

19

A WOBBLY FUTURE

A battered and bruised Christina gingerly pushed open the door to the Wobbly Dumpty Tavern and Inn and hobbled in. Her hair was singed and her face bright red in parts. They stood in sharp contrast to her new clothes, which consisted of a demure, beige, long-sleeve, frilly shirt and a dark brown skirt. In her hand was a small valise.

She'd been in many times over the years, and watched it change hands several times, but the Wobbly Dumpty always remained a haven to those standing between the Tub and the Fare.

The mouth-watering display of caramelized vegetables and a roasting bore drew her to the chimney in the middle of the tavern, as it did every time. It was a two-hundred-year-old tradition to have one roasting every day and drew people from all over. Her stomach growled for the first time in a long time.

Tables and chairs radiated from the chimney outwards, with a bar a few yards just over to her left. There was a disappointing number of patrons for evening, but all the better for her, given the circumstances.

She smiled warmly at the rich, honey brown floor, walls, and ceiling. They reminded her of the inn she'd grown up in. Even the standard crank lanterns that lined the walls seemed to give her a nod of nostalgia.

"Can I help you?" the bartender asked, offering a cocked, bushy eyebrow. He was bald, with a grand mustache and mutton chops.

Christina made her way over to the counter and leaned against it, grimacing and groaning in discomfort. Dropping the small suitcase she'd stolen, she turned to him. "Did you hear about Humpty?" she asked, with an intense look.

He straightened up, recognizing the coded cue. Plucking a wet glass from the water basin below the counter, and taking the cloth from his shoulder, he started drying it. "No, I didn't. What happened to him?"

"He had a bad fall. Rumor is it was the wall, bad construction." She put a hand on the counter, palm up.

He tapped her hand, confirming that they were on the same side. "In these parts there are some bad bricks, but we don't have any. At least, not today," he said, waving the cloth about. He put the glass down on the counter and got another one.

Christina nodded and gradually let her gaze sweep the room. There was indeed no one who stood out, no bad bricks as they called them. She looked up, scratching her neck. "I'm looking for some breakfast. Two eggs, one missing some yoke." She clasped her hands together. *Please let Angelina and Mounira have made it here.*

"Oh, yeah," he pointed at a far corner with his chin. "One sunny side up."

A Blond, good. That's Angelina.

"And a small egg, short a bit of yoke."

She smiled and tapped the counter.

"I had a late breakfast, probably about an hour ago."

"Oh." Christina sighed, disappointed.

"There's still some. I didn't clean my dishes."

She perked up and followed his gaze. "Thanks." Christina left the bar and made her way around the chimney.

As soon as the far corner's tables came into view, she saw Mounira spring out of her seat. Dodging several chairs, she charged Christina and grabbed her in a tight, one-armed hug.

Coughing and wincing, Christina patted Mounira on the shoulders. "Careful, I'm hurt all over."

Angelina stood up, a smile on her face. "You must be delirious with pain. You're wearing a skirt."

Christina rolled her eyes. "I have a friend who's a clothing merchant. This was all he had in my size."

"That's your witty comeback? This is serious." Angelina sat down. "What'd you do?"

Taking her seat at the table as Mounira did, Christina ran a hand through her hair. "Blew up the tomb."

"The old founder's tomb?" Mounira asked.

Christina nodded. "Yup."

"Wow." Angelina leaned back, chuckling. She pointed at Mounira. "Remember what I said about Rumpere? That's how one makes one's self a life's mission." She chuckled some more. "Holy moly. That's going to ripple through all of the Moufan world. You're going to be enemy number one, with Rumpere leading the charge."

"He was in the tomb," Christina added.

Angelina thought for a moment. "Oh. That might not be so bad then. If he's dead. Is he dead?"

Christina shrugged. "I nearly got killed myself. He was behind me somewhere. I don't know."

Mounira reached out and took Christina's hand. "I was counting down the minutes before we were going to have to come and rescue you."

Giving the hand a squeeze, Christina then let it go. "I'm okay and appreciate the thought." She looked at the empty plates and glasses on the table. "I am starved though." She waved at a server, flagging them down. "One plate of the pork dinner, with everything."

The server nodded and then left.

Christina sat back and looked at Mounira. "Your hair. What happened to it?"

Mounira looked at Angelina. "She said we don't want people knowing what we look like. She picked the clothes too."

"Well, that saves us a bit of time. Good thing, our coach leaves in two hours." Christina scratched the back of her hand. "There's still a lot to do before then."

Angelina frowned. "Two hours? The coach for Plance leaves in one, doesn't it?"

"The Moufan have a firm presence in Plance." Christina leaned forward. "I'm surprised you have the schedules memorized. Are you here often?"

"Often enough." Angelina replied. "Two hours, that means you want to head for Kondla. Planning on visiting the Grand Library?"

"Something like that." Christina sat back in her chair, staring at the table, her face stoic. *Either you know the schedule because you've been in Dery a lot, but never taken the time to see me or slip me a message, or you're up to something.* "I wanted to have enough time to have a real meal and then make it over to an apothecary I know. I need something to numb the pain in my shoulder and back."

"The one on Winston and Pei?" Angelina asked.

Christina raised her chin, thinking of where she'd just come from. "That's the one I had in mind." She was thankful that she'd resisted the urge to use the mint-scented rub, as it would have likely given her away. "Would you mind picking up the coach tickets and a jar of the soothing rub?" She looked at Angelina coldly, as if playing poker and keeping her cards glued to the table.

Angelina studied her for a moment before nodding. "You must be in some pain, I haven't seen you like this in a while."

"Collapsing a tomb has a way of being painful," Christina replied, cracking a half-hearted smile.

"Okay. I'll pick up a pair of coach tickets for you guys too," said Angelina standing up. "Meet you at the coach station in an hour and a half?"

"Sounds good." Christina watched quietly as Angelina left the tavern until the plate of food arrived.

Mounira brought Christina up to speed on how they'd escaped the Moufan compound, and Christina ate and nodded contently.

"I'm not sure if I should be proud or laugh that you guys got out of there that way." Christina wiped her mouth with a napkin. "That said, I'm one to talk. My plan was far worse, but I'll share later."

Mounira reached over and squeezed Christina's hand. "I haven't seen this edition of you in a long time. Not since before everything happened at Kar'm."

Christina raised an eyebrow, a sorrowful smile on her face.

"I feel like you're back," Mounira continued with a cheeky smirk.

"Not entirely." Christina wrinkled her nose and lowered her gaze, turning away from Mounira. "I'm getting there. I was stuck and couldn't move, but now that I'm moving I feel …," she sucked in a quiet breath and stared at Mounira's wise but adolescent face. "I couldn't have done it without you."

"When I lost my arm, I had to keep moving or the pain would overwhelm me," Mounira said. "You, Tee, Elly, all of you helped me through it. Now the pain's a part of me. It gives me strength or courage when I think I have none left."

Christina reached over, as if she was going to take Mounira's hand, and then patted it quickly before sitting up and putting her hands together in front of her. "The way you've always talked about your physical pain, it has been going through my mind for the past few hours," she shrugged off her other thoughts.

Reaching into her sleeve, Christina drew out the lock pick. "I was trapped in Christophe's room for a while."

"How?" Mounira asked.

"I'll tell you later, when we're on the coach. But, this," she waved the lock pick, "this somehow made me feel like he was there with me. Like Papa was trying to help." She closed her fist around the pick. "I don't know, it's stupid, right?"

Mounira's mouth was open, her eyes glossy and big. "You said Papa."

Christina grimaced.

"As an Augustan, I'd say he was with you. The pick to—"

"No," Christina said, pointing a finger at her. "This isn't some symbol, it's …," she slipped the pick back into her sleeve. Running a hand through her hair, she sighed. "I just wanted to show you." She studied the clock hanging on the wall nearby. "We need to get moving."

"Angelina only left ten minutes ago. Isn't it a little early to get going?" Mounira's words trailed off as she took in Christina's expression. "We're not going to Kondla, are we?"

"No, we're not. We're leaving in fifteen minutes."

"That valise you left at the bar, it's not just got clothes for you, does it?"

"No. One change of clothes for each of us, plus some money to get us to where we are going." Christina handed the plate off to the server. She then leaned forward, putting her elbows on the table.

Mounira copied her.

"I could see something in your eyes when Angelina was talking, something's bugging you. I've only seen that look when dealing with Moufan trainees or Franklin Watt. It's when you don't trust someone, or they're lying and you know it," said Christina.

Mounira drummed her fingers on the table, then scratched the back of her head. "There were a few things today. Hard to remember what exactly, but something feels off."

"It does." Christina looked at the clock again. "It's ten to eight, we have to go. I have the tickets in my pocket."

They got up from their table and headed for the valise, then the door.

"You bought them before you came? How did you know we'd be here?" asked Mounira.

"I didn't. I took a risk, and hopefully, everything plays out the way I need it to."

They left the tavern and headed down a street, the gas lights shining, making up for the dwindling sunlight.

"Oh, I remember something weird," Mounira said. "When I was with Angelina earlier, we went to the fountain at the center of the market. She pointed out the dub-dubs and explained all the Tub and Fare things about them. She also reached under the water and pulled a sack out of nowhere."

Christina shook her head. "Woo, what?"

"Oh, and we went to the Neumatic Tube Office. She made me wait outside." Mounira shrugged. "I don't know why."

Christina pinched the bridge of her nose. "Okay, I can't handle all of this right now. Let's get on the coach, then I'll break all of this down." She picked up the pace.

"What did I say?" Mounira said, nearly running beside her.

"It's everything you said. Angelina was a skilled mercenary with a good heart when I met and recruited her for Kar'm. But during that, the time we were together and then afterwards, I never got so much as a hint that she was a spy of any kind. The stuff you just talked about, you only learn that stuff when you're part of one of a few secret societies or work for someone who did. Something's more than a little off."

They stopped at a corner and waited for a procession of horse-drawn carriages to pass before continuing.

"Was Angelina being chummy? Complimenting you, telling you how good you were at things or how insightful you were?"

Mounira nodded.

Christina renewed her grip on the valise. "If my paranoid side's right, then she could have been trying to worm information out of you."

"What type of information? I don't know anything."

"You spent the most amount of time with Christophe of anyone. Some people could think that means you know or heard something." Christina shook her head. "I'm probably wrong." She glanced up at a flickering gas street lamp. "Hopefully."

They hurried down a street filled with theater goers, everyone dressed up.

"Excuse us," Christina kept repeating.

"Is that what a coach is? It looks like a carriage with two horses," Mounira said.

"Of course. Sometimes four horses, but you know that, don't you?" Christina stopped and frowned at her. "You've never ridden one?"

Mounira shook her head. "We didn't have them back home. At least, I never saw one. Everyone has their own horses and wagons." She looked across the street. "Why aren't we crossing? Isn't that the coach office over there?"

She followed Christina's gaze and then saw a brief flash.

"I just need a second. I have someone following me, a second set of eyes." Christina whistled twice and stretched.

A single whistle came back.

"Good, there's no one tailing us. I had to make sure

that nobody knew where we were going. Let's cross," Christina said.

As they past a sign on the side of a building that read: *Coaches this way.* Mounira turned to Christina. "Do you think Rumpere will come after us?"

Christina looked around and then squarely at Mounira. "If he's alive, he will. And if he's been martyred, then his disciples will come with a vengeance. But every day, I will protect you with my life, and every day, I will help make you stronger to get you ready to fight the battles yourself, should I ever fall."

Mounira's eyes welled up and she nodded. "You're family," she said, with a simple shrug and smile. "Now and forever."

"Now and forever," Christina repeated.

They walked until they came to a standalone ticket booth sitting at the edge of the road, with a single-story building behind it with an open barn door for an entrance.

The ticket booth looked like four wardrobes put together, with a hole cut into the upper half of one side. Inside sat a bald man on a chair with a dim crank lantern on a hook. He was engrossed in a novel.

Below the window were the painted words: *coach ticket office.* Above the open barn doors were the words: *waiting room - coaches through here.*

"Need tickets or have tickets?" the man asked in a

monotone voice without looking up. He then licked his finger and turned the page of his book.

"I have tickets." Christina reached into a side-pouch of her valise and handed over the thin, brown paper strips she'd got from the man earlier.

He glanced at them and then handed them back. "Go through the waiting room to the deck, you'll find the driver and coaches there. Yours leaves in three minutes, better hurry." Not a single word of his had any passion or interest.

Christina handed the tickets to Mounira and then walked into the waiting room. It had a gravel floor and bleached-white wainscoting along the walls, with a half-dozen benches surrounded by families. There were oil lamps hanging from hooks every few feet along the walls.

At the far end was another set of open barn doors from which the pungent smell of manure wafted in, accompanied by the sounds of impatient horses and drivers.

"How do you know Angelina's not going to show up here?" Mounira asked.

Christina pointed at the destinations board on one of the walls of the waiting room. "Notice anything?"

"Kondla's not listed." Mounira thought for a moment. "Is there another coach station on the other side of town that goes to Kondla?"

"It turns out, there is." Christina smiled.

Leaving the waiting room, they walked on to the wooden deck that split into several wooden plank paths, each one leading to a coach. Each one had a driver standing with a numbered wooden placard. Gas lamps shone down on each one of the drivers ominously.

"We want number seven," Mounira said. "The one over there on the left." She led the way, the planks creaking and wobbling beneath her feet, threatening to drop her into the muddy, filthy mess that was the ground.

As they passed the second carriage, Christina noticed a young girl being lifted into it by a handsome man in his late thirties. A woman about the same age, with a beautiful peach and white dress then climbed in.

"Christina?"

She stared at Mounira.

"Are you okay?" Mounira asked.

Christina nodded and continued walking. "Sorry, I was remembering something from long ago. I once had a friend named Jacky. We were close for a while. I put her on a coach with a couple like that, so she could have a good life. I don't know what ever happened to her."

"Tickets," the driver said as they approached.

"This is a nice-looking coach." Mounira looked at the other ones and then at theirs again. "Definitely the nicest."

"I thought a bit of comfort would be appreciated, after the day we had," Christina said.

Mounira handed the driver the tickets.

The driver had a beige blouse with rolled up sleeves, a floppy cap, and brown pants with suspenders. She checked the tickets and pocketed them, then opened the door to the carriage.

As she stepped out of Mounira's way to allow her to get in, Mounira stopped, looking at the driver's forearm.

The driver took Christina's valise and climbed up the ladder to attach it to the roof.

Christina stared at Mounira. "Get in."

"I thought I saw something on her arm," Mounira whispered to Christina, over her shoulder, switching her language to Frelish. "I didn't get a good look."

Christina rubbed her eyes. "I'm tired, what did you say?"

Mounira shook her head. "Don't worry about it. It was probably nothing."

"The more of the first part of this three-day journey to Yarbo we can get done sleeping, the better. I requested a stop at a mid-sized town on the way, so we can get new clothes and change things up if we need to," Christina said.

Mounira climbed in. "We're going to Yarbo? As in the coastal city? The one run by criminal gangs?"

Getting in, Christina sat on the bench opposite

Mounira. "Yes, it's coastal. But establishments are more sophisticated than gangs," she scratched the side of her head and then shrugged. "They're bigger, smarter, better organized, than gangs and usually have some level of political protection."

"Here's a crank if you need it," the driver said, putting a crank lantern on the floor between them and then closing the door.

"Thanks," Christina replied. "Another thing I did was I paid to ensure they don't take any more passengers for this ride. It'll just be the two of us."

Mounira smiled.

"There's been a lot of things I've thought about sharing over the past few months," Christina said, sighing uneasily. "And I'd like to start sharing those things with you, if you're interested." She picked up the crank lantern and gave its winding arm a few whirls, brightening the cabin up.

"I'd love it. Hey, why are we going to Yarbo?"

"Apart from the reason that it's the biggest city in the area with lots of easy access to then go anywhere? One of the benefits of it being run by establishments is that they loath the Moufan. I think one of the original establishments was founded by an ex-Moufan, and any they catch are sent back home, in a box."

"Oh," Mounira said, shocked.

"I need to show you something." Christina reached into her vest and pulled out a notebook. "Angelina gave me this when she showed up earlier today. I was planning for you and I to leave in a few days, to finally make the journey to take you home. Angelina's notebook has all the possible safe routes, contacts, and a lot of notes. I don't know if she made it, or got it from someone, but I now feel confident for the first time that we have a way to get you home without walking into a war zone."

Mounira held the notebook out in front of her, her eyes shining with wonder in the crank lantern light. "Can we trust it?"

Christina leaned back, putting a finger to her mouth. "We have time to figure that out."

"We do," Mounira said, as the coach started moving. "After we find out why Stein was at the compound. I know you're going to go after him."

Christina looked at Mounira.

"I spent a lot of time with your father. Sometimes, he told me about his fears and duty. He also told me how proud he was of you, and how he didn't have to worry about his inventions ruining the world because you would stop it."

Christina closed her eyes and put her fingers against her forehead.

"We are family, and I won't let you do this alone."

The coach rocked back and forth as the lights of the city went by.

Slowly, Christina nodded and opened her eyes. "I

ran into Stein, just before I was locked in Papa's room. But before I catch you up on my day, I wanted to tell you there's another reason we're going to Yarbo."

"Oh?"

"The second time I escaped from the Pieman's household, I made it to Yarbo. I lived there for two years; it was rough, but it was good. I made some close friends. Two of them grew up to run an establishment. A few times, when I've needed to disappear or think, or needed some help tracking something down without the Tub finding out, I've gone there. They're good people."

"Do you trust them?" Mounira asked, glancing at the notebook.

"I hope so, because we're going to need them."

20

TREACHERY DOWN THE TUBES

The copper bell above the door of the Neumatic Tube Office rang as Angelina entered.

A clerk looked up at her from the painted white counter. He had stacks of papers he was going through, a quill in his hand, and an ink well before him. Behind him was a wall of Neumatic glass cylinders, all neatly arranged in a shiny, brown set of shelves that ran to the ceiling. Each cylinder sparkled and had its shipping receipt pulled out and leaning against it.

"Sorry, miss, but we are closed for the evening."

Angelina pointed. "I can see—"

Without looking up, the clerk continued. "We are closed. Messages can be picked up tomorrow morning at nine, provided you have proof you are the recipient written on the shipping label." He waved the quill at the door. "Please see yourself out. I'm quite busy."

Angelina locked the door. "I'm not going anywhere." She turned around the wooden sign that hung in the window to say it was closed to the outside world.

The clerk glared at her and wiggled his greying mustache as she approached the counter. "This is most inappropriate behavior. I need you to leave, promptly."

Angelina pulled off her leather gloves and slapped them on the counter. Then, with a look that pushed the clerk onto his heels, she leaned forward. "Do you know how exhausting it is to search all over this massive city and then to discover there is only one NTO office? Not three like Doyono or Plance, but one single, solitary avenue for communicating with the entire continent. It's madness."

The clerk straightened up to his full height and towered over Angelina. "Miss, you need to leave now." He put the quill down and pointed sharply at the door. "Now."

Angelina reached across and grabbed the man's outstretched hand, bending his fingers back and forcing him down until he was lower than her. "I truly apologize, for I am rarely like this, but I am not in the mood." She pushed his fingers back further. "If you would like to keep your digits in good working order, then I recommend we do what's needed, and I can be gone within minutes. Do we understand one another?"

The clerk nodded, and Angelina let him go.

With a fearful gaze, the man stood up, rubbing his hands. He cleared his throat, "how am I to be of service?"

"You should have received a cylinder this morning. It had a blank shipping receipt and a black ribbon that ran along the inside. The ribbon had two red stitches at the top."

He furrowed his brow and then his eyes widened in surprise. "We did."

"May I have it?" she asked, glaring at him.

"I'll need to see some identification, for my log book. Sorry, standard procedure."

Angelina offered a toothy, threatening smile. "Really? I don't think so."

The clerk lowered his gaze. "I do—ah—believe in a case like this, we can make an exception." He then turned to the wall of cylinders and examined the ones on the bottom row. "Here it is. To be honest, we were of half a mind to just repurpose it."

Angelina took it from him and examined it thoroughly. She then rotated it by the window, making sure the light caught any hidden details. "Good, it's not been touched." She put it on the counter and opened it. Taking the black ribbon out, she turned it around and fed it back into the nearly invisible slot on the inside of the cylinder. She then removed the wax-sealed letter.

Opening it, she mumbled to herself as she read it, glaring up at the clerk occasionally to keep him at bay.

Angelina finished and tapped the letter on the counter, thinking.

"I'll just take care of this." The clerk put his hand on the cylinder and Angelina raised a finger at him, freezing him in place.

"No, sorry. My mistake, please go ahead," she said. She read through the letter again and then folded it up and stuffed it into a pocket. "May I have some stationery?"

With a quick nod, he handed her a sheet of paper and offered her the quill.

Angelina looked at the ceiling, mumbling to herself. Then, concentrating, she wrote out a message.

"I'm not familiar with that language."

"Be glad, for if you were, I might have to kill you." Angelina wrinkled her nose and bobbed her head from side to side playfully as if reconsidering the fake threat. "And I'm wearing the wrong type of outfit. So, best for the both of us really."

She folded the letter in half and put it back in the cylinder and screwed the lid on.

The clerk stared at the cylinder and then ran his hand along the side. "This seems to be misshapen. I've seen a few like this. We can't allow that through the system. Allow me to get you another."

"No," she said pushing the cylinder toward him. "Send this one, as is."

"Okay." The clerk picked up a shipping receipt. "And if you'd be so kind as to fill this in."

"Use it as is."

The clerk frowned, his bushy eyebrows merging about his confused eyes. "Um, I'm not sure you're aware how these things work. You see—"

She lifted her chin. "It'll get to where it needs to go."

The man nodded obediently. "Okay, well, I can't imagine how it'll work, but the lady knows best. For the record, the receiving stations forward messages on based on this slip of information."

"My friend will get it." She reached into a belt pouch and put three bills on the counter.

The clerk pointed at the money. "That's more than we charge."

"I need all of your receipts for receiving this cylinder, and I need you to turn your dial back two clicks. I can't have you counting the one I picked up, or the one I sent."

"Excuse me?"

She doubled the money. "I can't have any records of my being here or what I was here for, do you understand? I'd much rather take care of things this way, than have to burn this place down and kill you. As I said, I'm not in the clothes for it, never mind not in the mood."

The clerk glanced around, confirming there was no one around, and then pocketed the money. "Is there anything else I can do for you?"

"Not unless you know where my friend went, or why my boss wants me to find some guy named Oskar."

21

THE FUTURE GIANT SLAYERS

"Tea and tasties," Jacqueline said, arriving with a silver tray and setting it down on the hills of paper covering the desk. She took a moment to ensure that it was steady and turned around. "Francis?"

Her husband was asleep in the chair, one arm drooped down, the letter opener just beyond his fingers. In his lap were two opened letters, the third was crumpled up, sitting a foot from the fire.

She tucked the blanket around him and fetched another. "There you go. Now, what's made you scowl so much?" She kissed him on the cheek.

He smiled and rolled his head to the other side of the chair.

Bending down, she picked up the letters and turned up the desk crank lantern. Jacqueline then sat down and poured herself a cup of tea. "Now, let's see what people had to say, shall we?" She opened the crumpled letter. "Gold trimmed corners? This must be from the Royal Council."

As she read the letter, her cheeks flushed and she clenched her jaw. She then read the two letters sitting in Stein's lap. With each word, her blood boiled more and more until she finally finished, her face in a twisted snarl.

Taking a key from a desk drawer, she unlocked their filing cabinet and sifted through its contents. "Here we are—*Royal Council Correspondence*. Let's see how long this has been going on."

As the minutes ticked by, the picture became more and more clear, and the vicious, manipulative game being played became more apparent. She turned and stared at her husband, tears in her eyes. "Oh, Francis, why did you feel the need to carry this burden yourself?" She nodded to herself. "It's what you kept saying, wasn't it? That you believed I would become like the giants, the Creangles and Neumas, in that little lab we made for me."

Jacqueline turned to face the mechanical arm that hung on the far wall, a puzzle she still hadn't figured out. "You foolish, lovely man." Drawing in a deep breath, she stared at him, his chest rising and falling.

"Weaker men would not have returned," she said, the corner of her mouth turned up. "And I bet if I say nothing, you'll confess to everything in the morning, won't you? You'd come to me after my coffee, when I'm looking out at the garden. You'll have dark circles around your eyes, your face will be slack and sullen, and you'll have your heart in your hand. You will be a man defeated."

She dabbed at a loose tear. "And it will break you. The man who is my hope and light, the one who charges out into the realm of people, armed with a plan we have forged together, will be gone."

Jacqueline gently tugged her shirt down. "You once told me you lived a life of almosts until you met me. And I won't allow this moment to become another one. The question is, what haven't you tried? How can I change the morning to come, to put a bridge across that abyss of defeat you are probably torturing yourself over right now?"

Tapping her fingers, she noticed the ticking of the hand-sized windup clock sitting on a shelf. "It's early yet. That's a good sign."

She stood up and went over to the fire. Turning around, a hand on her chin, she gazed out at the room. "Think, Jacky. Think." The year-old painting was of Francis and her on the shore of the Southern Sea just outside Yarbo on their honeymoon. "We had a great time there, didn't we? Met some wonderful people." An idea sparked her mind and imagination to life.

Jacqueline walked over and picked the painting off

the wall. On the back was an envelope. Taking it, she pulled out the single piece of folded paper and stared at the list of names and addresses. "And I said you were an ornery fool for writing down their names, Francis. I was wrong." She looked at him, still slumbering. "There, I've admitted it. It's not my fault you were asleep for this once in a lifetime event."

She crouched down beside her husband. "The one thing you are remarkably bad at, Francis, is asking for help." Glancing over at the two brand new Neumatic Tube cylinders, she smiled and kissed him on his forehead. "Let the nightmares go, my love. The answers might just be in Yarbo."

A distinct floral smell pierced through the darkness of Rumpere's unconscious and roused him. With his eyes still closed, he drew in a painful breath.

It's familiar, but there's something specific. It's a floral. I know that scent. It's lavender.

Wheels squeaked nearby and in the distance there were the sounds of warriors yelling their battle cries in unison.

Lavender and training? I must be in the infirmary. But why?

He tried to make a fist, grimacing as he did so. *There*

was a blast. Creangle and the tomb ... I'm alive. My skin feels like I'm covered in a thousand fiery needles.

Grunting, Rumpere fought with his body until an eye opened and confirmed where he was.

Draped from the ceiling were light blue sheets with a woven Moufan prayer on them looking down on him.

"Who's there?" he croaked, his throat dry and lips cracking. "I see the edge of someone."

A black-hooded head popped into the edge of Rumpere's peripheral vision. "Hmm? He's awake. Get the Deputy. Rumpere has returned to us. Our leader lives," he said excitedly.

"Of course, I live." Contorting his face, Rumpere managed to crack the crust covering his other eye and opened it to a thin slit.

There was a Moufan-Man standing beside his bed, fists in the air in triumph. He pulled back his hood, revealing a youthful face. He couldn't have been more than eighteen years old. "We've been waiting for this moment."

Swallowing slowly, Rumpere nodded. "You called for my Deputy. He lived?"

The Moufan-Man frowned. "Oh, no. He died in the tomb. We followed your succession plan. There is a new Deputy."

"Ah." Rumpere nodded gently and relaxed in the bed. "I need water."

"Yes, sir." The Moufan-Man left and returned with a wooden mug full of water. He paused, his expression shifting from relief to apprehension. "Do you want me to—"

Rumpere glared at him angrily. "I am not an invalid." He wiggled his fingers, making them bleed.

Taking as big of a breath as he could muster, Rumpere grabbed hold of the wooden edges of the simple medical bed. Letting out the breath, and with a mix of stifled screams, he pulled himself up to a sitting position. Tears of anguish ran down his face as the newly-promoted Deputy and Rumpere's entourage entered the room.

"By Fate's fury, he's sitting up already?" The Deputy pulled his hood back, his face split in a huge grin. "Unbelievable. They said you would be out for days, at least."

"History waits for no one," Rumpere said, his audience all nodding in agreement. He motioned for the water with a shaking hand.

The attending Moufan-Man handed it to him and everyone watched, their anxiety playing out on their faces and in their eyes, as Rumpere spilled a third of it while drawing it up to his mouth.

After taking a sip, he shot a glare at the attendant, who promptly took the mug from him.

Rumpere's head drooped and he blinked wildly.

"You must lay back down, you've been badly

injured," one of the two women Moufan at his bedside said.

"Wise words," Rumpere whispered. Gingerly, he followed her recommendation, sighing at the end. "How bad are my injuries?"

The Deputy stepped forward and gazed down at him. "The burns were mostly to your face and chest and are said to be recoverable, though it will take some time. One of your legs was badly broken. It's not known whether or not it will heal properly."

"I will heal," Rumpere said, a tired fierceness in his voice.

"You've been reacting very well to the salves and medicines we've been administering for the past two days. Some of them have been banned for decades by Moufan law, but we figured you would understand."

"I do. How long have I been here?"

"Three days," the Deputy said. "They were giving you sleeping root, to help you heal."

"Ah." Rumpere nodded, licking his lips and then forcing a swallow. "Three days? That's unacceptable. You should have forced me awake."

He looked about, thinking, the room awaiting his next words eagerly. "How am I alive?"

"You were found in the stairwell. My predecessor shielded you with his body," said the Deputy.

"Hmm." Rumpere raised a finger in the air. "And what of our plans? The tomb?"

The Deputy looked at those around him and rubbed the back of his neck. "The tomb's destroyed. We lost everything, I'm afraid. But our morale is strong and the Moufan are still committed to your vision."

Shaking a finger back and forth, Rumpere dared a smile. "We did not lose everything."

"Pardon?" The Deputy leaned forward.

Rumpere's smile twisted into a painful, toothy sneer. "There's a secondary cache. I learned from dealing with the Fox before coming to this compound, that it's best to keep the truly prized items in a second, more secret location. It's small, but the weapons and items we have there are of real import, including a symbol of the Tub itself that will rally many to our cause." He coughed. "Our cupboard is not bare."

They all stared down in awe at their leader.

"I am tired," Rumpere said. "But one more thing. My mind, it's clearer now than ever. The fire burned away the impurities of my thoughts and my impatience. I feel like hardened steel drawn fresh from the forge."

"We should let you rest," the Deputy said. He and the others pulled their hoods up.

"You, wait." Rumpere pointed at the Deputy.

When everyone was gone, he wiggled his finger, drawing the man in close.

"I have your complete allegiance, do I not?" asked Rumpere.

"Of course you do. That is why you made me third in command."

"Then understand this," Rumpere grabbed the man's wrist, glaring at him, his face twisted in pain. "You will find me Creangle and that filthy Southerner rat. Why are you smiling?"

"I have received word from one of our agents, a coachman, who is with them as we speak."

"Excellent." Wiggling gently in his bed to get more comfortable, Rumpere closed his eyes. "Awaken me if there's anything important."

"Of course."

"And, a final thing. Tell the Moufan that I will speak to them at the start of the next month. I will not lie here while vultures swarm."

"Surely you will need more time to heal."

"Weakness is sickness, and I will not let our people fall ill. If they do not see me strong, we will have chaos, and the dream will die."

The End of Book 1

EPILOGUE

Several Weeks Later

I n the shadowy, flickering oil lamp light of the great hall, one hundred and twenty-eight black-hooded, red-sashed elite Moufan-Men stood at attention as their leader made his way to the center of the small stage.

Placing both of his hands on the silver cane, his fingers gripping its golden head tightly, he gazed out at the crowd.

"As I have risen from the ashes, so shall come a new era for the Moufan. We have worked too long, too hard to allow anything, even death itself, to stop us," Rumpere said, the light of the room only enough to outline his face and body.

"The Tub to which we were beholden has been

gone for two years, but only now are we united and able to step out of its shadow." Lifting his cane into the air, he continued. "This cane was the symbol and property of the last candlestick maker of the Tub. Let any doubt of their end be now washed away." He let the cane drop to the floor. As the end struck, two four-inch spikes sprung from the cane's golden head and electricity crackled.

Rumpere smiled as he felt the room lean in, eager to hear more.

He took a wobbly step to one side, planting the cane and rendering it dark. "Many of you have said that we should hunt down Creangle with all of our might and show the world our strength, but how strong is a man that smashes a table to kill a fly? Is it not weakness to allow the fly to distract one away from the call of destiny? We will watch our enemies, and we will wait, until we choose the fate they should be dealt."

There was a murmur among the crowd.

"With Creangle's failed attempt on my life, her failed attempt at destroying our trove of treasures, she gave me something vital. She gave me a clarity of vision and purpose. You see, one day soon children will sing songs about the Dery Plance Moufan-Men. They will go to sleep secure when they hear a rhyme about the Moufan of Doyono."

He made his way to the edge of the stage. "A

darkness is spreading, and we, the Moufan, are the only ones who can push it back. And we, not our enemies, will choose where and when we will engage. Today, we start on our path to a new world order, one led by the Moufan." He tapped the cane, bringing it to electrical life one more time. "The Moufan shall rise."

"The Moufan shall rise," the crowd thundered.

THANK YOU FOR READING

Reviews are powerful and are more than just you sharing your important voice and opinion, they are also about telling the world that people are reading the book.

Many don't realize that without enough reviews, indie authors are excluded from important newsletters and other opportunities that could otherwise help them get the word out. So, if you have the opportunity, I would greatly appreciate your review.

Don't know how to write a review? Check out **AdamDreece.com/WriteAReview**. Where could you post it? On GoodReads.com and at your favorite online retailer are a great start!

Don't miss out on sneak peeks and news. Join my newsletter at: **AdamDreece.com/newsletter.**

PLAYLIST

Here's what I listened to when I wrote the book:

Hell to the Liars - London Grammar

Brave Enough (album) - Lindsey Stirling

I don't know why - Imagine Dragons

Whatever it takes - Imagine Dragons

Believer - Imagine Dragons

Rise Up - Imagine Dragons

Oh Woman Oh Man - London Grammar

Lithium - Evanescence

Big Picture - London Grammar

Rooting for You - London Grammar

ABOUT THE AUTHOR

Off and on, for 25 years, Adam wrote short stories enjoyed by his friends and family. Regularly, his career in technology took precedence over writing, so he set aside his dream of one day, maybe, becoming an author.

After a life-changing event, Adam decided to make more changes in his life, including never missing a night of reading stories to his kids again because of work, and becoming an author.

He then wrote a personal memoir (yet unpublished) as every story he tried to write became the story of his life. With that out of the way, he returned to fiction and, with a nudge from his daughter, wrote *Along Came a Wolf* and created *The Yellow Hoods* series.

He lives in Calgary, Alberta, Canada with his awesome wife and amazing kids.

Adam blogs about writing and what he's up to at **AdamDreece.com.** He is on Twitter **@AdamDreece** and Instagram **@AdamDreece.** And lastly, feel free to email him at Adam.Dreece@ADZOPublishing.com.

ALSO BY ADAM DREECE

The Yellow Hoods

Discover the original, best-selling, young adult series that launched Adam Dreece's career and created the world of Mondus Fumus. Join Tee, Elly, Nikolas Klaus and their friends as their lives are turned upside in the pursuit of the first steam engine.

This gripping and snarky series is great fun for kids (9+) and adults.

Available in eBook, paperback, and audiobook formats.

The Wizard Killer

In the post-apocalyptic fantasy world of Mondus Inferno, where once flying cities ruled by Wizards dotted the skies, a man with no name fights to survive long enough to learn his past.

This high action, episodic series waits for no one. So buckle up and watch your back. For ages 12+.

Available in eBook, paperback, and audiobook formats.

The Man of Cloud 9

In the late 21st century, a brilliant inventor is on the verge of reshaping human history with his nanobot-cloud technology when an old enemy discovers his greatest secret. Will he be able to stop and save the lives of those closest to him, or will he risk everything and everyone for a chance to make it?

This sci-fi thriller will have you stopping and looking at the world around you, realizing that this future isn't that far away. For ages 14+.

Available in eBook and hardcover formats.

Survive
and
thrive as
an author.

With Indie Author
ADAM DREECE

You've got this.

ALONG CAME A PODCAST

Adam's got a great, new, audio podcast. Writing life can be daunting, from finding inspiration to get that special scene out, to marketing, to finding your voice again after a personal tragedy. Tune in and hear Adam's guests share their experiences, ideas, and the advice they received along the way.

AlongCameAPodcast.com